Up One Pair of Stairs

I WENT up One Pair of Stairs;
    Just like me!
I looked out the window;
    Just like me!
And there I saw a bigger world
    Than In the Nursery!

Up
ONE PAIR OF STAIRS
of
MY BOOKHOUSE

EDITED BY
Olive Beaupré Miller

PUBLISHERS
The BOOKHOUSE *for* CHILDREN
CHICAGO   TORONTO

———————————×———————————

Publishers of

My BOOKHOUSE
Six Volumes

My TRAVELSHIP
Three Volumes

My BOOK *of* HISTORY
Six Volumes

———————————×———————————

Printed in U.S.A.

List of Stories and Poems

LIST OF STORIES AND POEMS

LIST OF STORIES AND POEMS

LIST OF STORIES AND POEMS

Katharine Sturges Dodge

THE WONDERFUL WORLD*
WILLIAM BRIGHTY RANDS

Great, wide, beautiful, wonderful World,
With the wonderful water round you curled,
And the wonderful grass upon your breast—
World, you are beautifully dressed.

*Reprinted by the courteous permission of John Lane Company.

The Cap That Mother Made

A SWEDISH TALE

Once upon a time there was a little boy, named Anders, and he had a new cap. A prettier cap was never seen, for his mother herself had knit it; and who could ever make anything half so nice as Mother! The cap was yellow, except a small part in the middle. That was blue, for there had not been enough yellow yarn to make it all; and the tassel was blue.

Anders' brothers and sisters walked about admiring him; then he put his hands in his pockets and went out for a walk, for he was altogether willing that everyone should see how fine his mother had made him.

The first person he met was a farmhand walking beside a cart loaded with peat, and bidding his horse gee-up. When he saw Anders' new cap, the farmhand made a bow so deep that he bent nearly double, but

Anders trotted proudly past him, holding his head very high.

At the turn of the road he came upon Lars, the tanner's boy. Lars was such a big boy that he wore high boots and carried a jack-knife. But oh, when he saw that cap, he stood quite still to gaze at it, and he could not help going up close to Anders and fingering the splendid blue tassel.

"I'll give you my cap for yours," he cried, "and my jack-knife besides!"

Now this knife was a splendid one, and Anders knew that as soon as one has a jack-knife, one is almost a man. But still he would not for all the world give up, for the knife, the cap which Mother had made.

"Oh, no, I could not do that," he said. And then he nodded good-bye to Lars, and went on his own way.

Soon after this Anders met a queer little lady. She curtsied to him until her skirts spread out about her like a balloon and she said: "Lad, you are so fine, why do you not go to the king's ball?"

"Yes, why do I not?" thought Anders. "With this cap, I am altogether fit to go and visit the king."

And off he went.

In the palace yard stood two soldiers with guns over their shoulders and shining helmets on their heads. When Anders went to pass them, they both leveled their guns at him.

"Where are you going?" asked one of the soldiers.

"I am going to the king's ball," answered Anders.

"No, you are not," said the other soldier, trying to push him back. "Nobody can go to the king's ball without a uniform."

But just at this moment the princess came tripping across the yard, dressed in a white satin gown, with ribbons of gold.

"This lad has no uniform, it's true," she said, "but he has a very fine cap and that will do just as well. He shall come to the ball."

So she took Anders by the hand and walked with him up the broad marble stairs, past the soldiers who

stood on every third step, through magnificent halls
where gentlemen and ladies in silk and velvet were
waiting about. And wherever Anders went, all the
people bowed to him, for, as like as not, they thought
him a prince when they saw what it was that he wore
on his head.

At the farther end of the largest hall a table was
set with long rows of golden plates and goblets. On
huge silver platters were piles of tarts and cakes. The
princess sat down under a blue canopy with bouquets

of roses on it; and she bade Anders to sit in a golden chair by her side.

"But you must not eat with your cap on your head," she said, and she started to take it off.

"Oh, yes, I can eat just as well with it on," said Anders, and he held on to it with both his hands, for if it were taken away from him, he did not feel sure he would ever get it again.

"Well, well, give it to me," begged the princess, "and I will give you a kiss."

The princess was beautiful, and Anders would surely have liked to be kissed by her, but not for anything in this world would he give up the cap that Mother had made. He only shook his head.

Then the princess filled his pockets full of cakes; she put her own heavy gold chain around his neck, and bent down and kissed him.

"Now will you give me the cap?" she said.

Anders moved farther back in his chair, but he never once took his hands from his head.

Then the doors were thrown open and the king himself entered, accompanied by gentlemen in glittering uniforms and plumed hats. The king wore a mantle of blue velvet, bordered with ermine, and he had a large gold crown on his head.

When he saw Anders in the golden chair, he smiled.

"That is a very fine cap you have," he said.

"So it is," said Anders, "it is made of Mother's

best yarn, and she has knit it herself, and every one wants to get it away from me."

"But surely you would like to change caps with me," said the king, and he lifted his shining gold crown from his head.

Anders said never a word but when the king came nearer to him with his gold crown in one hand, and the other hand outstretched toward that beautiful cap, then, with one jump, Anders was out of his chair. Like an arrow he darted out of the hall, through the palace, down the stairs, and across the yard. He ran so fast that the necklace the princess had given him fell from his neck, and all the cakes rolled out of his pockets.

But he had his cap! He had his cap! He had his cap! With both hands he clutched it tight as he ran back home to his mother's cottage. "Well, Anders, where have you been?" cried his mother. So he told her all about what had happened.

All his brothers and sisters stood and listened with mouths wide open.

But when his big brother heard how he had

refused to give his cap in exchange for the king's golden crown, he cried out:

"Anders, you were foolish! Just think of all the things you might have bought with the king's gold crown! Velvet jackets and long leather boots and silken hose, and a sword. Besides, you could have bought yourself a much finer cap with a feather in it."

Anders' face grew red, very red. "I was not foolish," he answered. "I could never have bought a finer cap, not for all the king's crown. I could never have bought anything in all this world one half so fine as the cap my mother made me!"

Then his mother took him up on her lap, and kissed him.

DAME WIGGINS OF LEE

MARY E. SHARPE AND JOHN RUSKIN

Dame Wiggins of Lee
  Was a worthy old soul,
As e'er threaded a nee-
  dle, or washed in a bowl;
She held mice and rats
  In such antipathee,
That seven fine cats
  Kept Dame Wiggins of Lee.

      The rats and mice scared
        By this fierce whiskered crew,
      The poor seven cats
        Soon had nothing to do;
      So, as any one idle
        She ne'er loved to see,
      She sent them to school,
        Did Dame Wiggins of Lee.

The master soon wrote
  That they all of them knew,
How to read the word "milk"
  And to spell the word "mew."
And they all washed their faces
  Before they took tea:
"Were there ever such dears!"
  Said Dame Wiggins of Lee.

When spring-time came back,
  They had breakfast of curds;
And were greatly afraid
  Of disturbing the birds.
"If you sit, like good cats,
  All seven in a tree,
They will teach you to sing!"
  Said Dame Wiggins of Lee.

So they sat in a tree,
  And said, "Beautiful! Hark!"
And they listened and looked
  In the clouds for the lark.
They sang, by the fireside,
  Symphoniouslee,
A song without words,
  To Dame Wiggins of Lee.

They called the next day
  On the tomtit and sparrow,
And wheeled a poor sick lamb
  Home in a barrow.
"You shall all have some sprats
  For your humanitee,
My seven good cats,"
  Said Dame Wiggins of Lee.

While she ran to the field
  To look for its dam,
They were warming its bed
  For the poor sick lamb.
They turned up the clothes
  All as neat as could be.
"I shall ne'er want a nurse,"
  Said Dame Wiggins of Lee.

UP ONE PAIR OF STAIRS

She wished them good-night
  And went up to bed:
When, lo! in the morning,
  The cats were all fled.
The Dame's heart was nigh broke,
  So she sat down to weep,
When she saw them come back
  Each riding a sheep.

  The Dame was unable
    Her pleasure to smother,
  To see the sick lamb
    Jump up to its mother.
  The farmer soon heard
    Where his sheep went astray,
  And arrived at Dame's door,
    With his faithful dog Tray.

For the care of his lamb,
  And their comical pranks,
He gave them a ham
  And abundance of thanks.
"I wish you good-day,
  My fine fellows," said he;
"My compliments, pray,
  To Dame Wiggins of Lee!"

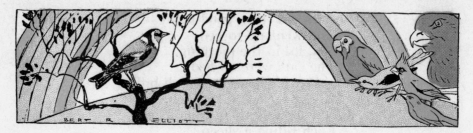

How the Finch Got Her Colors
A FLEMISH LEGEND

There was once a time when all the birds were gray and had no colors at all. Then the Great Bird, who ruled over them, called them all together, showed them the rainbow, and told them that he had decided to give each of them one of those splendid colors. At once they began pushing and shoving and crowding about him.

"Let me have first choice! I'll take green," screeched the parrot.

"Give me blue! I want blue!" piped the bluebird.

"I'll take yellow," cried the oriole.

And so it went. But during all this clamor and strife, there was one little bird who sat quietly back and waited her turn. That was the finch.

"Now you each have a splendid color," said the Great Bird, "and it's well you have all been provided for, for every single color is gone."

Just then he spied the finch.

"Come here, little finch," he cried. "Why have you asked for nothing?"

22

"I was waiting my turn," said the finch.

"But now all the colors are gone," said the Great Bird.

"Then must I go always in gray?" asked the finch.

Suddenly the Great Bird called all the other birds back as they were about to fly away.

"Go always in gray because you were too unselfish to push and shove!" he cried. "No! that you shall not!"

So he made all the other birds pass before him. From each he took a bit of color and gave it to the finch. Then lo and behold! she shone with all the tints of the rainbow; not one color alone was hers, but all— all, shading beautifully into each other, and blending together in one lovely whole!

Thus it came about that the most beautiful bird of the air was the little wee finch who waited her turn.

THE GOLDFINCH*
ODELL SHEPARD

Down from the sky on a sudden he drops
Into the mullein and juniper tops,
Flushed from his bath in the midsummer shine
Flooding the meadowland. . . .
Lightly he sways on the pendulous stem,
Vividly restless, a fluttering gem,
Then with a flash of bewildering wings
Dazzles away up and down, and he sings
Clear as a bell at each dip as he flies
Bounding along on the wave of the skies. . . .

*From *A Lonely Flute.* Used by permission of the publishers, Houghton Mifflin Company.

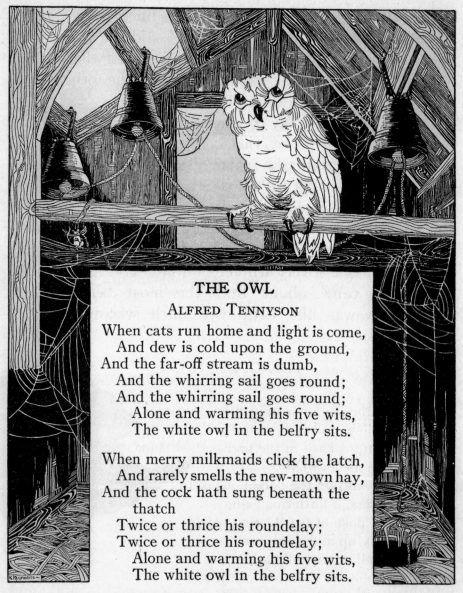

THE OWL

ALFRED TENNYSON

When cats run home and light is come,
  And dew is cold upon the ground,
And the far-off stream is dumb,
  And the whirring sail goes round;
  And the whirring sail goes round;
    Alone and warming his five wits,
    The white owl in the belfry sits.

When merry milkmaids click the latch,
  And rarely smells the new-mown hay,
And the cock hath sung beneath the
    thatch
  Twice or thrice his roundelay;
  Twice or thrice his roundelay;
    Alone and warming his five wits,
    The white owl in the belfry sits.

24

The Owl's Answer to Tommy*
JULIANA HORATIA EWING

One evening Tommy's grandmother was telling him and his little brother Johnny a story about a BROWNIE who used to do all the work in a neighbor's house before the family got up in the morning.

"What was he like, Granny?" asked Tommy.

"Like a little man, they say, my dear."

"What did he do?"

"He came in before the family were up, and swept up the hearth, and lighted the fire, and set out the breakfast and tidied the room, and did all sorts of house-work. But he never would be seen and was off before they could catch him. But they could hear him laughing and playing about the house sometimes."

"What a darling. Did they give him any wages, Granny?"

"No, my dear. He did it for love. They set a pancheon of clear water for him overnight, and now

*From *Brownies*, published by The Macmillan Company.

and then a bowl of bread and milk or cream. Sometimes he left a bit of money in the water. Sometimes he weeded the garden or threshed the corn. He saved endless trouble both to men and maids."

"O Granny! Why did he go?"

"The maids caught sight of him one night, my dear, and his coat was so ragged, that they got a new suit, and a linen shirt for him, and laid them by the bread and milk bowl. But when BROWNIE saw the things, he put them on and, dancing round the kitchen, sang,

" *'What have we here!   Hemten hamten!*
Here will I nevermore tread nor stampen.'
And away he danced through the door and never came back again."

"O Grandmother! But why didn't he come back?"

"The Old Owl knows, my dear, I don't. Ask her."

Now Tommy was a lazy boy. He wished that he could find a brownie to tidy the room, and fetch the turf, and pick up chips, and do all his work for him. So that night, while little Johnny was off in the land of dreams, growing rosier and rosier as he slept, Tommy lay wide awake, thinking of his grandmother's story.

"There's an owl living in the old shed by the lake," he thought. "It may be *the* Old Owl herself, and she knows, Granny says. When father's gone to bed and the moon rises, I'll go and ask her."

UP ONE PAIR OF STAIRS

By and by the moon rose like gold and went up into the heavens like silver, flooding the fields with a pale, ghostly light. Tommy crept softly down the ladder, through the kitchen and out on the moor. It was a glorious night, though everything but the wind and Tommy seemed asleep. The stones, the walls, the gleaming lanes, were so intensely still, the church tower in the valley seemed awake and watching, but silent; the houses in the village round it had all their eyes shut; and it seemed to Tommy as if the very fields had drawn white sheets over them, and lay sleeping also.

"Hoot! hoot!" said a voice from the fir wood behind him. Somebody else was awake, then. "It's the Old Owl," said Tommy; and there she came swinging heavily across the moor with a flapping, stately flight, and sailed into the shed by the lake. The old lady moved faster than she appeared to do, and

though Tommy ran hard she was in the shed some
time before him. When he got in, no bird was
to be seen, but he heard a sound from above, and
there sat Old Owl, blinking at him—Tommy—with
yellow eyes.

"Oh, dear!" said Tommy, for he didn't much like
it.

"Come up, come up!" said she hoarsely.

She could speak then! Beyond all doubt it was
the Old Owl, and none other.

"Come up here! come up here!" said the Old Owl.

Tommy had often climbed up for fun to the beam
that ran across the shed where the Old Owl sat. He
climbed up now, and sat face to face with her, and
thought her eyes looked as if they were made of
flame.

"Now, what do you want?" said the Owl.

"Please," said Tommy, "can you tell me where to
find the brownies, and how to get one to come and
live with us?"

"Oohoo!" said the Owl, "that's it, is it? I know
of two brownies."

"Hurrah!" said Tommy. "Where do they live?"

"In your house," said the Owl.

Tommy was aghast.

"In our house!" he exclaimed. "Whereabouts? Let
me rummage them out. Why do they do nothing?"

"One of them is too young," said the Owl.

"But why doesn't the other work?" asked Tommy.

"He is idle, he is idle," said the Old Owl, and she gave herself such a shake as she said it that the fluff went flying through the shed, and Tommy nearly tumbled off the beam.

"Then we don't want him," said he. "What is the use of having brownies if they do nothing to help us? But perhaps if you would tell me where to find them," said Tommy, "I could tell them what to do."

"Could you?" said the Owl. "Oohoo! oohoo!" and Tommy couldn't tell whether she were hooting or laughing.

"Of course I could," he said. "They might be up

29

and sweep the house, and light the fire, and spread the table, and that sort of thing, before Father came down. The BROWNIE did all that in Granny's mother's young days. And they might tidy the room, and fetch the turf, and pick up my chips, and sort Granny's scraps. Oh! there's plenty to do."

"So there is," said the Owl. "Oohoo! Well, I can tell you where to find one of the brownies: and if you can find him, he will tell you where his brother is. But all this depends upon whether you will follow my directions."

"I am quite ready to go," said Tommy, "and I will do as you tell me. I feel sure I could persuade them to come; if they only knew how every one would love them if they made themselves useful!"

"Oohoo! oohoo!" said the Owl. "Now pay attention. You must go to the north side of the lake when the moon is shining—('I know brownies like water,' muttered Tommy)—and turn yourself round three times, saying this charm:

'Twist me and turn me and show me the Elf—
I looked in the water and saw—'

When you have got so far look into the water, and think of a word that will rhyme with Elf, and at the same moment you will see the brownie."

"Is the brownie a merman," said Tommy, "that he lives under water?"

"That depends on whether he has a fish's tail,"

said the Owl, "and that you can see for yourself."

"Well, the moon is shining, so I shall go," said Tommy. "Good-by, and thank you, Ma'am," and he jumped down and went, saying to himself, "I believe he is a merman, all the same, or else how could he live in the lake?"

The moon shone very brightly on the center of the lake. Tommy knew the place well, for there was a fine echo there. Round the edges grew rushes and water plants, and turning himself three times, as the Old Owl had told him, he repeated the charm:

"Twist me and turn me and show me the Elf—
   I looked in the water and saw—"

Now for it! He looked in, —and saw his own face.

"Why, there's no one there but myself!" said Tommy.

"And what can the word be? I must have done it wrong."

"Wrong!" said the Echo.

Tommy was almost surprised to find the echo awake at this time of night.

"Much you know whether I'm wrong or not," said he. "Belf! Celf! Delf! Felf! Helf! Jelf! There can't be a word to fit the rhyme. And then to look for a brownie and see nothing but myself!"

"Myself," said the Echo.

"Will you be quiet?" said Tommy. "If you would tell me the word there would be some sense in your interference; but to roar 'Myself!' at me, which neither rhymes nor runs—it does rhyme, though, as it happens," he added: "how very odd! it runs, too—

'Twist me and turn me and show me the Elf—
I looked in the water and saw myself!'

Which I certainly did. What can it mean? The Old Owl knows, as Granny would say; so I shall go back and ask her."

And back he went. There sat the Old Owl as before.

"Oohoo!" said she, as Tommy climbed up. "What did you see in the lake?"

"I saw nothing but myself," said Tommy, indignantly.

"And what did you expect to see?" asked the Owl.

"I expected to see a brownie," said Tommy; "you told me so."

"And what are brownies like, pray?" inquired the Owl.

"The one Granny knew was a useful little fellow, something like a little man," said Tommy.

"Ah!" said the Owl, "but you know at present this one is an idle fellow, something like a little man. Oohoo! oohoo! Are you quite sure you didn't see him?"

"Quite," answered Tommy sharply, "I saw no one but myself."

"Hoot! toot! How touchy we are! And who are you, pray?"

"I'm not a brownie," said Tommy.

"Don't be too sure," said the Owl. "Did you find out the word that rhymed with Elf?"

"No," said Tommy, "I could find no word with any meaning that would rhyme, except, 'myself.' "

"Well, if 'myself' rhymes," said the Owl, "what more do you want?"

"I don't understand," said Tommy humbly, "you know I'm not a brownie."

"Yes, you are," said the Owl, "and a very idle one, too. All children are brownies."

"But I couldn't do work like a BROWNIE," said Tommy.

"Why not?" inquired the Owl. "Couldn't you sweep the floor, light the fire, spread the table, tidy the room, fetch the turf, pick up your own chips and sort your grandmother's scraps?"

"Please," said Tommy, "I should like to go home now and tell Johnny."

"Very well," said the Old Owl, "I think I had better take you."

"I know the way, thank you," said Tommy.

"Do as I say," said the Owl. "Lean your full weight against me and shut your eyes."

Tommy laid his head against the Owl's feathers. Down he sank and sank. He could feel nothing solid,—he jumped with a start to save himself, opened his eyes, and found that he was sitting in the loft with Johnny sleeping by his side. And what was odder still, it was no longer moonlight, but early dawn.

"Get up, Johnny, I've a story to tell you," he cried. And while Johnny sat up and rubbed his eyes, he told him all about it.

And after that Tommy and Johnny were the most useful little BROWNIES in that whole country.

AN EXPLANATION OF THE GRASSHOPPER*
VACHEL LINDSAY

The Grasshopper, the Grasshopper,
I will explain to you:—
He is the Brownies' racehorse,
The fairies' Kangaroo!

*Taken from *The Congo*. Used by permission of The Macmillan Company.

Snow-white and Rose-red

WILHELM AND JACOB GRIMM

A poor widow once lived in a little cottage that had a garden in front of it, and in this garden grew two beautiful rose-trees. One of these trees bore white roses and the other red. Now the good woman had two children who were just like the rose-trees. One was named Snow-white and the other Rose-red, and they were the sweetest, kindest, most industrious and cheerful little maids in all the world. Rose-red loved to run and skip over fields and meadows, picking nosegays of flowers and chasing the beautiful butterflies, but Snow-white was quieter and more gentle than her sister. She remained at home with her mother, either helping her with her work or reading aloud to her when their work was done. The two children loved each other so dearly that they always went hand in hand when-

ever they were out together, and if Snow-white said to her sister, "We will never leave each other," Rose-red always answered, "No, not while we live." Then the mother would add, "Whatever one has, let her always share with the other."

They often roamed together in the woods, gathering berries, and no beast ever even offered to hurt them. On the contrary, all the animals came up to them in the most trustful and affectionate manner. The little hare would nibble a cabbage leaf from their very hands; the deer grazed beside them; the stag leaped past them joyous and free, the birds never stirred from their branches at their approach, but sang to them in perfect security. No evil ever befell them. If night overtook them in the wood, they laid themselves down on the moss and slept until morning, and their mother was satisfied they were safe and was never anxious about them.

Once when they had passed the night in the woods and were awakened by the bright morning sun, they saw a beautiful child in a shining white dress sitting close by their resting place. She rose when they opened their eyes, and looked at them kindly, but she said not a word and vanished from their sight. When the children looked about them, they saw that they had slept on the edge of a precipice, over which they would certainly have fallen, had they gone two steps farther in the darkness. Their mother told them that the beautiful child must have been the angel who watches over good children.

Snow-white and Rose-red kept their mother's cottage

so clean and neat that it was a pleasure even to look into it. In the summer, Rose-red looked after the house, and placed by her mother's bed every morning before she awoke, a nosegay in which was a rose from each of the rose-trees. In the winter, Snow-white lit the fire and put the kettle on after scouring it so that it shone like gold. In the evening when the snow flakes fell, the mother said, "Snow-white, go and bolt the door." Then they drew round the fire and the good woman read aloud to the children from a large book while the girls listened and busied themselves at spinning. Beside them lay a lamb and behind perched a little white dove with its head tucked under its wing.

One evening as they all sat thus cozily together, a knock was heard at the door as if some one desired to enter.

"Quick, Rose-red, open the door," said the mother. "It must be some traveler in need of shelter."

Rose-red accordingly shot back the bolt expecting to see a poor man, but it was no such thing—it was a bear who thrust his great, black head in at the open door. Rose-red cried out and sprang back; the lamb bleated; the dove fluttered her wings, and Snow-white hid herself behind her mother's bed. But the bear began to speak and said, "Don't be afraid. I will do you no harm. I am half frozen and only wish to warm myself by your fire."

"Poor bear," said the mother, "lie down by the fire; only take care you don't burn your fur."

Then she called Snow-white and Rose-red to come out

of their hiding places. "This bear," she said, "is a good kind creature and will do you no harm." So the children obeyed and by degrees the lamb and the dove drew near too, and they all forgot their fear.

"Children," said the bear, "knock a little of the snow off my coat." So they fetched the broom and swept the bear's coat quite clean. After which he stretched himself out before the fire and growled quite happily and comfortably. Before long the children and the bear and the lamb and the dove were all good friends and Snow-white and Rose-red began to sport with their unexpected guest, tugging at his thick fur or putting their feet on his back and rolling him over and over. Then they took a thin hazel-twig and tickled him with it, and when he growled they laughed. The bear submitted to everything with the best possible good nature, only when they went a little too far, he cried, "Children, children, leave me an inch of my life!"

When night came and all prepared to go to bed, the widow said to the bear: "You can stay here and lie on the hearth all night if you like. It will shelter you from the cold and snow."

The bear accepted the offer gratefully, but as soon as the day dawned, the two children let him out and he trotted over the snow back into the woods.

From this time on, the bear came every evening at the same hour, laid himself down by the fire and let the children play whatever pranks they liked with him. Soon

they grew so attached to their strange playfellow that the door was never bolted of an evening until he had made his appearance. But when spring came and everything outside was green and bright, the bear said one morning to Snow-white, "I must leave you now and I will not be able to return all summer."

"Where are you going, dear bear?" asked Snow-white.

"I must go to the woods," answered the bear, "to protect my treasure from the bad dwarfs. In the winter when the ground is frozen hard, they are obliged to stay shut up underground and cannot work their way out, but now that the sun has thawed the earth, they find their way up to the surface and are ever on the watch for what they can steal, and whatever touches their hands or reaches their caves, rarely if ever sees daylight again."

Snow-white was very sorrowful when she took leave of the good-natured beast and unbolted the door that he might depart. In passing out, his fur was caught on a hook and as a bit was torn out, Snow-white fancied that she saw something shine like gold underneath it, but he passed out so quickly that she did not feel sure what it was, and in a twinkling he had disappeared among the trees.

A short time after this the mother sent her children out into the woods to gather sticks. They soon came upon a large tree which lay felled on the ground, and among its roots, half hidden by the grass, they saw something jumping and hopping about, but what it was they could not make out. When they drew nearer they saw it was a dwarf with an old withered face and a snow-white beard a yard long. The end of the beard was caught tight in a cleft in the tree and the little fellow was springing backwards and forwards like a dog at the end of a rope, but he could not get free. He glared at the children with his fiery red eyes and screamed out, "What are you standing there for? Can't you come and help me?"

"What have you been doing, little man?" asked Rose-red.

"You silly goose," cried the dwarf, "I wanted to split the tree that I might get shavings for our kitchen. Those great thick logs such as are needed to cook the great mountains of provisions that are devoured by coarse, greedy folk like you, would quite burn up the little food we cook. I had successfully driven in the wedge and should soon have done what I wanted, when the wedge sprang unexpectedly out of the cleft, which closed again quickly over the end of my beautiful white beard. So here I am stuck fast and I cannot get away. Stupid simpletons, why do you stand there and laugh and do nothing?"

In spite of the little 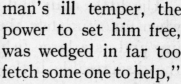 man's ill temper, the girls did all in their power to set him free, but in vain—the beard was wedged in far too firmly. "I will run and fetch some one to help," said Rose-red. "Idiot!" screeched the dwarf. "Why go and fetch more dunderheads? Here are two too many already! Can't you think of anything better?"

"Don't be so impatient," said Snow-white. "I will try to do something else." And taking out her scissors, she snipped the end off the dwarf's beard, thus setting him free at once. But for all that did he say thank you? No! never a bit of it!

"Drat you, you ninnies, for cutting my beautiful beard," he cried as soon as he felt himself free. And seizing a bag full of gold which was hidden among the roots of the tree, he made off into the woods without even so much as a backward look at the children who had helped him.

Shortly after this Snow-white and Rose-red went out to fish in the brook. As they drew near the water, they saw something that looked like a great grasshopper jumping toward the stream as though just about to leap in. They ran to see what it could be and recognized the very same old dwarf.

"Where are you going?" asked Rose-red. "Surely you can't mean to jump into the water."

"I'm not such a fool!" screamed the dwarf. "Don't you see that that horrid fish is pulling me in?"

The little man had been sitting on the bank fishing when unfortunately the wind entangled his beard in the line and as a large fish directly afterwards took the bait, the disagreeable little fellow was not strong enough to pull the creature out, so the fish got the upper hand and was dragging the dwarf in after it. Though he caught at every stick and twig within reach, that did not help

him much; he was forced to follow every move of the fish and was in continual danger of being drawn into the water. The girls came up just in time and did all they could to disentangle his beard from the line, but in vain. Nothing was left to do, but use the scissors again. So Snow-white cut off a very small piece of the beard. But when the dwarf saw what the girls were about, he cried in a rage, "Is this the way you ruin a fellow's face? Blockheads! I wish you had lost your way before ever you came this road. Was it not enough to shorten my beard before but you must be spoiling it altogether?"

Then he fetched a bag of pearls that lay among the brushes, hobbled away and vanished behind a stone.

It happened soon after this that the mother sent her children to town to buy thread, needles, ribbons and lace. Their road led over a heath where great rocks lay scattered about. As they trudged along, their attention was soon drawn to a huge bird that hovered about above them. It circled nearer and nearer the earth till at last it dashed suddenly down among a mass of rocks. At once they heard a sharp, piercing cry and running to the spot, they saw, to their horror, that the eagle had pounced upon their old acquaintance, the dwarf, and was about to carry him off. The tender-hearted children did not for a moment hesitate. Taking firm hold of the little man, they struggled stoutly to free him from the eagle, and after much rough handling on both sides, the dwarf remained at last safe in the hands of his courageous little friends, while the great bird flew away. But for all that, did the little old man say thank you? No! never a bit of it! When he had in a degree recovered from the shock he cried in his thin cracked voice, "Couldn't you have handled me more gently? Look at my little coat. It's all torn to shreds, you useless, awkward hussies."

He then seized a sack of precious stones and vanished under the rocks. The girls were by this time quite accustomed to his thankless manner, so they went on their way and did their errands in town. On their way home, as they were again passing the heath, they once more came unexpectedly upon the ugly dwarf. He had emptied out his sack of precious gems and was counting them over, for he never thought anyone would be crossing the heath so late. The setting sun shone on the brilliant stones and they gleamed and glittered so beautifully that the children stood still to admire them. The face of the dwarf grew scarlet with rage as he saw them.

"Greenhorns! What are you standing there gaping at?" he cried, and was about to make off to his cave when a loud growl suddenly stopped him. Out of the woods came a great black bear. The dwarf in a fright once more tried to escape to his hiding place, but the bear was right upon him. Then the little man cried out in terror, "Dear Mr. Bear, I beg you spare me. I'll give you all my treasure. Only look at all those beautiful gems. What pleasure would you get from gobbling up such a little fellow as I? You wouldn't even get a taste of me! But look at those

44

two wicked girls. There, lay hold of them! They would be tender morsels and are as fat as quails—pray take them, good Mr. Bear, and let me go!"

The bear, however, was not to be moved by his words. He gave the evil little creature one blow with his paw and that was the end of him once and for all.

In the meantime, the girls had run away towards home, but the bear called after them, "Snow-white, Rose-red, stop! Don't be afraid. I will go with you." Then they recognized his voice and stood still and when the bear had come near them, the bear-skin suddenly fell to the ground and there stood before them a handsome young man dressed in gold.

"I am a king's son," said he, "but was doomed by that wicked dwarf who stole my treasure to run about the woods in the form of a bear until I should be set free by his death. Now he has got his well-earned punishment." Snow-white married the prince and Rose-red his brother; and they  divided between them the great treasure which the dwarf had collect- ed in his cave. The good mother lived for many years peacefully with her children. But when she left her cottage she car- ried with her the two rose-trees and they stood before her window and continued every year to bear the most beautiful red and white roses.

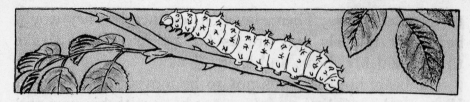

The Story of a Caterpillar*
KATHARINE PYLE

A caterpillar had crawled up on a twig. It looked the twig over, then fastened itself tightly to it by its hind legs and began twisting itself and moving its head up and down with a weaving motion. Every time the caterpillar's head moved, it left behind it something that looked like a glistening thread of silk.

An ant that was crawling along the branch stopped and stared with wonder. "What in the world are you doing?" it asked.

The caterpillar paused to rest for a moment. It was hard work, bending and doubling itself in that way. "I'm making a house," it said.

"Making a house!" cried the ant.

A bee that had lighted close by began to buzz with laughter. "Will you tell me, if you please, what sort of a house that is?" he cried.

"The only sort of house I know how to make," the caterpillar answered humbly.

"I never heard of anything so absurd. Why don't you hunt about and find a hollow tree, or a good hive, and live in that? Then you would be safe."

*From *Stories of Humble Friends* by Katharine Pyle. Copyright, 1902. American Book Company, publishers. Used by special permission.

"Or you might find a hole under a stone," added the ant. "That's a very good place."

The caterpillar shook its head. "This is the only sort of house I know how to make," it repeated. Then it set to work again.

As for the bee and the ant they went their ways. "A poor sort of a house indeed," each one thought to itself. But the caterpillar went on working.

Up and down, up and down its head moved, weaving and weaving. Now the silk was like a thin, silvery veil about it. Through the veil you could still faintly see the caterpillar moving.

At last the veil grew so thick that you could not see the caterpillar at all. You could only guess that it might still be at work inside.

After a while the bee came by that way again.

It stopped and looked the little house all over. Then it flew down to the ant-hill. "Miss Ant, Miss Ant, come out here," it buzzed. "I've such a joke to tell you."

The little ant stuck its head up from the hill.

"Such a joke! That caterpillar we were watching has finished its house, and has forgotten to leave any door," and the bee buzzed very hard.

"That is too bad," said the ant, "I'm afraid it will starve."

But the caterpillar did not die. It was not even hungry. It was fast asleep in its little cocoon house. While it slept the sun shone or the rain beat, but the little house let in neither sun nor rain. It was snug and dark.

UP ONE PAIR OF STAIRS

If anyone had opened the cocoon now he would have found a wonderful thing. Inside the hard, gray outside shell was a lining as soft as silk, and still inside of this was something — what was it? Not a caterpillar, not a moth either, though if one looked carefully one could see what looked like tiny wings folded closely down each side of folded legs, and the shape of feathery antennae such as moths have, but these, too, folded closely down. All were sealed together in what looked like a brown, soft skin. This thing was what we call a pupa.

Days and nights passed and at last what had once been the caterpillar began to stir and wake.

"How strange I feel! How strange I feel!" said the thing to itself. "I must have light and air."

One end of the cocoon was very soft and loose. It was through this end that what had once been the caterpillar pushed its way out into the air.

Oh, how weak it felt! Fastened to it on each side were two crumpled wet things, which it began to move feebly up and down. As it moved them it felt its strength returning and the crumpled things began to spread and dry. Broader and broader they spread until they were strong, velvety wings, two on each side. They were of the most beautiful soft brown color, with a pinkish border along the edges. In the middle of each of the lower wings was a glistening spot like the "eye" spot on a peacock's feather.

This thing was no caterpillar; it was a beautiful winged moth.

Presently it walked from the twig down upon the gray cocoon, within which it had lain so long. Then it spread its wings and floated softly off through the air and down to the earth. It did not fly far, for it had not its full strength as yet.

When it alighted, where should it be but on the ant-hill! The little ant was very busy there, tugging at twigs and leaves, and hunting for food. It stopped its work to stare with awe at the wonderful stranger. "You beautiful thing," it said, "where did you come from?"

"Don't you remember the caterpillar that made itself a house on the twig above?"

"Oh yes, poor thing, it must have died long ago," said the ant. "I went up there once or twice to see if I could help it, but there was no sound nor stir."

"I am that caterpillar," said the moth gently.

The ant stared and wondered. "I was once a pupa myself," it cried. "But I did not hatch out with such wings as those."

Just then who should come buzzing by but the very bee that had laughed at the caterpillar's house. It, too, stopped to gaze at the wonderful stranger. When it learned that this moth was that very caterpillar it buzzed for wonder. "Well, well!" it said, "so that was what you were about, was it; growing wings in your queer house!"

But the moth stirred itself. "Now I must go," it said. "I must find a shelter under a rock or in some hollow tree until the sun goes down. But tonight—ah, tonight! Then I shall come out to fly wheresoever I will."

So it waved its great wings and flew softly and noiselessly away out of sight.

The ant and the bee sat looking after it. "And to think," cried the bee, "that we should not have understood what that caterpillar was doing! After all, every one knows his own business best."

TO A BUTTERFLY
WILLIAM WORDSWORTH

I've watched you now a full half-hour,
Self-poised upon that yellow flower;
And, little Butterfly! indeed
I know not if you sleep or feed.
How motionless!—not frozen seas
More motionless! and then
What joy awaits you, when the breeze
Hath found you out among the trees,
And calls you forth again!

The Brooklet's Story*

MARGARET SIDNEY LOTHROP

The Silly Little Brook awoke and opened its eyes to the sun and the world. "Oh, how do you do?" said the Sun, laughing as the Silly Little Brook blinked its eyes at him.

"Who are you?" asked the Silly Little Brook. "I never saw you before."

"Of course not," said the Sun, laughing more than ever, "because you have never been awake before. Come, now, it is time for you to get to work; you have been a long time asleep. Look back of you."

The Silly Little Brook did just as the Sun told her and looked back of her. "I don't see anything," she said, "except a black hole in the ground."

"Of course you don't," said the Sun, "because that is all there is to see. You have just come out of that hole where you have been asleep all your life. Now look ahead!"

The Sun said this so loudly and stared at her face so long that the Silly Little Brook began to feel quite uncomfortable; so she winked and blinked, and said nothing.

"Look ahead," commanded the Sun sharply. And this time she obeyed. There was a tiny, wee little stream of clear, white water trickling away like a thread down the mountain. It was the Silly Little Brook.

*From *Stories Polly Pepper Told*. Reprinted by the courteous permission of the author and the publishers Lothrop, Lee & Shepard Co.

UP ONE PAIR OF STAIRS

"Now, hurry!" said the Sun; by this time he was very fierce for his face had been getting rounder and bigger every minute, "and set to work, for you have a great deal to do. Be a useful little brook, and don't stop on your way, but make every one glad that you woke up. Good day." And the Silly Little Brook felt her feet give way before her, and in a minute she was slipping and sliding down, down the mountain side.

"I'm not going to be sent down in this fashion," she grumbled, as soon as she could catch her breath, while she rested a bit in a hollow. "I shall choose my way and what I will do. And I am not going to work all the time either, and the cross old Sun need not think that he can command me to do it. I am going to play as much as I want to."

With that the Silly Little Brook rested in the hollow all that day, and the next and the next.

The first day the birds came to see the Silly Little Brook, and they sang sweet songs over her head and they told her pretty stories, and they dipped their beaks in her clear little pool of water in the hollow. And the Silly Little Brook said to herself, "Oh, what a beautiful time I am having. How glad I am that I didn't pay any attention to what the cross old Sun said to me when he told me not to stop. I shall stop here as long as I please." And she did.

And the next day the birds came and everything was pleasant, and the Silly Little Brook went to sleep at night and dreamed of all sorts of beautiful things. But the day after she looked up and saw to her astonishment a flock of birds that was whirring along over to the top of the mountain side, pause when they came to her, and look down. Then they whispered together and presently off they flew, twittering, "Oh, no, no! We'll not stop there."

What to make of it the Silly Little Brook did not know; she only rustled and grew angrier and angrier and said that she did not care. But she went to sleep, crying as hard as she could that night and her pillow, a clump of moss, was wet with tears.

At last, as morning broke, the Silly Little Brook heard a voice close to her ear, saying, "Oh, dear Brook, wake up! I have something to say to you." And there was Robin Redbreast.

The Silly Little Brook at that opened her eyes. "What is it?" she asked sadly.

"Don't you know why the birds are flying over your head to seek other streams, without so much as giving you a gentle word, and no one remains to tell you the truth but me?" asked the Robin.

"No, I don't," said the Silly Little Brook. "Tell me, Robin."

"Look for yourself," said Robin Redbreast.

So the Silly Little Brook turned her eyes to look at herself in the little hollow where she had rested and, lo and behold, instead of the clear, white water, with only the

shadows of the violets to color it, why, there was a dark, dirty pool of water with a little green scum coming all over the top of it.

"Why, where have I gone?" screamed the Silly Little Brook. "That is not I!"

"Oh, yes it is," said Robin Redbreast. "You have turned into this ugly pool because you stayed still. Oh, dear Brook! Why did you not obey the good Sun and go on?"

"I will now," said the Silly Little Brook, bursting into a torrent of ripples; and she tried to start. But her feet were all tangled up in a mass of leaves and green weeds and she could not move an inch.

"I'll help you," said Robin Redbreast kindly, and jumping down he picked patiently all the sticks and leaves he could in his bill and carried them out of the way of the Silly Little Brook, so she could once more start to run down the mountain side.

But as fast as he picked the leaves and the sticks out of the way of the Silly Little Brook, ever so many more would come blowing down from the trees and choke up her course again. So at last poor Robin Redbreast had to sit down, quite tired out, and declare that he could do no more. Then the Silly Little Brook began to rush about and cry more loudly than ever; and the sticks and leaves flew around her thick and fast, for it was a very windy day. The birds flew over her head, never so much as giving her a glance, and it was very dreadful indeed.

The Silly Little Brook mourned and the wind in the trees sobbed above her. Robin Redbreast let his head droop on his pretty red bosom. But suddenly he hopped up, and he trilled out loud and clear, while he flapped his wings, "Stop crying, dear Brook; I will fly and bring some help," for he had heard what the Silly Little Brook had not been able to hear—the notes way up in the sky of some little birds that he knew. So off he flew, post-haste, and back he came with a whole troop of Robin Redbreasts who were on a journey together. There were so many of them that they picked out every stick and leaf before the new ones had a chance to choke up the way and pretty soon, "Start now!" they twittered.

The Silly Little Brook started. Then away she went slipping, and sliding, and trickling, and running like a mad little thing down the mountain side.

"Don't ever stop again," called every one of those Robin Redbreasts after her, "but go on—and on—and on!"

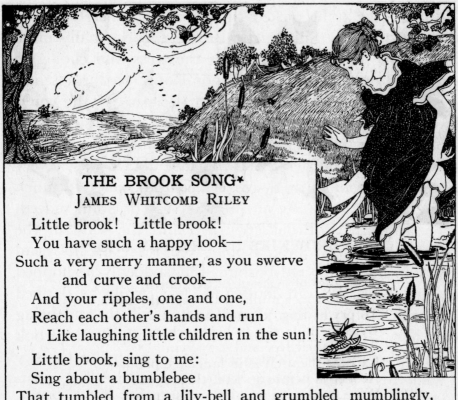

THE BROOK SONG*
JAMES WHITCOMB RILEY

Little brook!   Little brook!
You have such a happy look—
Such a very merry manner, as you swerve
        and curve and crook—
    And your ripples, one and one,
    Reach each other's hands and run
        Like laughing little children in the sun!

Little brook, sing to me:
Sing about a bumblebee
That tumbled from a lily-bell and grumbled mumblingly,
    Because he wet the film
    Of his wings and had to swim,
        While the water-bugs raced round and laughed at him.

Little brook—sing a song
Of a leaf that sailed along
Down the golden-braided center of your current swift and strong,
    And a dragon fly that lit
    On the tilting rim of it,
        And rode away and wasn't scared a bit.

*Copyright used by special permission of The Bobbs-Merrill Company.

THE BROWNIES IN THE TOY SHOP*
PALMER COX

As shades of evening settled down,
The Brownies rambled through the town,
To pry at this, to pause at that,
By something else to hold a chat,
And in their free and easy vein
Express themselves in language plain.
At length before a store, their eyes
Were fixed with wonder and surprise
On toys of wood, and wax, and tin,
And toys of rubber piled within.
Said one, "In all our wandering 'round,
A sight like this we never found.
When such a passing glimpse we gain,
What wonders must the shelves contain!"
Another said, "It must be here
Old Santa Claus comes every year
To gather up his large supply,
When Christmas Eve is drawing nigh."
A third remarked, "Ere long he may
Again his yearly visit pay;

*From *The Brownies, their Book.*   Used by the permission of The Century Co.

58

UP ONE PAIR OF STAIRS

Before he comes to strip the place,
We'll rummage shelf, and box, and case,
Until the building we explore
From attic roof to basement floor."
Not long were they content to view
Through dusty panes those wonders new;
And, in a manner quite their own,
They made their way through wood and stone.
And then surprises met the band,
In odd conceits from every land.
Well might the Brownies stand and stare
At all the objects crowded there!
Here, things of gentle nature lay
In safety, midst the beasts of prey;
The goose and fox, a friendly pair,
Reposed beside the lamb and bear;
There horses stood for boys to ride;
Here boats were waiting for the tide,
While ships of war, with every sail
Unfurled, were anchored to a nail;

PALMER COX

There soldiers stood in warlike bands;
And naked dolls held out their hands,
As though to urge the passers-by
To take them from the public eye.
This way and that, the Brownies ran;
To try the toys they soon began.
The Jack-in-box, so quick and strong,
With staring eyes and whiskers long,
Now o'er and o'er was set and sprung
Until the scalp was from it flung;
And then they crammed him in his case,
With wig and night-cap in their place,
To give some customer a start
When next the jumper flew apart.
The trumpets, drums, and weapons bright
Soon filled them all with great delight.
Like troops preparing for their foes,
In single ranks and double rows,
They learned the arts of war, as told
By printed books and veterans old;
With swords of tin and guns of wood,
They wheeled about, and marched or stood,
And went through skirmish drill and all,
From room to room by bugle-call.
The music-box poured forth an air
That charmed the dullest spirits there,
Till, yielding to the pleasing sound,
They danced with dolls a lively round.
The rocking-horse that wildly rose,
Now on its heels, now on its nose,
Was forced to bear so great a load,
It seemed to founder on the road.
Thus, through the shop in greatest glee,
They rattled 'round, the sights to see,
Till stars began to dwindle down,
And morning crept into the town.
And then, with all the speed they knew,
Away to forest shades they flew.

A PICTURE BY A LITTLE GIRL AND
A POEM BY A LITTLE GIRL
"THERE'S DOZENS FULL OF DANDELIONS
down in the FIELD:
little GOLD pLATES,
LITTLE GOLD DISHES IN THE GRASS.
I CANNOT COUNT THEM,
BUT THE FAIRIES KNOW EVERY ONE."

This poem was written by a little girl named Hilda Conkling when she was five years old, and she has written many more beautiful poems. Pamela Bianco was also a little girl when she drew this pretty picture. The poem is reprinted from *Poems by a Little Girl* by Hilda Conkling. Copyright, 1920, by Frederick A. Stokes Company. The picture is from *Flora* by Pamela Bianco. Courtesy J. B. Lippincott Company, Publishers, Philadelphia.

THE SONG SPARROW*
HENRY VAN DYKE

There is a bird I know so well,
   It seems as if he must have sung
   Beside my crib when I was young;
Before I knew the way to spell
   The name of even the smallest bird,
   His gentle-joyful song I heard.
Now see if you can tell, my dear,
What bird it is that, every year,
Sings "Sweet—sweet—sweet—very merry
   cheer."

A lofty place he does not love,
   But sits, by choice, and well at ease,
   In hedges, and in little trees
That stretch their slender arms above
   The meadow-brook; and there he sings
   Till all the field with pleasure rings;
And so he tells in every ear,
That lowly homes to heaven are near,
In "Sweet—sweet—sweet—very merry
   cheer."

The Tongue-Cut Sparrow*
TERESA PEIRCE WILLISTON

In a little old house in a little old village in Japan, lived a little old man and his little old wife.

One morning when the old woman slid open the screens which form the sides of the Japanese houses, she saw on the doorstep a poor little sparrow. She took him up gently and fed him. Then she held him in the bright morning sunshine until the cold dew was dried from his wings. Afterward she let him go, so that he might fly home to his nest; but he stayed to thank her with his songs.

Each morning, when the pink on the mountain tops told that the sun was near, the sparrow perched on the roof of the house and sang out his joy.

The old man and woman thanked the sparrow for this, for they liked to be up early and at work. But near them lived a cross old woman who did not like to be wakened so early. At last she became so angry that she caught the sparrow and cut his tongue. Then the poor little sparrow flew away to his home. But he never could sing again.

*From *Japanese Fairy Tales*. Published by Rand McNally & Company.

When the kind woman knew what had happened to her pet she was very sad. She said to her husband, "Let us go and find our poor little sparrow." So they started together, and asked of each bird by the wayside: "Do you know where the tongue-cut sparrow lives? Do you know where the tongue-cut sparrow went?"

In this way they followed until they came to a bridge. They did not know which way to turn, and at first could see no one to ask.

At last they saw a bat, hanging head downward, taking his day-time nap. "O, friend Bat, do you know where the tongue-cut sparrow went?" they asked.

"Yes. Over the bridge and up the mountain," said the bat. Then he blinked his sleepy eyes and was fast asleep again.

They went over the bridge and up the mountain, but again they found two roads and did not know which one to take. A little field mouse peeped through the leaves and grass, so they asked him, "Do you know where the tongue-cut sparrow went?"

"Yes. Down the mountain and through the woods," said the field mouse.

Down the mountain and through the woods they went, and at last came to the home of their little friend.

When he saw them coming the poor little sparrow

UP ONE PAIR OF STAIRS

was very happy indeed. He and his wife and children all came and bowed their heads down to the ground to show their respect. Then the sparrow rose and led the old man and the old woman into the house, while his wife and children hastened to bring them boiled rice, fish, and cress.

After they had feasted, the sparrow wished to please them still more, so he danced for them what is called the "sparrow dance."

When the sun began to sink, the old man and woman started home. The sparrow brought out two baskets. "I would like to give you one of these," he said. "Which will you take?" One basket was large and looked very full, while the other one seemed very small and light. The old people thought they would not take the large basket, for that might have all the sparrow's treasure in it, so they said, "The way is long, so please let us take the smaller one."

They took it and walked home over the mountain and across the bridge, happy and contented.

When they reached their own home they decided to open the basket and see what the sparrow had given them. Within the basket they found many rolls of silk and piles of gold, enough to make them rich, so they were more grateful than ever to the sparrow.

The cross old woman who had cut the sparrow's tongue was peering through the screen when they opened their basket. She saw the rolls of silk and piles of gold, and planned how she might get some for herself.

The next morning she went to the kind woman and said, "I am so sorry that I cut the tongue of your sparrow. Please tell me the way to his home so that I may go to him and tell him I am sorry."

The kind woman told her the way and she set out. She went across the bridge, over the mountain, and through the woods. At last she came to the home of the little sparrow.

He was not so glad to see this old woman, yet he was very kind to her and did everything to make her feel welcome. They made a feast for her, and when she started home the sparrow brought out two baskets as before. Of course the woman chose the large basket, for she thought that would have even more wealth than the other one.

It was very heavy, and caught on the trees as she was going through the wood. She could hardly pull it up the mountain with her, and she was all out of breath when she reached the top. She did not get to the bridge until it was dark. Then she was so afraid of dropping the basket into the river that she scarcely dared to step.

When at last she reached home she was tired out, but she pulled the screens close shut, so that no one could look in, and opened her treasure.

Treasure indeed! A whole swarm of horrible creatures burst from the basket the moment she opened it. They stung her and bit her, they pushed her and pulled her, and scratched her.

At last she crawled to the edge of the room and slid aside the screen to get away from the pests. The moment the door was opened they swooped down upon her, picked her up, and flew away with her. Since then nothing has been heard of the old woman.

LITTLE MAID OF FAR JAPAN*
ANNETTE WYNNE

Little maid upon my fan,
Did you come from far Japan?
What a tiny oval face!
Do you like this other place?

Do you miss the cherry trees
Where you know the little breeze,
Where you heard the cuckoo sing
In the spring?

Then you crossed your lattice floor,
Flung aside your paper door,
Joined the other maids at play,
Far away.

Now you live upon my fan,
Little maid of far Japan,
Still, you have a merry face—
Do you like this other place?

*From *For Days and Days*. Reprinted by the courteous permission of Frederick A. Stokes Company.

The Foolish, Timid, Little Hare

AN EAST INDIAN FABLE

Once upon a time there was a foolish, timid, little Hare, who was always expecting something awful to happen. She was forever saying, "Suppose the earth were to crack and swallow me up! O dear me! Just suppose!" She said this over and over again till at last she really believed the earth was about to crack and swallow her up.

One day she was asleep under a palm tree when some Monkeys above dropped down a cocoanut. As soon as the little Hare heard the noise, up she jumped and cried, "O dear me! the earth is surely cracking!" Then she ran away as fast as she could, without ever looking behind her.

Presently she met an older Hare, who called out after her, "Why are you running so fast?"

The foolish, timid, little Hare answered, "The earth is cracking

69

and I'm running away, so as not to be swallowed up!"

"Is that it?" cried the second Hare. "Dear me! Then I'll run away too!" and off he dashed beside her. Soon they met another Hare; they told him the earth was cracking, and off he dashed beside them. So it went on, till at last there were a hundred thousand Hares all running away as fast as they could.

By and by the Hares met a Deer.

"Why are you all running so fast?" asked the Deer.

"The earth is cracking!" they wailed. "We're running away so as not to be swallowed up!"

"The earth is cracking? O dear me!" cried the Deer, and she bounded after the crowd as fast as she could go.

A little farther on, they passed a Tiger.

"Why are you all running so fast?" called the Tiger.

"The earth is cracking!" the fearful ones wailed. "And we're running away so as not to be swallowed up!"

"The earth is cracking? O dear me!" howled the Tiger, and he sprang away after the crowd as fast as he could go.

In a few minutes more they met an elephant.

"Why are you all running so fast?" asked the Elephant.

"The earth is cracking!" the fearful ones wailed. "And we're running away so as not to be swallowed up!"

"The earth is cracking? O dear me!" trumpeted the Elephant, and he lumbered off after the crowd as fast as he could go.

At last the wise King Lion saw the animals running pell-mell, head over heels in a crazy crowd, and he heard them cry, "The earth is cracking!" Then he ran out boldly before them and roared three times till they halted.

"What is this you are saying?" he cried.

"Oh, King!" they answered. "The earth is cracking! We'll all be swallowed up!"

"The earth is cracking?" roared King Lion. "Hoity-toity! Wait a minute! Let's just take time to find out if such a thing could be true. Who was it that saw the earth crack? I pray you, tell me that!"

"Not I," said the Elephant. "Ask the Tiger! He must have seen it crack, for it was he who told me."

"Not I," said the Tiger. "Ask the Deer! She must have seen it crack, for it was she who told me!"

"Not I," said the Deer. "Ask the Hares! They must have seen it crack, for it was they who told me!"

So every single animal said he had not been the one to see the earth crack and he pointed out some one else who had told him all about it. Thus King Lion came at last to the Hares and the Hares all pointed to the one foolish, timid, little Hare who stood by shivering and shaking, more afraid than before. "She told us," they all cried.

Then the Lion said, "Little Hare, what made you say the earth was cracking?"

"I heard it crack," said the Hare.

"You heard it?" asked the Lion. "Where did you hear it crack?"

"By the big palm tree. I was fast asleep, and I woke up and thought, 'O dear me! Suppose the earth should

crack and swallow me up!' Just then I heard a cracking noise, as loud—as loud as thunder—and away I
ran as fast as I could."

"Well then," said the Lion, "you and I will go back to
the place where the earth is cracking and see what is the
matter."

"No, no, no!" cried the foolish, timid, little Hare. "I
would not go there again for anything in the world."

"But," said the Lion, "I will take you on my back."
So at last the foolish, timid, little Hare got up on the
Lion's back and away they went like the wind, till they
came to the Palm Tree. No sooner had they arrived, than
they heard a loud thud—the Monkeys threw down another cocoanut! And there they had it at last. At last

the Hare understood how nothing but a falling cocoanut had made her think that the earth was cracking. So the foolish, timid, little Hare went back to the other animals and she stood up before them all and said, "The earth is *not* cracking."

"Well! Well! Well!" said the Elephant. "You don't say! So the earth is *not* cracking after all!" And he turned around and lumbered off into the forest.

"Well! Well! Well!" said the Tiger. "So the earth is *not* cracking!" And he turned around and trotted off into the forest.

Thus every one of the animals turned around and went back into the forest, and that was the end of the earthquake.

MY BOOK HOUSE

A SONG OF THE CANADIAN LUMBERJACK

A FOLK-SONG TRANSLATED FROM THE CANADIAN FRENCH

O, all the raftsmen, where are they?
To winter camp they've gone away,—
    Bang on the ring!
Make way! Let pass the raftsmen!
Bang on the ring! Bang, bang!

They've stopped at Bytown on the way,
To dress themselves in clothing gay,—
    Bang on the ring!
Make way! Let pass the raftsmen!
Bang on the ring! Bang, bang!

They've put small boots on their big feet
At Ma'am Gauthier's they dance and eat,—
    Bang on the ring!
Make way! Let pass the raftsmen!
Bang on the ring! Bang, bang!

In bark canoes they paddle gay,
Up Ottawa's stream they steer their way:
    Bang on the ring!
Make way! Let pass the raftsmen!
Bang on the ring! Bang, bang!

They've come to winter camp, hooray!
They've cut axe-handles straight away—
    Bang on the ring!
Make way! Let pass the raftsmen!
Bang on the ring! Bang, bang!

Amazed, the Ottawa's waters stay,
Such noise those axes make all day,—
   Bang on the ring!
Make way! Let pass the raftsmen!
Bang on the ring! Bang, bang!

When camp is over, where are they?
They've gone back home without delay—
   Bang on the ring!
Make way! Let pass the raftsmen!
Bang on the ring! Bang, bang!

They kiss their wives and sweethearts gay,
They're glad to be back home to stay,—
   Bang on the ring!
Make way! Let pass the raftsmen!
Bang on the ring! Bang, bang!

This picture was taken from an old print in the Chateau de Ramezay, Montreal.

NURSE'S SONG
WILLIAM BLAKE

When the voices of children are heard on the green,
    And laughing is heard on the hill,
My heart is at rest within my breast,
    And everything else is still.

"Then come home, my children, the sun is gone down,
    And the dews of the night arise;
Come, come, leave off play, and let us away
    Till the morning appears in the skies."

"No, no, let us play, for it is yet day,
    And we cannot go to sleep;
Besides in the sky the little birds fly,
    And the hills are all covered with sheep."

"Well, well, go and play till the light fades away,
    And then go home to bed."
The little ones leaped, and shouted, and laughed,
    And all the hills echoéd.

The Honest Woodman
ADAPTED FROM LA FONTAINE

A poor Woodman was once cutting down a great tree by the edge of a lake. He was a strong man and he made the chips fly as he flung his axe over his shoulder and sent it ringing against the wood. Keeping time to each stroke, he sang merrily:

"Ring, axe, ring!
Stout heart, sing!
My little ones, they must be fed;
My axe and I will earn their bread!

"Fly, chips, fly!
Leap up high!
My little ones, they must be warm;
My axe will house them from the storm!

"Fall, tree, fall!
Oak tree tall!
Oh, hear the even, ringing stroke
Of my good axe on solid oak!"

But as he sang, just then the bright steel head of his axe flew off the handle, went whizzing, whirring through the air, and fell with a mighty splash into the blue waters of the lake.

The Woodman stood for a moment too much astonished to move, watching the bubbles and circles that swirled out ever wider from the spot where his blade had sunk from sight. Then he sat himself sadly down by the grassy shore of the lake with the useless wooden handle by his side.

"Alas! Alas!" he cried, "what shall I do? What shall I do?" For he was too poor to buy another axe and the lake was too deep for him to hope he could ever find the one he had lost. He thought of his children at home. Their bread, their firewood, the very roof that covered them, all depended on his earning a living with the axe. But as he cried, "Alas! Alas!" there suddenly rose before him in the lake a beautiful lady in white, with golden hair and a crown of white and yellow water lilies on her head.

"Do not be sad," she cried in a voice that rippled like tiny wavelets, "here is your axe." The sunlight gleamed from the blade which she reached out toward him, and the Woodman joyously sprang to his feet to take it. But as his hand was almost upon it, he noticed it was not his own steel axe she was holding up, but a very much richer golden one.

"Oh no!" he cried sorrowfully, seating himself again, and dropping his outstretched hand. "That is not my axe. That one is made of gold and is much finer than mine. Mine was only steel."

At that, the lady in white, with the crown of lilies, disappeared beneath the water, leaving the Woodman still more sorrowful for the moment of hope he had had. But in an instant, up rose her golden head again.

"Do not be sad," her voice tinkled and rippled

even more musically than before, "here is your axe."
Once again the Woodman sprang joyously to his
feet, for the blade she held up this time, did indeed

look like his own. But just as his hand was almost upon it, he noticed that it was not steel after all, but silver.

"Oh no!" he cried, sinking down as before, "that is not my axe. That one is made of silver and is much finer than mine. Mine, as I told you, was only steel."

The lady disappeared, but when she rose for a third time from the lake, all the joy of laughing water was in her voice.

"Honest Woodman," she cried, "here is your own steel axe, and here are the gold and silver ones beside. These are yours all three, because, no matter how great was your need, you would not take what was not your own!"

One by one, she tossed the three blades onto the soft green slope beside him, then she sank once more and forever gently out of his sight.

Joyously the honest Woodman took up his own steel axe and the other two, and so rich were the gold and silver ones, that with them he knew he could buy all that was needed for his little ones at home.

Thereafter, when his good steel blade rang out once more in the forest, he sang more merrily than before:

> "Ring, axe, ring!
> Stout heart, sing!
> My little ones are richly fed,
> An honest heart has won their bread!"

Chanticleer and Partlet

RETOLD FROM THE NUN'S
PRIEST'S TALE BY CHAUCER

A widow had a cottage near a grove within a little dale, and in a yard fenced round about with sticks, she kept a cock called Chanticleer. In all the land of crowing there was not his peer! His voice was like an organ in the church, his crowing was more sure to tell the time of day than any clock. His comb was redder than the coral fine; his bill was black as jet; his color was burnt gold.

This gentle cock had seven hens to do his bidding, and of these the fairest was Dame Partlet. So mannerly, so wise and gay was she, that Chanticleer loved none among the hens one half so well, and it was joy to hear the n sing together when the sun began to shine.

Now it befell one morn as Chanticleer slept on his perch by fair Dame Partlet's side, that he began to groan like one who has been troubled by some horrid dream.

"O my dear heart," Dame Partlet cried. "What aileth you?"

He answered her: "My love, I pray you, be not troubled by my groaning, but, alack, I dreamt that I was in a sorry case. Methought I roamed within our yard when there I saw a beast, like to a hound, who would have seized me by the throat. His color was betwixt a yellow and a red. His tail and both his ears were tipped with black. His snout was small, and round and glowing were his eyes. Of him I was afeared."

"For shame!" Dame Partlet cried. "How dare you say unto your love that anything can make you feel afeared! Have you no manlike heart, and yet you have a beard? What means a dream? Why nothing, certainly."

Her words bring shame to Chanticleer. He heeds his dream no more but cries: "My lady Partlet fair, I have such bliss when that I see the beauty of your face, you are so scarlet red about the eye, it maketh all my fear to die."

With that he flew down from the beam, and, clucking, gan his hens to call.

> Royal he was; he was no more afeared.
> He looketh as it were a grim lion.
> And on his toes he roameth up and down;
> Him deigneth not to set his foot to ground,
> He chucketh when he hath a corn y-found,
> And to him rennen then his wivies all.

But suddenly a sorry thing befell. A sly old fox that had been living in the grove for three long years, that very night had found a passage through the hedge and burst into the yard. There in a bed of cabbages he hid himself and lay in wait till it was past the noontide of the day, biding his time to fall on Chanticleer.

Fair in the sun, Dame Partlet and her sisters lay, to bathe them in the sand. The sun shone bright and Chanticleer sang merry as a mermaid in the sea. But, as he cast his eyes upon a butterfly that flitted o'er the cabbage bed, he was aware of this false fox that lay full low. Then had he ne'er a wish to crow, but cried anon: "Cluck, cluck," and up did start as one that was affrighted in his heart. He would have fled but that the fox cried out:

"Now gentle sir, alas, where will you go? Be not afraid of me that am your friend. I am not come to do you harm. In truth, I only came to hear you sing. You have a voice as lovely as the angel's song. My lord your father—bless his soul!—and likewise your good mother have been guests of mine and visited my house. So certainly I wish to please you, too. But when men speak of singing, I am wont to say, 'Save Chanticleer, I never heard one sing as did his father of a morning. He would stand upon his tiptoes, stretch his neck both long and small, and, that he might give forth the fulness of his voice, would close his eyes, and then how he would sing! Ah, there was never any cock in this land or another that could equal him in wisdom and in song.' Now, sir, for holy charity, shut fast your eyes and let me hear if you can sing as did your father in his day."

At this, great Chanticleer was filled with vanity and

pride, and he began to beat his wings as one that could not see the fox's sly and cunning lie, so charmed was he with silly words of flattery. He stood high on his toes; he stretched his neck, and ah, he held his eyes fast closed, that he might cry his loudest for the nonce.

Then up the fox did start while that the cock had still no opened eye to see. He seized him by the throat and bore him off in triumph, prisoned fast between his teeth.

Alack! such cry was never made by ladies in that sorry day when Troy was conquered, as those hennies made when they had sight of Chanticleer; and louder than them all Dame Partlet cried.

The widow and her daughters heard the hennies cry and make such woe, and out of doors they ran to see the fox slip toward the grove, the cock fast in his mouth. They cried, "Out harrow! Well away! Ha, ha, the Fox!" And after him they ran. With sticks and staves, came many another too. There Collie ran, the dog, and Malkin with a distaff in her hand.

> Ran cow and calf and eek the very hogs,
> So were they feared for barking of the dogs,
> And shouting of the men and women eek;
> They ran as though they thought their hearts would break!

They yelled like fiends; the duckies cried; the geese for fear flew over trees; out of their hive came a swarm of bees.

The cock, meanwhile, thought out a plan and thus at length, in spite of fears, he spake:

"If I were you, good sir, I would not let this rout of

knaves put me to shame by howling all unanswered at my heels. I'd turn about and cry, 'A murrain take you all! In spite of you, I'll carry off this cock and eat him in the wood!' "

So Chanticleer did wake the pride in Master Fox. "In faith," quoth Master Fox, "I'll tell them who I am!"

But, as he dropped his jaws to let the words come forth, all suddenly he loosed the cock who thus broke free and flew up high into a tree. And now the fox beheld how that his prize was gone. Sore was his grief and yet he thought: "I'll fool that cock again."

"Alas!" quoth he. "O Chanticleer, alas! I have done wrong to make you so afeared. But, sir, I did it of no bad intent. Come down and let me tell you what I meant. I'll speak the truth, God help me so!"

"Nay then," quoth Chanticleer. "Beshrew me, if you fool me any oftener than once. You shall no more through silly flattery get me to wink and close mine eyes.

<blockquote>
For he that winketh when he ought to see,
God will never save from thee!"
</blockquote>

The Battle of the Firefly and the Apes*
A FILIPINO TALE

When the sun goes down in the Philippine Islands, darkness comes quickly, and there begin at once to glimmer here and there, in among the trees and tall ferns, and high up in the air, the myriad little lamps of the fireflies.

One evening a firefly was on his way to visit a friend. As he flew quietly along, carrying his little lamp and minding his own affairs, he met an ape. Said the ape:

"Ho, ho, Mr. Firefly, why do you always carry a light?"

"I carry a light so that I can see the mosquitoes and keep out of their way," answered the firefly.

"Keep out of the way of the mosquitoes!" cried the ape. "You're a coward then! You're afraid of the mosquitoes!"

"I am not a coward, and I am not afraid of the mosquitoes!" said the firefly. "I go my way and mind my own affairs, and I leave the mosquitoes alone to go their way. That's why I carry a lamp."

But the ape insisted that the firefly was afraid, or he would not carry a light and try to avoid the mosquitoes. The next day Mr. Ape told all his ape friends that the firefly carried a lamp because he was a coward. So Mr. Ape and all his ape friends

*Adapted from *The Ape and the Firefly*. Used by the kind permission of American Folk-Lore Society.

laughed and made every manner of sport of the firefly.

Now the firefly soon heard what Mr. Ape had said, and how all the apes were laughing at him, so he resolved to teach them a lesson. He hurried off at once to Mr. Ape's house. Mr. Ape was asleep, but the firefly flashed his lamp in his face and wakened him with a start.

"Why did you tell everyone that I was a coward?" he demanded. "Tomorrow come to the plaza and there, in the sight of all, we will prove whether or not I am a coward!"

"Ho, ho, ho!" laughed the ape, "so you're offering to fight with me? Well, who are you going to bring to help you? One of your size will scarcely stand up alone against such a powerful creature as I."

"I shall come alone," said the firefly quietly.

Then the ape, seeing he could not make the firefly give up his idea in this way, suddenly grew very fierce and thought to frighten him out of it.

"Well," he cried, "I shall bring a whole company of apes! I shall have a thousand at least, each one as big as myself! We shall see then what will happen to you if you dare to come alone!"

So Mr. Ape called all his ape friends together, ordered each one to get a great club and meet him on the plaza at six o'clock the next evening. Just before six they all came in a crowd, as he had commanded, but they found the one small firefly already waiting.

Mr. Ape drew his company up in line and put himself at their head; then he fiercely gave the order to go forward against the firefly. But the firefly suddenly lit on the great ape's nose. The ape who stood next him struck savagely at his little foe. The firefly darted swiftly and nimbly out of reach of his blow, so the huge club missed him altogether and fell square on the great ape's nose! Flat fell Mr. Ape to the ground!

Then the firefly hurried to the second ape's nose. The third ape struck at his foe, but the firefly dodged out of the way as before, and the blow fell square on the second ape's nose! He, too, fell flat to the earth! Then the firefly flew to the nose of the third ape; the story was repeated. Flat fell the ape to the ground! So it went on down the line, each ape aiming his huge club at the firefly on his neighbor's nose, missing the firefly, and knocking his neighbor flat. Over they bowled, one after another, like a row of ninepins. At last the firefly was left victorious over every one of his fallen foes.

"Who now can say that the firefly is afraid?" he cried.

The apes cowered, shame-faced, on the ground with never a word to say. But the firefly flew quietly away, to mind his own affairs as before.

TWINKLING BUGS

When the sun sinks under the world's red rim,
And the river fades till its shores are dim,
And the trees are dark where the shadows lie,
Then they go by,
By,
By—
The twinkling bugs go by.

WHO CAN CRACK NUTS?*

MARY MAPES DODGE

Rut-a-tut-tuts!
Who can crack nuts?
Squirrels, can you?
"That we can, true—
Rut-a-tut-tuts,
We can crack nuts!"
Chicketty-chack,
Cracketty-crack,
"Pooh!" said the hammer,
"Silence your clamor,
Rut-a-tut-tuts—
Who can't crack nuts?"

*From *Rhymes and Jingles;* copyright, 1874, by Scribner, Armstrong & Co.; 1904, by Charles Scribner's Sons. By permission of the publishers.

The Nutcracker and Sugardolly Stories*

CAROLYN SHERWIN BAILEY

I

Once upon a time there were an old peddler and his wife going to town to market, and the peddler had a bag full of all sorts of nuts, and the woman had a basket of eggs upon her head.

The day was warm and sunny, and because the high road was so hot, they decided to go through the woods, a new way. As they went, they came to a beautiful shady path under the trees, a path they had never traveled before. On and on it went, until it ended all at once at a wonderful garden—a garden with a silver fence and a gold lattice gate all set with jewels, and over the gate was written a name in letters, "The Fairy Honeymouth."

*From *Firelight Stories*. Used by the permission of Milton Bradley Company.

91

The lattice gate was tightly closed, but behind it one could see gay flowers, and hear beautiful birds singing loudly in trees all made of sugar. On either side of the gate stood a great tree, and one tree bore large green nuts, nuts as large as hen's eggs, and the other was a sugar tree, dropping sugar plums down upon the path below.

"We must go inside," said the peddler, dropping his nuts. "We must indeed," said his wife, setting down her eggs. So they both climbed the lattice gate, and dropped down on the other side, although the birds in the garden sang loudly to them, "Don't do it. Don't do it."

Then the two buried their hands in the white sugar that filled the garden walks and smelled of the flowers that were all made of sugar, and at last the peddler said, "I must have one of those great green nuts. It would sell for more at the market than all the nuts I can gather in a twelve-month."

"Don't do it. Don't do it," called the birds, but the peddler paid no attention to them. He climbed the tree beside the gate and put one of the great green nuts in his pocket.

"See what I have found," called his wife, who had climbed the sugar tree. There in a nest lay a huge white egg.

"We will put this egg under our hen whose nest is beneath the front stairs. It will hatch into a wonderful fowl which we will sell for much money."

"Don't do it. Don't do it," sang the birds, but the woman took the large egg.

Then the two climbed the gate again and went away from the garden of the Fairy Honeymouth, carrying with them her great white egg, and one of her great green nuts, which, of course, they should never have done. When they reached home, they put the egg under their hen who had her nest beneath the front stairs, and the peddler laid the great green nut upon the table and got out his hammer, because he had decided to crack it.

Bang, bang, he pounded. The nutshell fell apart, but instead of a kernel inside, there on the table stood a strange little dwarf no bigger than your hand. He wore a wig, and yellow trousers and a hussar's jacket, with big buttons, quite tidy and complete. He had a huge head, and thin legs, and such a wide mouth that it seemed as if his head would come in two. He stepped out of the nutshell, and yawned, and, jumping into a basket of nuts, he began cracking them as fast as he could with his teeth.

But while this was happening, there came a great cackling from under the front stairs where the hen had her nest. The great white egg had hatched and out of it, upon the floor, hopped the daintiest little girl. She wore little silk skirts, and hose, and dancing shoes. Her hair was all curled in rings, and she picked up her petticoat and began whirling and dancing all

around the room. The hen went out to the barnyard in a tiff, because she had hatched no chick, but
the peddler and his wife looked in wonder at the little
dwarf, cracking nuts with his huge mouth, and the
little lady in her dancing shoes, flying about the floor.
Then they whispered together, and they said:

"We have no children. We will keep these little
ones, and they shall be our children, and we will name
them Nutcracker and Sugardolly."

So that is how Nutcracker and Sugardolly came in
the first place and lived with the peddler and his wife.

II

The peddler soon found that he had a very bad bargain. Nutcracker was a naughty little dwarf. All day
long he did no good to anyone—only mischief. He got
into the nuts that were ready to go to market, and he

cracked every one with his great mouth. Then he climbed the nut trees outside, and threw shells at the people passing by. When the peddler's wife tried to catch him with her broom, out from under it he would slide, and jump to the shelf and hide inside the clock, or he would dance a little way ahead of the broom and make faces at the peddler's wife.

He had only two friends—the great big barnyard cock who took him for rides about the garden, and little Sugardolly whom he loved very dearly.

Now Sugardolly was almost as much trouble as Nutcracker, for she would do no work, and she could eat nothing but honey and sweets from the flowers; and if she could not have all the flowers in the garden she would sit in a corner and cry. It was Nutcracker who brought her sweets, and Nutcracker who comforted her when she cried. But at last, when Nutcracker had eaten all the nuts that were gathered in the house, and

all that grew in the garden, he decided to run away, for the peddler's house no longer amused him. So early one morning he buttoned his little soldier jacket tightly about him, hopped on the cock's back, the cock spread his wings, and they went over the wall and far, far away. Nutcracker had decided to make a home for Sugardolly somewhere else.

III

The old peddler awoke in the morning, and he found the house very, very still. No cock in the garden crowed, and no little dwarf Nutcracker was about, rattling nuts. And Sugardolly sat in a corner and cried all day long, nor would she be comforted by all the sweets in the garden, because Nutcracker had gone away. The old peddler took Sugardolly upon his knee, and got down the sugar bowl for her to eat from, but she still cried. For many, many days she sat in the chimney corner, and grew more and more thin.

At last the white hen, who had a nest beneath the front stairs, took pity on Sugardolly, and told her that Nutcracker had gone away on the cock's back.

"Oh, take me away, too," cried poor little Sugardolly. So the white hen, with Sugardolly on her back, early one morning flew over the garden wall and across the meadow to find Nutcracker.

At first they were not sure which way to go. No one had seen Nutcracker and the cock. But one day they found one of the cock's red tail feathers by the roadside, and a bit farther on they came to another, and then, when they had entered a deep, deep wood, they came to the cock himself, strutting proudly about, and gathering hazel nuts.

"Where, oh, where is my dear Nutcracker?" asked Sugardolly of the cock.

"That I do not know," said the cock. "He climbed a great tree, and that was the last I saw of him."

And when the white hen saw the cock, she decided to go no farther; so Sugardolly went on by herself to hunt for Nutcracker.

The woods were very dark when it came night, but Sugardolly carried a bright glow-worm for a lantern. In the morning she was asked to breakfast by some bees, who fed her all the honey she could eat.

"Have you seen Nutcracker—a little dwarf in a brown soldier's jacket?" she asked of the bees.

Oh, yes the bees had seen Nutcracker, but it had been many days before that he had passed by.

"Buzz, buzz, buzz, buzz,
Over grasses and flowers,
Nutcracker has gone
Through the wood's green bowers,"

hummed the bees, so Sugardolly hurried on.

She called to the birds as she went, "Have you seen my Nutcracker—a little dwarf with thin legs, and a very wide mouth?" And the birds sang back to Sugardolly:

"Pick, pick, pick, pick,
Be quick, be quick,
Yonder Nutcracker springs,
And rushes and rushes
Through the green bushes,
Be quick, be quick."

Sugardolly did hear a rustling, but when she crept beneath the bushes to see, she found only a squirrel who chattered and threw shells in her face.

Poor little Sugardolly! She called to the bluebells:

"Little bell flowers so blue,
Did Nutcracker pass you?"

But the wind shook the bluebells, and they answered not a word.

Sugardolly would have cried then, if she had not come, all at once, upon the fairy palace of the Queen Rosebush. The palace was made of green leaves, with thorns at the corners to keep out the crickets, and there came a sound of music and singing from inside.

"Is it a party?" asked Sugardolly of a gold bug.

"It is a party," said the gold bug. "I will take you in."

So Sugardolly went inside the palace with the gold bug and she saw the Queen in a rose-leaf dress and a veil of spider's net, sitting upon the throne, and the young princesses in bright, shining, golden dresses, sitting beside her. The birds were the orchestra.

"You may spend the night with us," said Queen Rosebush graciously.

UP ONE PAIR OF STAIRS

So Sugardolly slept in a pink rosebud all night, and breakfasted from ambrosia in the morning, and thanked the Queen for her kindness and started once more to look for Nutcracker.

As she went on her way through the forest, she came to a singing brook, and she sat down beside it to rest. And she listened, for the brook was singing to her as it flowed along its pebbles:

"From mountains I come,
Where the dwarfs have their home.
In the cave whence I spring,
Nutcracker is King.
To him swiftly flee;
His queen thou shalt be."

"I shall find my Nutcracker! I shall find my Nut-cracker!" said Sugardolly, jumping up. She ran and ran by the edge of the brook far, far along, as far as the brook flowed, calling, "Nutcracker, Nutcracker," but no Nutcracker answered.

At last she came to the place where the brook started from a deep cave, and as she called, "Nutcracker," the rocks answered back, "Nutcracker," and that was all—no little dwarf came out. So Sugardolly sat down on the rocks, very much discouraged, and tired, and after a while she fell fast asleep.

IV

I do not know how long Sugardolly slept by the cave where the brook started, but when she awoke, there at her side, underneath a water plant, sat a little brown dwarf, busily fishing for pearls. He looked very much like Nutcracker, except for his mouth, which was smaller, and his jacket, which was green instead of red.

"Good-day, little lady," said the dwarf to Sugardolly, and Sugardolly, who was a polite little lady, said "Good-day" in reply. Then the dwarf rolled up his net, and put his pearls in the little sack that hung by his side, and blew a shrill blast upon his tiny silver trumpet.

Out from all the cracks and crevices of the rocks came other, and still other little dwarfs, and they joined hands and danced about Sugardolly, and told her what a pretty little lady she was, and they asked her to be their queen.

"Have you seen my Nutcracker—a little dwarf in yellow trousers?" asked Sugardolly.

Then all the dwarfs began shaking their little fists and stamping their little feet, and scowling in a terrible rage.

"Nutcracker was a wicked king," said one of the dwarfs.

"He ate all of our nuts that we had gathered for the winter," said another.

"He stole our bag of gold nuts," said a third, "and he threw them into the brook because he broke his tooth trying to crack one."

"We drove him away from our home," said the first dwarf.

Then Sugardolly began to cry, but the dwarfs forgot their rage to see her so unhappy. They brought her a tiny scepter, and a glittering crown all set with jewels, so Sugardolly decided to be their queen.

And Sugardolly was happier than she had been in a long time. The dwarfs found a fairy baker who brought her every morning jars of honey, and sugar rolls, and sweet, sweet cakes in his basket—all she could eat. The dwarfs made a set of tiny furniture for her, a bed and a chair and a table of sea shells, inlaid with real gold.

And while the dwarfs were away all day at their work, creeping into the cracks and holes of the earth for gold and silver and jewels, Sugardolly did their housekeeping. She dusted, and polished their dishes, and made their beds, and she always had their tea brewed

when they came home with their stores. One day she found their gold nuts in the brook, which made them very happy. Then, at night, the dwarfs sat about their fire, crosslegged on the floor, warming their toes, and they sang songs to Sugardolly upon her throne, and they told her stories. So, after a while, Sugardolly forgot to be lonely for Nutcracker, and she was very happy indeed, being queen of the dwarfs.

V

Now all this time Nutcracker was lost in the deep, deep woods. He had been most ungrateful, and he had hidden himself in a tree because he wished all the nuts of the forest for his own little self, and he wanted the cock, who had been so very kind to him, to go home again. So the cock did go home, as you know, with the white hen, after eating a great many hazel nuts, and selfish little Nutcracker was left alone with all the forest to wander about in.

For a while in the sunny, pleasant weather, Nutcracker had a good time. He climbed all the trees, and sampled all the different sorts of nuts. Never before had he been able to eat all the nuts he wanted, so he cracked hazel nuts, and walnuts, and butternuts, and filberts, and he made a pile of empty shells as high as a berry bush; but alas, the frosts came!

Nutcracker's jacket and his yellow trousers were not warm enough for the chill nights and the keen, frosty mornings. He longed for the peddler's kitchen and the warm porcelain stove. He wished to hide himself beneath the cock's wings or creep into the nest of the white hen under the front stairs, but none of these things could Nutcracker do, for he had forgotten the way home.

At the foot of a large oak tree lived a great red

squirrel, who was chief of all the squirrels in the woods. It was he who divided the forest into parts, and every squirrel had his own trees and his own holes in which to live. The red squirrel walked out often to see that no other squirrel gathered the nuts which belonged to his neighbor, and he had a fine fur great-coat which he wore to keep himself warm.

Now Nutcracker had seen the red squirrel, and had admired his fur coat, and had thrown nut shells at him; and one night Nutcracker went stealthily to the oak tree where the chief squirrel lived and he stole the fur coat while the squirrel was sleeping.

It exactly fitted Nutcracker, and he turned up the collar and danced about quite gayly. But the chief squirrel awoke and missed his coat. In a rage he sent word to all the squirrels of the forest to rise and make war upon Nutcracker, which they did.

They followed Nutcracker wherever he went, and took away his nuts. His sword, that was no bigger than a cambric needle, was of no avail to drive them away. He was obliged to hide under the dry leaves, and he grew very, very thin. One day, as he sat shivering and hungry, he heard a sound of feet and a crunching upon the leaves. A great four-legged creature nearly stepped upon him, and as he cried out, a boy, whose dog it was that had frightened him, came along, and Nutcracker told him all his troubles.

"You shall go home with me," said the boy. "We

have a nut tree in the garden and you shall live in the chimney corner and be my playfellow." So Nutcracker went home with the boy and the dog, and his troubles were over for a while at least.

VI

Every evening Sugardolly, Queen of the Dwarfs, counted the little men, as they sat about the fire, to see if they had all come home, and one night a little dwarf was missing. So Sugardolly counted them all over again—one, two, three; yes, one was certainly missing. Then all the other dwarfs ran about crying, and wringing their hands, and looking under the beds and beneath the tables, and, as they looked, the door opened and in ran the little lost dwarf, very much out of breath and tired.

He had a bundle of moss upon his back, which he dropped upon the floor, and he told them all how he had been gathering the moss from a castle hedge, and how he had been attacked by a cat which charged him from the castle kitchen, and the cat was driven by none other than Nutcracker, their old king.

"Oh," cried Sugardolly, "may I not go to the castle? May I not see my dear Nutcracker? I have been your queen for a long time. May I not be released?"

So the dwarfs saw that Sugardolly would be no longer happy with them, in spite of the honey, the gold furniture, and the stories, so they bowed their heads sadly and said, "Yes," to her.

"But you must not go alone," they said, "we will take you as far as the castle hedge, and guard you from the cat and leave you there, Sugardolly."

So, early in the morning, a wonderful procession set out for the castle. At the head marched the dwarf who knew the way to the place where Nutcracker had been seen. Behind, marched three other dwarfs, carrying Sugardolly on their shoulders, and last of all came the rest of the dwarfs with their swords at their sides, ready to attack the fierce cat.

But they did not meet the cat, and they reached the lodge in safety. There they set Sugardolly down, very carefully, and said, "Good-by," to her very sadly, for they were sorry indeed to lose their queen.

Then Sugardolly crept under the castle hedge, and hurried across the garden to the kitchen, and tried the kitchen door, but it was locked. So she went in the cellar window, and climbed the cellar stairs, and many more stairs, until she found herself in a great warm room. There was a wide fireplace, and a white bed where a little girl lay fast asleep, as it was still early morning. In the corner of the room there rose a little figure, wearing a hussar's jacket and having a huge and wide mouth.

"Ah, my dear Nutcracker," said Sugardolly, running over to him, with her arms spread wide.

"My dear little Sugardolly," cried Nutcracker, taking her tenderly in his arms.

Just then the little girl awoke, and sat up in bed, and rubbed her eyes to see the little lady in her silk skirts and dancing shoes. Sugardolly began to dance for joy, and the little girl clapped her hands.

"Such a tiny, pretty little thing," said the little girl. "You shall live with us, and be my doll."

So that is how Sugardolly found Nutcracker.

VII

The castle children loved Sugardolly dearly. She sang them all the songs she had learned from the bees, and the birds, and the gold bugs. She told them about the party at the palace of the Fairy Rosebush, and her housekeeping in the cave of the dwarfs.

And Nutcracker, for once in his life, was useful. He was able to climb up to the high places in the garden and fetch down the toys when they were lost—the hoop, the ball, and the shuttlecock. So the children fed

Nutcracker all the nuts he could eat, and Sugardolly all the sugar she wished, and matters went very well for a while. But, after a little, the time drew near to Christmas. In the corner cupboard of the castle play-room there was a mouse hole, and through the mouse hole for weeks before Christmas came the Fairy Honey-mouth, bringing chains of sugar corn, and silver cobwebs, and gold nuts for the Christmas tree.

Now, the castle children never opened the door of the corner cupboard, for they knew that they should not. But Nutcracker and Sugardolly grew very curious, and, because they had not good manners, one night, when the whole castle was asleep, they opened the door. They saw the gold nuts and the silver cobwebs, and they found the mouse hole.

"Let us go through this dark passage," said Nut-cracker, "and see where it ends."

So the two squeezed themselves through the mouse hole and hurried along until they reached the end of the passage. And there they found themselves in the most beautiful place—the garden of their god-mother, the Fairy Honeymouth. There was the same silver fence, and the gold lattice gate, the tree with the great green nuts on one side, and the sugar tree on the other, the birds singing, and sugar, sugar everywhere.

They forgot all about the castle children who had been so kind to them. Nutcracker began pulling out the birds' tail feathers to stick in his cap. He climbed the trees, and shook down all the nuts. Sugardolly filled her pockets and her shoes with sugar, and began tearing up by their roots the sugar flowers.

"Don't do it. Don't do it," sang the birds sadly, as they had sung once before to the peddler and his wife, but Nutcracker and Sugardolly did not heed them. They went on spoiling the garden.

Then, out of her palace in a rage came their godmother, the Fairy Honeymouth.

"Naughty Nutcracker, naughty Sugardolly, to run away so often," said the Fairy Honeymouth. She touched them with her wand. "You," she said to Nutcracker, "shall be turned to wood, and crack nuts all your life, but never eat another." And to Sugardolly she said, "You shall be turned to a sugar doll." And that is what happened to Nutcracker and Sugardolly.

Upon Christmas morning the castle children opened the door of the corner cupboard. Oh, the wonder of it! All the old toys were gone, and new ones stood in their places. In glittering splendor stood the Christmas tree hung with sugar chains, and silver cobwebs and gold nuts. And listen! On the tip top of the tree stood Sugardolly, her hair still curled, her skirts still outspread, and she was still wearing her dancing shoes, but her hair, and her skirts, and her shoes were made of pink sugar. And beneath Sugardolly, his great head peering out from the branches, his jacket tidily buttoned, and his wide mouth open, ready to crack the Christmas nuts that he might never eat, hung Nutcracker, all made of wood.

The news reached the cock who lived in the peddler's barnyard, and he mounted to the highest church steeple in town to try to see what had become of his old friend Nutcracker. And the cock stands there still, blown by all the winds of heaven, for he was not able to climb down again. And when the nights are chill and frost flies, when the storms beat against the window-pane, little children sit by the fire and tell the true stories of Nutcracker and Sugardolly, who had so many adventures, and who will hang on the Christmas tree as long as children believe in fairies.

A CHILD IN A MEXICAN GARDEN*
GRACE H. CONKLING

My garden-ground is very green,
With little streaks of light between,
And walls all made of white and red
Hold up the sky above my head.

I think sometimes that walls so high
Will never let the clouds get by;
But always, somehow and at last,
Over they slide and travel past.

*Taken from *Everybody's Magazine*.

III

The Right Time to Laugh*

An Australian Tale

In a dense Australian thicket, a lyre-bird that had been scratching and pecking about in a little round hillock, once found a choice bit of food. So he spread out his beautiful tail and began to rejoice.

Just then, along came a great, green frog.

"Good morning, my friend," said the frog, and he sat very solemnly by, waiting to be asked to share the feast. But the lyre-bird, instead of asking the frog to dine with him, took his food and flew up into the branch of a tree.

At last the great, green frog said:

"My friend, yesterday you dined at my house; have you not a small morsel to spare today for me?"

"Oh, yes!" said the lyre-bird, for he did not wish to appear so greedy as he was, "certainly you may have a bite of my food. Come right up here and help yourself."

"But how can I come up to you?" said the frog. "I have no wings with which to fly, and my feet were not made for climbing."

Looking about him, the lyre-bird spied a vine hanging down from the tree on which he was perched, and trailing one end on the ground.

"Oh, take hold of that vine," said he, "and I will pull you up."

So the great, green frog caught hold of the vine

and the lyre-bird pulled him up slowly till he was on a level with the branch where the lyre-bird was sitting.

"I thank you, my friend," said the frog, and was just about to hop down beside the food he desired, when the lyre-bird suddenly loosened his hold of the vine and let the frog down, plump! to the ground.

Then the lyre-bird, thinking he had played a very fine joke on his friend, laughed and laughed, and ate up his dinner all by himself.

But the great, green frog who had been badly shaken up and greatly disappointed, sat down below and thought of the injury done him till he could see nothing else.

"The lyre-bird played a wicked prank at my expense," said he, "and I shall repay him as he deserves."

So he hopped off to the neighboring river where the lyre-bird got his water, and drank and drank. He drank till he swallowed not only all the water in that river, but all the water in all the rivers and lakes in Australia! Then he sat, quite puffed out with what he had done, and solemnly blinked his eyes.

Soon the lyre-bird was in great distress for want of water, and sufficiently punished to be very sorry for what he had done. And alas! not only was he punished for his fault, but all the rest of the birds and beasts on the whole continent were made to suffer, too.

One by one, they went to the great, green frog and begged him to give out the waters again. Dingo, the wild-dog, went; Spiny, the ant-eater, went; Flying-fox, the great bat, went; Brush-tail, the opossum, went. And they said:

"Great frog, the lyre-bird has done you wrong, but now he is sorry for what he has done, and you are making all of us suffer who did you no wrong at all. Give forth the waters again, we pray you."

Still the great frog answered never a word.

Then the lyre-bird himself went before him and humbly begged his pardon.

But the frog held as stubbornly as ever to the thought of the wrong the lyre-bird had done, and would not forgive him. He sat as puffed up as before, and solemnly blinked his eyes.

Then the great, black swan went before him, and the white eagle, and the emu, and the parrots, and all the other birds and beasts. But, no matter how they besought him, he would not give back the water.

So at length the birds and the beasts got together and said:

"If the old frog only knew how ridiculous he is, sulking away, he would laugh at himself, and then the waters would gush from his mouth."

"Ah!" cried the ant-eater. "If that is the case, let us *make* him laugh and give up the rivers."

So they all stood in a circle about the solemn old frog and performed their funniest antics. First they brought out the duck-billed mole and they backed him up to the frog. When, from the mole's furry back, Mr. Frog was expecting the face of a beast, they turned him quickly around, and showed his absurd flat bill like a duck's, in the place where his snout ought to be! It was enough to make one scream with laughter, but the great, green frog never smiled the least little smile. He sat there as silent as ever and solemnly blinked his eyes.

Then they brought out the kangaroo. He leaped and jumped about on his long hind legs, with his short fore-legs pawing the air in the most ridiculous way, but still the solemn old frog never smiled the least little smile.

At last, at last they brought out an eel. The eel stood up on the very tip of his tail and danced. At that, the corners of the frog's mouth began to turn up; his lips began to twitch, his nose began to wrinkle, and then, all of a sudden, he opened his mouth and let out a mighty laugh. "Hah, hah! Hah, hah! Hah,

hah!'' He laughed and he laughed and he laughed, and, as he laughed, the waters gushed forth from his mouth and filled up the rivers and lakes.

"I was a silly old frog to sulk!" he cried.

Then the lyre-bird, and the wild-dog, and the ant-eater, and the flying-fox, and the opossum, and the black swan, and the white eagle, and the emu, and the parrots, and the duck-billed mole, and the kangaroo all hurried to get the drink which they had so sorely needed.

Legend of the Water Lily
An Ojibway Tale

A long, long time ago the great forests were filled with happy Indians. All the red men did what was right, so there were no wars among them, and the wild animals were tame, for no man thought to harm them. There was no winter then, but only one long summer; every tree and bush yielded fruit; the earth was covered with brilliant flowers; bright birds made music in the trees; and no man needed anything, for all men's wants were richly supplied.

In those happy times, the Indians sat outside their wigwams every night on the broad prairies and watched the stars. They loved to follow with their eyes those shining wanderers in the great dusky vault of the sky.

One night the red men noticed a star that shone far, far more brightly than all the others. Suddenly it seemed to leave the sky and drop half way down to the earth. There it stopped and hung like a bird of fire over a mountain peak to the southward. Night after night the Indians watched that star and knew not what it could mean. At last they sent out a number of braves to see if they could reach it. The braves made the journey, but they returned to say: "Though the shining thing does indeed hang in the top of a great pine tree on the mountain, we could learn nothing more about it."

For one whole moon the Indians wondered. Then it happened that a certain brave had a dream. A lovely maiden, white and silvery as the star, seemed to stand at his side and she said:

"This is a beautiful world in which you live, young brave. I love your birds and your flowers, your smiling lakes, your rushing rivers, your leaping waterfalls. I love your tall, green mountains, but best of all, I love your people and the little children that play in your villages. So I have left off wandering in the sky, and am come to find rest and a home among you. Ask your wise men what form I shall take, and where I shall dwell, that your people may love me always."

The young man awoke. The maiden had vanished, but as he stepped to the door of his wigwam, he saw the star just where it had been before, hanging over the mountain top.

So the young brave called all the older men to the council, and when they were sitting about on the ground in a circle, he told them his dream.

"The star would dwell among us," they said. "She

is welcome. Let her choose what form she will. She may live in the top of the pine tree or in the heart of a flower. Her home shall be wherever she finds rest."

Then they filled their peace pipes with sweet-smelling herbs, and sent up the fragrant smoke as a greeting to the star. The next night five young braves set out to welcome the shining maiden to the earth. When they returned, she was trailing softly behind them, and all through the night till the break of day, she hovered above their wigwams, flooding the village with a soft, gentle light.

With the dawn, she crept into the heart of a rose on the mountain side and said, "This shall be my home." But ere many days had passed, she learned that up there on the mountain she was too far away from the people she loved; the children seldom visited her. So she rose again and floated down to dwell in a flower on the prairie. Alas! There on the prairie great herds of buffalo came rushing by; the star was always a-tremble at the sound of their trampling hoofs. "Here is no place to rest," she said.

Then the wise men saw her rise once again and they feared lest she would go back after all to the sky. But, as the soft breeze bore her over the lake, she saw her own reflection floating peacefully on the quiet waters, and beside it, so peaceful, too, the reflections of her sisters who lived up above and wandered about in the sky.

"Ah, sisters, sisters, come down! come down to these quiet waters with me!" she cried. "Here let us be at rest—here where the gliding canoes of the people we love float by, and the children play all the day. Come down! Come down!"

The next morning the Indians found hundreds of beautiful white water lilies floating bright on the surface of the lake.

"The stars have come down to live with us!" cried the children. They handled the lilies gently and said: "We will make them glad that they chose their homes on the earth."

INDIAN CHILDREN*
BY ANNETTE WYNNE

Where we walk to school each day,
Indian children used to play—
All about our native land,
Where the shops and houses stand.

And the trees were very tall,
And there were no streets at all,
Not a church and not a steeple—
Only woods and Indian people.

Only wigwams on the ground,
And at night bears prowling round—
What a different place to-day
Where we live and work and play!

*From *For Days and Days*, published by Frederick A. Stokes Company.

121

DUCKS' DITTY*
KENNETH GRAHAME

All along the backwater,
Through the rushes tall,
Ducks are a-dabbling,
Up tails all!

Ducks' tails, drakes' tails,
Yellow feet a-quiver,
Yellow bills all out of sight,
Busy in the river!

Slushy green undergrowth
Where the roach swim—
Here we keep our larder,
Cool and full and dim.

Every one for what he likes!
We like to be
Heads down, tails up,
Dabbling free!

*From *Wind in the Willows;* copyright, 1908, 1913, by Charles Scribner's Sons.

Clytie*

FLORA J. COOKE

Clytie was not always a sunflower, turning on her stem to watch the journeying sun.

Long ago she was a water nymph and lived in a cave at the bottom of the sea. The walls of the cave were covered with pearls and lovely pink sea shells. The floor was made of snow-white sand, and the chairs were of amber, with soft, mossy cushions.

On each side of the cave opening was a forest of coral and sea fans. Behind the cave were Clytie's gardens. Here she spent long hours taking care of her sea anemones, her star lilies, or in planting rare kinds of seaweed. Clytie kept her favorite horses in the garden grotto. These were the swift-darting gold fish and the slow-moving turtles.

For a long time she was very happy and contented.

*From *Nature Myths and Stories*, copyrighted and published by A. Flanagan Company, Chicago.

The sea nymphs loved Clytie, and wove for her dresses of the softest of green sea lace. They told her all their best stories.

One day they took her to the mermaid's rock to hear the mermaid sing. Clytie liked one song best of all. It told of a glorious light which shone on the top of the water. After Clytie heard this song, she could think of nothing else, but longed day and night to see the wonderful light. But no ocean nymph dared take her to it, and she grew very unhappy. Soon she neglected her garden and all her sea treasures.

In vain the nymphs begged her to forget the enchanting light. They told her no sea nymph had ever seen it, or ever could hope to see it. But Clytie would not listen, and to escape them she spent more and more of her time in her shell carriage, riding far away from her cave. In this way she could dream, undisturbed, of the glorious light which the mermaid had called the "sun."

Now it happened that late one summer night, when the sea was warm and the turtles were going very slowly, Clytie fell asleep. Unguided, the turtles went on and on and up and up, through the green waters, until they came out at last close to a wooded island.

As the waves dashed the carriage against the shore, Clytie awoke. Trembling and filled with wonder she climbed out of the shell and sat down upon a rock.

It was early dawn, and the waking world was very beautiful. Clytie had never seen the trees and the

flowers. She had never heard the birds chirping, or the forest wind rustling the leaves. She had never smelled the fragrance of the meadows, or seen the morning dew upon the grass.

She was dazed by all these wonders, and thought she must be dreaming, but soon she forgot all about them, for the eastern sky blazed suddenly with light. Great purple curtains were lifted, and slowly a great ball of dazzling fire appeared, blinding her eyes with its beauty. She held her breath and stretched out her arms toward it, for she knew at once that this was the glorious light she had dreamed about and longed for. This was the sun.

In the midst of the light was a golden chariot, drawn by four fiery steeds, and in the chariot sat a wonderful, smiling King, with seven rays of light playing around his crown.

As the steeds mounted higher and higher in their path, the birds began to sing, the plants opened their buds, and even the old sea looked happy.

Clytie sat all day upon the rock, her eyes fixed upon the sun with a great love and longing in her heart.

She wept when the chariot disappeared in the west and darkness came over the earth. The next day from sunrise to sunset she gazed upon the sun, and at night she refused to go home. For nine days and nights she sat with her golden hair unbound, tasting neither food nor drink, only longing more and more for the smile of the glorious King. She called to him and stretched out her arms, yet she had no hope that he would ever notice her or know of the great love that filled her heart.

On the tenth morning, when she leaned over the water, she was amazed, for instead of her own face, a beautiful flower looked up at her from the sea. She gazed long, and at length in wonder she knew the truth. Her yellow hair had become golden petals, her green dress had turned into leaves and stems, and her little feet had become roots which fastened her to the ground. Clytie had become the small and humble image of the sun.

The next morning, when she lifted her face to the beautiful light, it was so radiant with happiness that the great King himself seemed to smile back kindly at the happy little flower.

And so Clytie began her life upon the earth, and she became the mother of a large family of flowers with bright faces like her own. Her children are called sunflowers, and you may find them scattered all over the country, even in the dry and dusty places where other flowers will not grow.

And if you care to, you may find out for yourselves whether or not it is true that all the sunflowers in the world turn upon their stalks, from sunrise until sunset, so that they may always keep their faces toward the sun.

How the Brazilian Beetles Got Their Gorgeous Coats*

ELSIE SPICER EELLS

In Brazil the beetles have beautiful, coloured, hard-shelled coats upon their backs like precious stones. Once upon a time, years and years ago, they had ordinary plain, brown coats. This is how it happened that the Brazilian beetle earned a new coat.

One day a little brown beetle was crawling along a wall when a big grey rat ran out of a hole in the wall and looked down scornfully at the little beetle. "O ho!" he said to the beetle, "how slowly you crawl along. You'll never get anywhere in the world. Just look at me and see how fast I can run."

The big grey rat ran to the end of the wall, wheeled around, and came back to the place where the little beetle was slowly crawling along at only a tiny distance from where the rat had left her.

*Taken from *Fairy Tales from Brazil*. Copyright, 1917, by Dodd, Mead & Company, Inc.

"Don't you wish that you could run like that?" said the big grey rat to the little brown beetle.

"You are surely a fast runner," replied the little brown beetle, politely. Her mother had taught her always to be polite and had often said to her that a really polite beetle never boasts about her own accomplishments. The little brown beetle never boasted a single boast about the things she could do. She just went on slowly crawling along the wall.

A bright green and gold parrot in the mango tree over the wall had heard the conversation. "How would you like to race with the beetle?" he asked the big grey rat. "I live next door to the tailor bird," he added, "and just to make the race exciting I'll offer a bright coloured coat as a prize to the one who wins the race. You may choose for it any colour you like and I'll have it made to order."

"I'd like a yellow coat with stripes like the tiger's," said the big grey rat, looking over his shoulder at his gaunt grey sides, as if he were already admiring his new coat.

"I'd like a beautiful, bright coloured, new coat, too," said the little brown beetle.

The big grey rat laughed long and loud until his gaunt grey sides were shaking. "Why, you talk just as if you thought you had a chance to win the race," he said, when he could speak.

The bright green and gold parrot set the royal palm

tree at the top of the cliff as the goal of the race. He gave the signal to start and then he flew away to the royal palm tree to watch for the end of the race.

The big grey rat ran as fast as he could. Then he thought how very tired he was getting. "What's the use of hurrying?" he said to himself. "The little brown beetle can not possibly win. If I were racing with some-body who could really run, it would be very different." Then he started to run more slowly, but every time his heart beat, it said, "Hurry up! Hurry up!" The big grey rat decided that it was best to obey the little voice in his heart, so he hurried just as fast as he could.

When he reached the royal palm tree at the top of the cliff he could hardly believe his eyes. He thought he must be having a bad dream. There was the little brown beetle sitting quietly beside the bright green and gold parrot. The big grey rat had never been so sur-prised in all his life. "How did you ever manage to run fast enough to get here so soon?" he asked the little brown beetle as soon as he could catch his breath.

The little brown beetle drew out the tiny wings from her sides. "Nobody said anything about having to *run* to win the race," she replied, "so I *flew* instead."

"I did not know that you could fly," said the big grey rat in a subdued little voice.

"After this," said the bright green and gold parrot, "never judge any one by his looks alone. You never can tell how often or where you may find concealed wings.

You have lost the prize and the beetle has won it."

Until this day, even in Brazil where the flowers and birds, and beasts, and insects have such gorgeous colouring, the rat wears a plain, dull grey coat.

Then the parrot turned to the little brown beetle who was waiting quitely at his side. "What colour do you want your new coat to be?" he asked.

The little brown beetle looked up at the bright green and gold parrot, at the green and gold palm trees above their heads, at the green mangoes with golden flushes on their cheeks, lying on the ground under the mango trees, at the golden sunshine upon the distant green hills. "I choose a coat of green and gold," she said.

From that day to this, the Brazilian beetle has worn a coat of green, with golden lights upon it.

For years and years the Brazilian beetles were all very proud to wear green and gold coats like that of the beetle who raced with the rat.

Then, once upon a time, it happened that there was a little beetle who grew discontented with her coat of green and gold. She looked up at the blue sky and out at the blue sea and wished that she had a blue coat instead. She talked about it so much that finally her mother took her to the parrot who lived next door to the tailor bird.

"You may change your coat for a blue one," said the parrot, "but if you change you'll have to give up something."

"Oh, I'll gladly give up anything if only I may have a blue coat instead of a green and gold one," said the discontented little beetle.

When she received her new coat she thought it was very beautiful. It was a lovely shade of blue and it had silvery white lights upon it like the light of the stars. When she put it on, however, she discovered that it was not hard like the green and gold one. From that day to this the blue beetles' coats have not been hard and firm.

From the moment that the little beetle put on her new blue coat she never grew again. From that day to this the blue beetles have been much smaller than the green and gold ones.

When the Brazilians made their flag, they took for it a square of green, the colour of the green beetle's coat. Within this square they placed a diamond of gold like the golden lights which play upon the green beetle's back. Then, within the diamond, they drew a circle to represent the round earth and they coloured it blue like the coat of the blue beetle. Upon the blue circle they placed stars of silvery white like the silvery white lights on the back of the blue beetle. About the blue circle of the earth which they thus pictured they drew a band of white, and upon this band they wrote the motto of their country, *"Ordem e Progresso,"*—order and progress.

UP ONE PAIR OF STAIRS

Little Goody Two-Shoes

AN INCIDENT from the Story
ASCRIBED TO OLIVER GOLDSMITH

All the world must know that Two-Shoes was not her real name. No; her father's name was Meanwell and he was for many years a farmer in the parish where Margery was born; but Margery and her little brother Tommy, were early left alone to the wide world.

It would have done your heart good to have seen how these two little ones were so fond of each other, and how hand in hand they trotted about.

They were both very ragged, and Tommy had no shoes, and Margery had but one. They had nothing, poor things, to support them but what they picked from the hedges, or got from the poor people, and they lay every night in a barn.

Mr. Smith was a very worthy clergyman, who lived in the parish where Little Margery and Tommy were born; and having a relation come to see him, who was a charitable, good man, he sent these children to him. The gentleman ordered Little Margery a new pair of shoes, gave Mr. Smith some money to buy her clothes, and said he would take Tommy and make him a little sailor.

After some days the gentleman intended to go to London, and take little Tommy with him.

The parting between these little children was very affecting. Tommy cried, and they kissed each other a hundred times; at last Tommy wiped off his sister's tears with the end of his jacket, and bid her cry no more, for that he would come to her again when he returned from sea.

As soon as Little Margery got up the next morning she began crying for her brother. However, at this instant, the shoemaker came in with the new shoes, for which she had been measured by the gentleman's order.

Nothing could have helped Little Margery to bear the parting with her brother but the pleasure she took in her two shoes. She ran out to Mrs. Smith as soon as they were put on, and, stroking down her ragged apron, thus cried out, "Two shoes, ma'am, see two shoes." And so she behaved to all the people she met, and by that means obtained the name of Goody Two-Shoes.

Little Margery was very happy in being with Mr. and Mrs. Smith.

She saw how good and how wise Mr. Smith was, and concluded that this was owing to his great learning, therefore she wanted of all things to learn to read. For this purpose she used to meet the little boys as they came from school, borrow their books, and sit down and read till they returned. By this means she got more learning than any of her playmates, and laid the following scheme for instructing those who knew less than herself. With her knife she cut out of wood ten sets of these letters:

a b c d e f g h i j k l m n o p q r s t u v w x y z

And having got an old spelling book, she made her companions set up all the words they wanted to spell.

I once went her rounds with her, and was highly diverted.

It was about seven o'clock in the morning when we set out on this important business, and the first house we came to was Farmer Wilson's. Here Margery stopped, and ran to the door, tap, tap, tap. "Who's there?" "Only Little Goody Two-Shoes," answered Margery, "come to teach Billy." "Oh! Little Goody," says Mrs. Wilson, with pleasure in her face, "I am glad to see you. Billy wants you sadly, for he has learned his lesson." Then out came a little

boy. "How do, Doody Two-Shoes," says he, not able to speak plain. Yet this little boy had learned all his letters; for she threw down this alphabet mixed together thus:

b d f h k m o q s u w y x j a c e g i l n p r t v z

and he picked them up, called them by their right names, and put them all in order thus:

a b c d e f g h i j k l m n o p q r s t u v w x y z.

The next place we came to was Farmer Simpson's.

"Bow, wow, wow," says the dog at the door. "Sirrah," says his mistress, "why do you bark at Little Two-Shoes? Come in, Madge; here, Sally wants you sadly, she has learned all her lesson." "Yes, that's what I have," replied the little one, in the country manner; and immediately taking the letters she set up these syllables:

ba be bi bo bu,   ca ce ci co cu,
da de di do du,   fa fe fi fo fu,

and gave them their exact sound as she composed them.

The next place we came to was Gaffer Cook's cottage. Here a number of poor children were met to learn, who all came round Little Margery at once. Having pulled out her letters, she asked the little boy next her what he had for dinner. He answered, "Bread." "Well, then," says she, "set up the first letter." He put up the B, to which the next child added r, and the next e, the next a, the next d, and it stood thus, Bread.

"And what had you, Polly Comb, for your dinner?" "Apple pie," answered the little girl; upon which they set up these words with many others, till the game of spelling was finished. Margery then set them another task, and we proceeded.

So Little Goody Two-Shoes kept herself busy, learning and teaching, until her brother Tommy, after many adventures, returned to her again from sea, and brought back treasures enough to make them both comfortable and happy.

THE WANDERER'S NIGHT SONG
JOHANN WOLFGANG VON GOETHE

Over all the hilltops
Is peace;
In all the treetops
Noises cease;
There's scarce a breeze;
The birds in the woods are still;
Wait then until
You, too, shall sleep.

137

The Story of Li'l' Hannibal*

TRANSCRIBED BY CAROLYN SHERWIN BAILEY

Once on a time, 'way down South, there lived a
little boy named Hannibal, *Li'l'* Hannibal.   He lived,
along with his gran'mammy and his gran'daddy in a
li'l' one-story log cabin that was set right down in a cotton
field.   Well, from morning until night Li'l' Hannibal's
gran'mammy kept him toting things.   As soon as
he woke up in the morning it was:

"Oh, Li'l' Hannibal, fetch a pine knot and light the
kitchen fire."

"Oh, Li'l' Hannibal, fetch the teakettle to the well
and get some water for the tea."

"Oh, Li'l' Hannibal, mix a li'l' hoecake for your gran'-
daddy's brea'fus'."

"Oh, Li'l' Hannibal, take the bunch of turkeys' feathers
and dust the hearth."

And from morning until night Li'l' Hannibal's
gran'daddy kept him toting things, too.

"Oh, Li'l' Hannibal," his gran'daddy would say, "fetch
the corn and feed the turkeys."

"Oh, Li'l' Hannibal, take your li'l' ax and chop some
light wood for your gran'mammy's fire."

"Oh, Li'l' Hannibal, run 'round to the store and buy
a bag of flour."

"Oh, Li'l' Hannibal, fetch your basket and pick a
li'l' cotton off the edge of the field."

*Used by the courteous permission of *Good Housekeeping.*

So they kept poor little Hannibal toting 'most all day long, and he had only four or five hours to play.

Well, one morning Li'l' Hannibal woke up and he made up his mind to something. Before they could ask him to light the kitchen fire, or fill the teakettle, or mix the hoecake, or dust the hearth, or feed the turkeys, or chop any wood, or go to the store, or pick any cotton, he had made up his mind that he was not going to tote for his gran'mammy and his gran'daddy any longer. He was going to run away!

So Li'l' Hannibal got out of bed very quietly. He put on his li'l' trousers and his li'l' shirt and his li'l' suspenders and his li'l' shoes—he never wore stockings. He pulled his li'l' straw hat down tight over his ears and then—Li'l' Hannibal ran away!

He went down the road past all the cabins. He went under the fence and across the cotton fields. He went through the pine grove past the schoolhouse, stooping down low so the schoolmistress wouldn't see him, and then he went 'way, 'way off in the country.

When he was a long way from town Li'l' Hannibal met a Possum, loping along by the edge of the road, and the Possum stopped and looked at Li'l' Hannibal.

"How do? Where you goin', Li'l' Hannibal?" asked the Possum.

Li'l' Hannibal sat down by the side of the road and he took off his straw hat to fan himself, for he felt quite warm, and he said:

"I done run away, Br'er Possum. My gran'mammy and my gran'daddy kep' me totin', totin' for them all the time. I doesn't like to work, Br'er Possum."

"Po' Li'l' Hannibal!" said the Possum, sitting up and scratching himself. "Any special place you boun' for?"

"I don't reckon so," said Li'l' Hannibal, for he was getting tired and he had come away without any breakfast.

"You come along of me, Li'l' Hannibal," said the Possum; "I reckon I kin take you somewhere."

UP ONE PAIR OF STAIRS

So the Possum and Li'l' Hannibal went along together, the Possum loping along by the side of the road, and Li'l' Hannibal going very slowly in the middle of the road, for his shoes were full of sand and it hurt his toes. They went on and on until they came, all at once, to a sort of open space in the woods and then they stopped. There was a big company there—Br'er Rabbit, and Br'er Partridge, and Br'er Jay Bird, and Br'er Robin, and Ol' Miss Guinea Hen.

"Here's Po' Li'l' Hannibal come to see you," said the Possum. "Li'l' Hannibal done run away from his gran'mammy and his gran'daddy."

Li'l' Hannibal hung his head like as if he was ashamed, but nobody noticed him. They were all as busy as ever they could be, so he just sat down on a pine stump and watched them.

Each one had his own special work and he was keeping at it right smart. Br'er Robin was gathering all the holly berries from the south side of the holly tree and singing as he worked:

"Cheer up, cheer-u-u!"

Br'er Partridge was building a new house.

Br'er Jay Bird was taking corn Down Below. You know that is what Br'er Jay Bird does all the time: takes one kernel of corn in his bill to the people Down Below and then comes back for another. It is a very long trip to take with one kernel of corn, but Br'er Jay Bird doesn't seem to mind.

Ol' Miss Guinea Hen was about the busiest of the whole company, for she was laying eggs. As soon as ever she had laid one she would get up on a low branch and screech, "Catch it! Catch it! Catch it!" like to deafen everybody. But Li'l' Hannibal was most interested to see what Br'er Rabbit was doing. Br'er Rabbit had on a li'l' apron, and he kept bringing things in his market basket. Then he cooked the things over a fire back in the bushes, and when it got to be late in the afternoon he spread a tablecloth on a big stump and then he pounded on his stew pan with his soup ladle.

"Supper's ready," said Br'er Rabbit.

Then Br'er Robin and Br'er Partridge and Br'er Jay Bird and Br'er Possum and Ol' Miss Guinea Hen all scrambled to their places at the table and Li'l' Hannibal tried to find a place to sit at, but there wasn't any for him.

"Po' Li'l' Hannibal!" said Br'er Rabbit as he poured out the soup. "Doesn't like work. Cyan't have no supper!"

"Catch him! Catch him!" said Ol' Miss Guinea Hen, but no one did it. They were all too busy eating.

They had a grand supper. There was breakfast strip, and roast turkey, and fried chicken, and mutton,

and rice and hominy, and sweet potatoes, and peas, and beans, and baked apples, and cabbage, and hoe-cake and hot biscuit, and corn muffins, and butter cakes, and waffles, and maple syrup.

When they were through eating it was quite dark, and they all went home, even Br'er Possum, and they left Li'l' Hannibal sitting there all by himself.

Well, after a while it began to get darker. Br'er Mocking Bird came out, and he looked at Li'l' Hannibal and then he began to scream, just like Ol' Miss Guinea

Hen: "Catch him! Catch him! Catch him! Catch him!"

Br'er Screech Owl looked down from a tree and he said very hoarsely:

"Who! Who! Who-oo!"

Then all the frogs began to say, loud and shrill, "Li'l' Hannibal! Li'l' Hannibal!"

So Li'l' Hannibal got up from his pine stump and he said, "I reckon I better go home to my gran'mammy."

Well, Li'l' Hannibal started for home, slowly, because his feet hurt and he was hungry. When he came to the pine grove by the schoolhouse the shadows came out from behind the trees and followed him, and that was much worse than seeing the schoolmistress. But Li'l' Hannibal got away from them all right. He crawled under the fence and ran across the cotton field and there in the door of the cabin was his gran'-daddy with a lantern. His gran'daddy had been out looking for Li'l' Hannibal.

"Why, Li'l' Hannibal, where you been all day?" asked his gran'daddy.

"Why, Li'l' Hannibal," said his gran'mammy, "here's your corn mush. I kep' it warm on the hearth, but afore you eat your supper, Li'l' Hannibal, jus' take your li'l' basket and run roun' to the chicken house for a couple of eggs."

So Li'l' Hannibal took his li'l' basket and he started off for those eggs, singing all the way. You see, he reckoned he was mighty glad to be at home and toting again.

A Story about the Little Rabbits*

Joel Chandler Harris

"Fine um whar you will en w'en you may," remarked Uncle Remus with emphasis, "good chilluns allers gits tuck keer on. Dar wuz Brer Rabbit's chilluns; dey minded der daddy en mammy fum day's een' ter day's een'. W'en ole man Rabbit say 'scoot,' dey scooted, en w'en ole Miss Rabbit say 'scat,' dey scatted. Dey did dat. En dey kep der cloze clean, en dey ain't had no smut on der nose nudder."

Involuntarily the hand of the little boy went up to his face, and he scrubbed the end of his nose with his coat sleeve.

"Dey wuz good chilluns," continued the old man heartily, "en ef dey hadn't er bin, der wuz one time w'en dey wouldn't er bin no little rabbits—na'er one. Dat's w'at."

"What time was that, Uncle Remus?" the little boy asked.

"De time w'en Brer Fox drapt in at Brer Rabbit's house, en didn't foun' nobody dar ceppin' de little Rabbits. Ole Brer Rabbit he wuz off some'rs raidin' on a collard patch, en ole Miss Rabbit she wuz tendin' on a quiltin' in de naberhood, en wiles de little Rabbits wuz playin' hidin'-switch, in drapt Brer Fox. De little Rabbits wuz so fat dat dey fa'rly made his mouf water, but he 'member 'bout Brer Wolf, en he

*From *Uncle Remus, his Songs and his Sayings.* Used by permission of D. Appleton & Company.

skeered fer ter gobble um up ceppin' he got some 'skuse. De little Rabbits, dey mighty skittish, en dey sorter huddle deyse'f up tergedder en watch Brer Fox' motions. Brer Fox, he set dar en study w'at sorter 'skuse he gwinter make up. Bimeby he see a great big stalk er sugar-cane stan'in' up in de cornder, en he cl'ar up his throat en talk biggity: 'Yer! you young Rabs dar, sail 'roun' yer en broke me a piece er dat sweetin' tree,' sezee, en den he koff.

"De little Rabbits, dey got out de sugar-cane, dey did, en dey rastle wid it, en sweat over it, but twan't no use. Dey couldn't broke it. Brer Fox, he make like he ain't watchin', but he keep on holler'n':

" 'Hurry up dar, Rabs! I'm a waitin' on you.'

"En de little Rabbits, dey hustle 'roun' en rastle wid it, but dey couldn't broke it. Bimeby dey hear little bird singin' on top er de house, en de song w'at de little bird sing wuz dish yer,

" 'Take you toofies en gnyaw it,
Take you toofies en saw it,
Saw it en yoke it,
En den you kin broke it.'

"Den de little Rabbits dey git mighty glad, en dey gnyawed de cane mos' fo' ole Brer Fox could git his legs oncrosst, en w'en dey kyard 'im de cane, Brer Fox, he sot dar en study how he gwinter make some more 'skuse fer nabbin' un um, en bimeby he git up en git down de sifter w'at wuz hangin' on de wall, en holler out:

" 'Come yer, Rabs! Take dish yer sifter, en run downt' de spring en fetch me some fresh water.'

"De little Rabbits, dey run down t' de spring en try ter dip up de water wid de sifter, but co's hit all run out, en hit keep on runnin' out, twell bimeby de little Rabbits sot down en 'gun ter cry. Den de little bird sittin' up in de trees he begin fer ter sing, en dish yer's de song w'at he sing:

147

" 'Sifter hole water same ez a tray,
Ef you fill it wid moss en dob it wid clay;
De Fox git madder de longer you stay—
Fill it wid moss en dob it wid clay.'

"Up dey jump, de little Rabbits did, en dey fix de sifter so 'twon't leak, en dey kyar de water ter ole Brer Fox. Den Brer Fox he git mighty mad, en p'int out a great big stick er wood, en tell de little Rabbits fer ter put dat on de fier. De little chaps dey got 'roun' de wood, dey did, en dey lif' at it so hard dey could see der own sins, but de wood ain't budge. Den dey hear de little bird singin', en dish yer's de song w'at he sing:

" 'Spit in yo' han's en tug it en toll it,
En git behine it, en push it, en pole it;
Spit in yo' han's en r'ar back en roll it.'

"En des 'bout de time dey got de wood on de fier, der daddy, he come skippin' in, en de little bird, he flew'd away. Brer Fox, he seed his game wuz up, en 'twa'nt long 'fo' he make his 'skuse en start fer ter go.

" 'You better stay en take a snack wid me, Brer Fox,' sez Brer Rabbit, sezee. 'Sense Brer Wolf done quit comin' en settin' up wid me, I gettin' so I feels right lonesome dese long nights,' sezee.

"But Brer Fox, he button up his coat collar tight en des put out fer home. En dat w'at you better do, honey, kase I see Miss Sally's shadder sailin' backerds en for'ds 'fo' de winder, en de fus' news you know she'll be spectin' un you."

Jamie Watt and the Tea Kettle

Jamie Watt, a little Scotch boy, sat by the great fireplace in his grandmother's kitchen. Above the rosy flames there hung an old-fashioned tea kettle.

Jamie had been whittling a piece of wood and making a cart with wheels, but now he dropped his work in his lap. Something had happened to the tea kettle that caught his eye, and he began to watch it closely, for he never let anything strange pass by without finding out the reason for it. The water in the kettle had begun to boil and a little white column of steam was puffing out from its spout. Pretty soon, S-s-s! S-s-s! Piff! Piff! Piff! the lid of the tea kettle began to rattle. S-s-s! S-s-s! Piff! Piff! Piff! something lifted the lid right up in the air!

"O Grandma! Grandma!" cried the boy in great excitement. "What is there inside of your tea kettle?"

Grandma was busy laying the table for supper.

"Nothing but water, Jamie!" she answered.

S-s-s! S-s-s! Piff! Piff! Piff! Up popped the lid again. The boy watched it, breathless with interest.

"But, Grandma, there must be something inside the kettle," he insisted. "See! Something keeps lifting the lid!"

"Ho, ho!" laughed his grandmother. "Perhaps it's a brownie or a pixie you're thinking is in the kettle! No, no! It's only the steam that does the lifting! See clouds of it are puffing out all around the lid."

Now Jamie wasn't thinking at all that it was a brownie or a pixie that was in the kettle. But he was thinking

DONN P. CRANE

that he wanted very much to know what this thing called steam was, that had so much strength and power. Carefully he leaned over and lifted the lid to look inside. Nothing at all could he see but boiling, bubbling water.

"Grandma," he asked, "where does the steam come from? How did it get into the kettle?"

Grandma was used to his questions; he was always wondering about things.

"Why, dearie," she answered, "steam always rises from water whenever water boils."

The boy stood studying the kettle for a little longer, then he sat down again, and while he was thinking he began absent-mindedly spinning the wheels on the little cart he was making. At last he burst out:

"Grandma, if the steam in that kettle is strong enough to lift the lid, why couldn't steam from a great deal more water lift much heavier things? Why—why couldn't it push wheels around?"

"Push wheels around!" Grandma did not even try to answer so absurd a question. Jamie had strange and idle dreams, she thought, and she wished he would spend his time thinking of something more useful than pushing wheels around with steam. But Jamie never left off wondering about the steam just the same, nor was his wondering so idle and useless as his grandmother supposed.

"That steam has the strength of a giant," he used to say to himself. "If I could only find out how to make use of it, it would not only lift heavy weights, but it would make machinery go, and do all sorts of work for men."

So Jamie went on studying and working as he grew to be a man. Many times he made experiments with steam engines and his engines failed to go, but he always learned something new from each failure. Other people thought him foolish and laughed at him.

"Ho, ho! Jamie Watt is going to harness up the clouds that puff out of his granny's tea kettle and make them do the work of a giant!" they would jeer. But in spite of all this, Jamie worked on year after year until at last he did indeed make what no one had thought he could—a steam engine that was a success. And that was the little Scotch boy's great gift to the world.

It was Jamie's engine that made possible the engines that draw trains, push steamboats and turn machinery. Men had lived for thousands of years beside that great giant, Steam, and yet not one of them ever learned how to harness it and make its mighty power of service to man, till one small boy began to wonder how it lifted the lid off the tea kettle in his granny's kitchen.

The Battle of the Frogs and Mice*
RETOLD FROM A CLASSIC GREEK POEM

Hark, while I sing of that dread war between the Mice and Frogs, which caused the heavens to shake as in the days when giants strove on earth.

Once on a time, a gentle mouse, all out of breath and tired with fleeing from a monstrous cat, dropped down to cool his thirst, and dipped his whiskers in a little pool.   Thereat, a frog from out the water popped his head and hoarsely cried:

"Who are you, stranger, and why have you come hither, panting for your breath? If you will tell me truly, you shall find in me a friend. I'll grant you entrance to the pleasures of this lake and you shall wander o'er my palace grounds and feast with me. This silver kingdom of the Pool and all the frogs obey me as their King. Great Swell-the-cheeks am I. My father was King Mud. And you, your form and manner, make me know that you, too, are a a King, son of some warrior-hero. Tell me who you are."

The frog thus ceased to speak and thus the mouse replied: "My name is known to beasts and men and all

*This amusing parody on the martial epic of the Iliad was for years attributed to Homer, but is now believed to have been written a century or so after his time.

the birds that fly. Prince Steal-the-grain am I. My father is King Nibbler-of-the-bread. But now, since you and I are both so different in our natures, how can we be friends? No cheese, nor honey cake, nor gilded bacon, nay, nor bread, can hide itself from me. But stalks and water herbs and all that frogs delight to eat, have no delights for me. Such food no mouse of any taste can bear. And so, farewell."

The downy Prince thus spoke his mind, but still the croaking King did urge:

"Fair stranger, you speak well, yet know that we, the frogs, not only sport in water, but likewise dance on land, and in both places gather food. So trust yourself to make a visit to my kingdom. I myself will bear you through the waters. Only jump up on my shoulders, and I swear that you shall safely reach my marshy court."

He spoke and leaned his back in readiness. Thereon, the mouse, persuaded, lightly leapt with nimble bound, and round the Frog King's neck he clasped his arms. Now, wondering, he glides away and gladly looks about to see the sights on every side. But O alack, when curling waves begin to rise and wet his downy sides, his thoughts grow sad and full of woe. How then he sorrows for the shore! Alack, he cannot swim! His tears flow down; he tears his hair and lifts his trembling feet above the water's angry roll. He sighs and trails his tail behind him in the waves, an oar with which he tries in vain to steady his wild plunging boat.

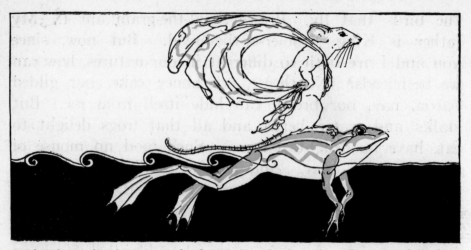

And as he sorrowed thus, lo, from the deep a hissing water snake arose, to roll his bloodshot eyes and dart with active rage along the surface of the pond. The Frog King now beheld that snake, and, all confused at such a sight, he dived to hide himself beneath the waves. Forgetful frog! He took no thought for that new friend whom he was bearing on his back, but pitched him headlong in the deep. Unskilled in swimming and so far from shore, the princely Mouse flings out his arms in vain. He, plunging, sinks and, struggling, mounts again, and sinks and strives, but strives in vain. And these last words from his pale lips resound:

"O traitor, traitor-frog! To fling me floundering from your back! Ye mice, arise and punish this false foe!"

This said, he sank to rise no more.

But now it chanced a gallant mouse, young Lick-the-dish, was loitering on the flowery bank and basking idly in

the sun's bright beams. He sees Prince Steal-the-grain
go down and shrieks aloud. The shores re-echo to his
cries, and thus the Nibbling Nation learns the fate that
has befallen him, their hero-prince. Sad, sorry grief is
now in every mouse's heart. Deep murmurs sound. From
lodge to lodge the sacred heralds run, and summon all
to come at sunrise to the council where in glory reigns
great Nibbler-of-the-bread, their King.

When rosy-fingered morn had tinged the clouds, the
Nation gathered round about their King. Slow he arose
and spoke with heaving breast: "For our lost prince
the father's tears are mine, but public grief is yours.
Plunged in the lake by Swell-the-cheeks, he drowned.
Rouse all our mice to war, my friends. To arms! To arms!"

His words awake a fire in every breast. The mice

WILLY·POGANY

begin to arm. The empty hulls of peas for buskins on their legs they bind, large shells of nuts for helmets on their heads. 'Tis needles that for lances serve the throng. They seize their shields, and so they stalk across the plain, while sunlight glints from all their points of steel. Dreadful in arms the marching mice appear.

And now the wondering frogs perceive a tumult near, and, leaping from the waters, form a ring to hearken whence the noises come. Too soon they see the marching crowd of mice, and there advancing to the fore, the valiant chief, Sir Creeper-into-pots, who bears the sacred herald's scepter in his hand, and thus he speaks:

"Ye frogs, we mice advance to punish your foul crime, for by the hand of Swell-the-cheeks, your King, our hapless Prince was slain. See there all decked in armor how we shake the shining lance! Then arm your host, the doubtful battle try, lead forth those frogs that have the soul to die!"

The chief draws back; the frogs the challenge hear, and, proudly swelling, much resent. Yet still they blame their King who by his thoughtless deed has brought this danger on their heads; but he, unwilling to admit his coward's act, now rising, speaks to clear his name with lies.

"O friends," he cries with false, deceiving tears, "I'm not to blame because their Prince lies drowned beneath the wave. He was a vain, conceited youth who tried our art of swimming out of pride, and being all unable to perform the feat, he sank. It was his fault alone that he was drowned. But now his people shower their anger on my guiltless head. Come, we will turn this war to victory, for I am innocent of any wrong. Now by the water's edge in armor bright we will await the battle shock. Bright shall the waters flash; loud shall the shores resound in honor of the victory of the frogs!"

His warriors hear and take his lies for truth, and so decide to offer battle to the mice.

Green is the suit his arming heroes choose; their glossy helmets are of shells, and tapering sea-reeds form their polished spears. Thus, dressed for war, they take the appointed height.

> *Now front to front the marching armies shine,
> Halt e'er they meet and form the lengthening line;
> The chiefs conspicuous seen and heard afar,
> Give the loud sign to loose the rushing war.
> Their dreadful trumpets, deep-mouthed hornets sound.
> The sounded charge remurmurs o'er the ground.

First to the fight, Loud-brawler-frog now flies, and with his spear he slays brave Lick-stick who with generous flame stands forth before his comrades in the mously line. The luckless warrior of the mice with javelin in breast, falls thundering to the ground. Alack! all soiled in dust his lovely tresses lie!

Now Scamper-into-holes has pierced the great frog hero, Stick-in-mud, a dreadful stroke that strikes dark fear straight to the heart of Cabbage-eater-frog. In headlong flight doth Cabbage-eater run, a frog long used to feasts and dainty fare, but less prepared for trials of pluck

*From Parnell's Translation.

and skill. In headlong flight he runs, and, stumbling o'er the brink, falls in the lake.

And now that mighty mouse, great Robber-of-the-granaries, in glory shines afar. At sight of him the mighty Croaker, Prince of Frogs, takes from the lake a monstrous mass of mud to hurl it at his foe. The cloud of dirt falls showering o'er the warrior mouse, dishonoring his face and blinding his bright eyes. Enraged and wildly spluttering, from the shore the hero Robber grasps a stone immense of size, a stone so great that but to lift its weight would take ten weak, degenerate mice of modern days. He hurls the stone upon his foe and strikes him down.

> Then nobly towering o'er the rest, appears
> A gallant prince, far taller than his years,
> His father's pride, the glory of his house,
> And more a Mars in battle than a mouse,
> His action bold, and strong his powerful frame,
> And Mer-i-dar'-pax his resounding name.
> This warrior, standing forth from out the crowd,
> Boasts the dire honors of his arms aloud;
> Then, strutting near the lake, with looks elate,
> Threats all its nations with approaching fate.

Ah, then it seemed as though the mice would make an end of all the frogs, and leave unpeopled those fair silver lakes. It seemed that all that valiant, green, and freckled race must perish for the sin of one alone, their coward King. Such sorrow had he wrought by treachery and lies.

But he whom men call father Jove, who made both frogs

and mice as well as men, and shows his grace no less to frogs than to the human race, felt softest pity rising in his soul. That mice and frogs should make such worlds of slain! Alack, what gentle croakers lay there dead! Alack, what pretty nibblers would arise no more. And to what end? What purpose had been gained? No end at all, but only sorrow, tears and shame. Thus are the sorry ways of war. So Jove, in pity, hurled the lightning down to bid those warriors stay their horrid fight.

Deep lengthening thunders roll. The hills and mountains quake. But little heed the mice. Still stubborn, they advance, nor even for a thunderbolt will stay their dread design. And since the lightning cannot move those stubborn hearts, great Jove sends other aid.

From out the neighboring shore, he calls a sudden throng.

There comes a band of unexpected warriors pouring o'er the plain. Deformed to view, in suits of armor strong, they come with sidewise wheeling march. Their limbs have harpy claws; dread scissors guard the passage to their mouths; broad spread their shining backs; their round black eye-balls roll within their savage chests. On eight long feet and either way they go, now forward and now back, for at each end they seem to have a head. These warriors men agree to call the crabs.

Now with their harpy claws, they seize the heroes by their tails; they nip their legs; they clip their arms. Confusion falls on all, confusion wild and mad. And from that armored host, in headlong flight, run frogs and mice alike. Across the plain they flee, nor do they stop for breath till they have crept in holes and safely hid themselves from sight.

And thus came to an end the sorry struggle that arose from one unthinking act of treachery. Thus in a single day a war was fought, a whole sad Iliad in the space of one revolving sun.

Doll i' the Grass
A Norse Folk Tale

Once upon a time there was a King who had twelve sons. When they were grown up he told them that they must go out into the world and find themselves wives. These wives, he commanded, must all be able to spin, weave, and make a shirt in a day, else he would not have them for daughters-in-law. He gave each of his sons a horse and a new suit of armor, so they set out into the world to look for brides.

When they had traveled a bit on the way, they said that they would not take Ashiepattle, their youngest brother, with them, for he was good for nothing. So they left the poor youth behind. Ashiepattle did not know what he should do or whither he should turn. He got off his horse, sat down in the grass and began to weep.

When he had sat there a while, lo! one of the tussocks among the grass began to stir and move, and out of it came a small white thing. Ashiepattle's mouth fell open with astonishment. But as the white thing came nearer, he saw it was a charming little lassie, such a tiny bit of a thing, so very, very tiny.

She came up to him and asked him if he would go below with her and pay a visit to the Doll i' the Grass.

Yes, that he would; and so he did. When he came down below, the Doll i' the Grass was sitting in a chair, dressed very finely and looking very beautiful. She asked Ashiepattle whither he was going and what was his errand.

He told her that he was one of twelve brothers, and that the King had given them each a horse and a suit of armor, bidding them go out into the world and find themselves wives.

"But," said he, "each wife must be able to spin, weave, and make a shirt in a day. If you can do that and will become my wife, I will not go a step farther."

So the Doll i' the Grass set to work at once to get the shirt spun, woven, and made, but when it was done, it was so tiny, no bigger than—so.

Ashiepattle took it and returned home. When he brought it out to show his father, he felt very shy because it was so small. But for all that it was perfectly made, so the King said he would have the lady who had made it for his daughter-in-law. You can imagine how happy and joyful Ashiepattle was then.

The road did not seem long to him as he set out to fetch his little bride. When he came to the Doll i' the Grass he wanted to take her up before him on his horse; but no, that she wouldn't; she said she would sit and drive in a silver spoon, and she had two small white horses which would draw her. So they set out, he on his horse and she in the silver spoon, and the horses which drew her were two small white mice.

Ashiepattle always kept to one side of the road, so that he would not ride over her; she was so tiny.

When they had traveled a bit on the way they came to

a large pond; there Ashiepattle's horse shied and upset the spoon, so that the Doll i' the Grass tumbled into the water. Ashiepattle was most sorrowful, for he did not know how he could get her out again; but after a while up came a merman with her. And now she had become just as big as any other grown-up person and far lovelier than before. So Ashiepattle placed her before him on his horse and rode home.

When he got there all his brothers had also returned, each with a bride, but, though they had thought themselves so much better than Ashiepattle and left him behind, they had all chosen brides who were ugly, ill-favored, and bad-tempered. On their heads these young misses had hats which were painted with tar and soot, and this had run down their faces, making them still uglier to behold.

The King was so overjoyed with Ashiepattle and his bride that he sent the others about their business, and said Ashiepattle should be King after him. So Ashiepattle and Doll i' the Grass held the wedding feast and they lived long and happily together.

FRIENDS*

ABBIE FARWELL BROWN

How good to lie a little while
  And look up through the tree!
The Sky is like a kind big smile
  Bent sweetly over me.

The Sunshine flickers through the lace
  Of leaves above my head,
And kisses me upon the face
  Like Mother, before bed.

The Wind comes stealing o'er the grass
  To whisper pretty things,
And though I cannot see him pass,
  I feel his careful wings.

So many gentle Friends are near
  Whom one can scarcely see,
A child should never feel a fear,
  Wherever he may be.

*Quoted by special permission of Houghton Mifflin Company.

Cinderella

ADAPTED FROM PERRAULT

Once upon a time there was a gentleman who married for his second wife, the proudest, vainest, and most selfish woman that ever was seen. She had two daughters, who were exactly like her in all things. The gentleman had also a daughter, but she was a young girl of the rarest sweetness and goodness. The mother could not bear the goodness of this young girl because it made the pride and ill-temper of her own daughters appear all the more ugly, so she gave her the hardest work in the house to do, in order that none of their visitors might notice her. She had to scour the dishes, scrub the floors, and clean the whole house from top to bottom. She had to sleep in the attic, upon a wretched bed of straw, while her sisters lay in fine rooms, on the very softest beds.

The young girl bore all this patiently, nor would she make her father unhappy by complaining to him of her lot. When she had done her work, she used to go into the chimney corner, and sit down among the cinders; hence, though her name was Ella, she was called by her sisters, Cinderella. Cinderella had only the poorest rags for clothes, but the sweetness and goodness that shone in her face, made her a hundred times more beautiful than her sisters, however richly they might be dressed.

It once happened that the King's son gave a very grand ball, to which all the great people of the kingdom were invited. Our young misses were highly delighted to re-

ceive an invitation. At once they began to busy themselves in choosing the gowns, petticoats and head-dresses which they should wear. Poor little Cinderella was not invited; yet, as she worked to get her sisters ready to go, they talked the whole day long of nothing but what they should do at the ball.

"For my part," said the elder, "I shall wear my red velvet suit with French trimmings."

"And I," said the younger, "shall wear my old skirt, but then to make up for that, I shall put on my gold-flowered mantle and my splendid diamond stomacher."

At last the happy day came. Though Cinderella was sad to think she must stay at home, she offered very sweetly to dress her sisters' hair, and even as she worked, they said unkind things to her.

"Cinderella, don't you wish you could go to the ball? How people would laugh to see a cinder-girl at a ball!"

Cinderella made no answer. She went on arranging their hair. So at last she had them looking as well as two young misses could, whose faces expressed nothing but pride and ill-temper. They paraded up and down before the long mirrors in their rooms, and then they got into the family coach and drove away to court.

Cinderella looked after them until they were far out of sight; then she crept into her corner by the chimney and fell softly a-crying. But Cinderella, like all good girls was watched over by a fairy godmother, and as she sat there in tears, her good fairy appeared before her.

MARGUERITE DAVIS

"My dear, dear child," said the queer little old lady, "why are you crying?"

"I wish—I wish I could—," Cinderella could not finish for sobbing.

"You wish," said the fairy, "that you could go to the ball. Is not that so?"

"Yes! O yes!" answered Cinderella, sighing.

"Well," said the Fairy, "be but a good girl, and I will see that you go." Then she commanded the dear child to run into the garden and bring her a pumpkin. Cinderella went obediently and gathered the finest she could find, though she hadn't the smallest idea how a pumpkin could help her get to the ball. Her fairy godmother scooped out all the inside, leaving nothing but the rind; then she struck it with her wand and behold! the pumpkin became a splendid gilded coach!

Next, the fairy godmother went to look into the mouse-trap, where she found six mice. She ordered Cinderella to lift the trap door, and, as each mouse ran out, she gave it a tap with her wand. At once the mouse was changed into a horse, till before them stood six fine horses of a beautiful, mouse-colored gray. Then she had Cinderella bring her the rat-trap. In that was a very large rat with splendid whiskers and she turned him into a coachman. Last of all, she said:

"Go into the garden, Cinderella, and bring me the six lizards you will find behind the watering pot."

No sooner had Cinderella done as she was commanded,

than the lizards became six footmen in gold embroidered coats. They skipped up at once behind the coach and sat there as grandly as though they had done nothing all their lives but serve in such a position.

The fairy then said to Cinderella, "Now you see a carriage fit to take you to the ball."

"Oh, yes, thank you!" cried Cinderella,

And the godmother touched her with her wand, and, at that same moment, her clothes were turned into cloth of gold and silver, all decked with jewels. Then the fairy gave her a pair of the prettiest glass slippers in the world, and said, as she stepped joyously into the carriage:

"This one command only you must obey. Do not on any account stay at the ball after midnight. If you do, your coach will become a pumpkin again, your horses mice, your coachman a rat, your footmen lizards, and your clothes the same rags you wore before."

Cinderella promised to obey and then she drove away. The King's son, being told that a great princess whom nobody knew was come to the ball, ran out to receive her. He gave her his hand as she alighted from the coach, and led her into the hall where the company was gathered. At once when she appeared, there fell over all a deep silence; every one left off dancing and the violins ceased to play. On all sides ladies and gentlemen whispered, "How beautiful she is!"

The King's son conducted her to the seat of honor, and afterwards led her out to dance. She danced so

gracefully that all admired her. She was kind and
courteous, too, even to her ill-tempered step-sisters,
who did not for a moment recognize in this lovely
princess their little cinder-girl. At last a splendid
feast was served, but in the midst of it all, Cinderella
heard the clock strike the quarter before twelve. She
rose and said farewell. Then she hastened away.

When she got back home, she found her godmother
waiting. Gratefully she thanked the little old lady for
what she had done. But as she was telling her all
that had happened, her two sisters knocked at the door.
Then the fairy changed Cinderella's brocaded gown to
rags again and disappeared in a twinkling. In her poor
old clothes Cinderella opened the door.

"If you had been at the ball," said one of her sisters, "you would have seen the finest, most beautiful Princess that ever your eyes looked on. She was very kind to us, too, and showed us much attention. But a little cinder-girl like you could never even dream of such beauty!"

Cinderella asked if they knew the name of the Princess.

"No," the step-sisters answered, "no one knows her name, but the King's son would give all the world to know!"

The next night the Prince asked everyone again to a ball that he might once more see the beautiful Princess. Cinderella's two sisters went, and when they were gone and the house was still, her godmother came as before and made Cinderella ready. The dress she wore on the second night was even more lovely than

the one she had had at first. The King's son welcomed her with beaming eyes and was always by her side. They danced with the same grace and beauty to the same lovely music. And they feasted as before. But when the clock struck a quarter to twelve Cinderella remembered her godmother's words and went obediently home.

The third night the King's son gave still another ball; once again the two sisters went and after them, Cinderella. Not a thing was less fine and splendid, not a person less kind and courteous than on the two nights preceding. Indeed the music was so beautiful; the movements of the dance were such wonders of harmony and grace; the room was so bright, and everything was so full of joy, that Cinderella never once thought how time was flying.

Suddenly the great clock of the palace began to strike twelve. One! Two! Three! Four! When she heard, Cinderella fled. Nimbly as a deer she ran. Five! Six! Seven! Eight! She was on the broad steps outside the palace. Nine! Ten! One little glass slipper fell from her foot, but she dared not stop to pick it up. Eleven! Twelve! Her clothes all turned to rags! Her coach disappeared! Mice, lizards and rat scampered off in the darkness.

As fast as she could, Cinderella ran home. All she had left of her finery was one little glass slipper, the mate to the one she had lost.

In great dismay, the Prince ran out from the palace

after her. Not a sign of her was anywhere to be seen. The guards at the gate said no splendid Princess had passed them. They had seen nobody but a poorly-dressed country girl, who ran as if for her life.

The Prince was very sorrowful and he had a search made everywhere. But all he could find of the beautiful Princess was the one little glass slipper she had dropped. For days and days he searched; then at last he had his servitors march up and down through the length and breadth of his kingdom, giving notice with sound of trumpet that every lady in the land should try on the little glass slipper. So small it was, he knew that none but the rightful princess could wear it. Hence he gave orders that whoever could get her foot into it, should straightway become his bride.

They began by trying the slipper on the princesses, then on the duchesses, and then on the other ladies of the court; not one of them did it fit. At last it was brought to Cinderella's two proud sisters, who each did all she could to squeeze in her foot; they pinched up their heels and drew in their toes, but in vain. Cinderella meantime stood by and watched what was going on. She knew her slipper and when her sisters had failed, she said to them modestly:

"Let me see if it will not fit me."

The sisters burst out laughing. "Could a cinder-girl wear such a slipper?" they cried. But the messenger who was sent out on the search, finding Cinderella

very beautiful, said it was but fair she should try it.

So Cinderella sat down and the gentleman put the slipper to her foot. Behold! it went on easily and fitted her like wax. The two sisters were dumb with amazement, but their amazement was greater still when Cinderella pulled out of her pocket the mate to that beautiful slipper. Thereupon, in came her good fairy, who touched the girl's clothes with her wand, and lo! they became more magnificent than any she had worn before.

And now her two sisters found her to be that beautiful lady who had been so kind to them at the ball. They threw themselves at her feet to beg pardon for all their ill treatment of her. Cinderella lifted them up, kissed them, and said she forgave them with all her heart.

She was conducted to the young prince, dressed as she was. He thought her more charming than ever. A few days later he led her, as his bride, to live with him at the palace. Cinderella, who was as good as she was beautiful, gave her two sisters a home at court. Henceforth they were kinder women.

UP ONE PAIR OF STAIRS

JUDGING BY APPEARANCES*

EMILIE POULSSON

An old Jack-o'-lantern lay on the
   ground;
He looked at the Moon-man, yellow
   and round.

The old Jack-o'-lantern gazed and he
   gazed,
And still as he looked he grew more
   amazed.

Then said Jack-o'-lantern,
   "How can it be
That fellow up there looks so much
   like me?

"I s'pose he must be a brother of
   mine,
And somebody cut *him, too,* from the
   vine.

"He looks very grand up there in
   the sky;
But I know just how 'twill be, by
   and by.

"He's proud of his shining, I have
   no doubt,
But just wait until *his* candle goes
   out!"

*From *Through the Farmyard Gate.* Used by the courteous permission of Lothrop, Lee & Shepard Co.

175

The Twelve Dancing Princesses

A GERMAN FOLK TALE

There was once a King who had twelve beautiful daughters and they slept in twelve beds, all in one room. When they went to bed, the doors were shut and locked, but every morning their shoes were found to be quite worn through as if they had been danced in all night long; yet nobody could ever find out where the maidens had been.

At last the King made it known to all the land that if any young man could discover the secret he should have the princess he liked best for his bride; but whoever tried and did not succeed after three nights, should be driven out of the kingdom in disgrace.

A King's son soon came. He was well entertained, and in the evening was taken to the chamber next to the one where the princesses lay in their twelve beds. There he was to sit and watch. In order that nothing might pass without his hearing it, the door of his chamber was left open. But the King's son soon fell asleep. When he awoke in the morning he found that the princesses had all been dancing, for the soles of their shoes were full of holes, yet he knew no more than before where they had been. The same thing happened the second night and the third. Each time the Prince fell asleep and learned nothing, so the King ordered him to be beaten and driven out of the kingdom. After him came several others, but they all went to sleep just as he had done and did not learn the secret, so they, too, were driven away in disgrace. In fact, so severely were these sons of Kings punished for their failures, that soon no more presented themselves to undertake the task.

Then it happened that a plain man, who was not a King's son, but was used to work for his living, came to the country where this King reigned. As he was traveling through a wood, the youth met an old woman who asked him where he was going. "I am passing through this land looking for work," said the youth, "but I should very much like to go to the castle and find out where it is that the princesses dance; then I might win one of them for my bride."

"Well," said the dame, "that seems to be a very hard task. But this is the secret of it—keep awake! Keep awake and watch!"

Then she gave him a cloak which she carried over her arm, and she said, "If you are listening carefully, you will hear the noise of their going. Then put on this coat; it will make you invisible and you will be able to go straight through the wall and follow them. Only mind you, do not let sleep overcome you or you will be lost." The youth listened well to this good counsel, then he went to the King and said he was willing to undertake the task.

He was as well received as the others had been, and the King ordered splendid royal robes to be given him in place of his plain garments. When the evening came he was led to the outer chamber. The princesses heard him come into the room and they laughed heartily. The eldest said, "This fellow will do as the rest have done. In a moment he will be snoring!" But the youth did nothing of the kind. He waited, every moment on guard. It was about midnight when the twelve princesses rose, opened their drawers and boxes, took out all their fine clothes, dressed themselves at the glass, and skipped about, eager to begin dancing. The youth listened till he heard the noise of their preparations cease, as though they were ready to go, then he quickly put on the cloak which the old woman had given him, and hurried into their chamber. Just as he arrived in the room, the eldest went up to her own bed and clapped her hands; at that the bed sank into the floor and a trap door flew open. Then the youth saw the twelve princesses go down through the trap door one after another, the eldest leading the way. He followed them so closely that in the middle of the stairs along which they were passing, he trod on the gown of the youngest princess and she cried out to her sisters, "All is not right, some one took hold of my gown."

"You silly creature," said the eldest, "it is nothing but a nail in the wall." So down they all went, and at the bottom, they found themselves in a most delightful grove of trees; the leaves were all of silver that

glittered and sparkled beautifully. The youth wished
to take away some token of the place to show the
King, so he broke off a little branch and there came
a loud noise from the tree. Then the youngest princess
said again, "I am sure all is not right—did not you
hear that noise? That never happened before." But
the eldest said, "It is only our princes shouting for
joy at our approach." Soon they came to another
grove of trees where all the leaves were of gold, and
afterward, to a third with leaves of glittering diamonds.
The youth broke a branch from each; and every time
he did so, there came a loud snapping, which made
the youngest princess cry out that something was

the matter. But in spite of her words, they all kept on till they came to a great lake. At the side of the lake there lay twelve little boats and in the boats were twelve handsome princes, who seemed to be awaiting the princesses.

One of the princesses stepped into each boat and the youth in the coat that made him invisible, got into the boat with the youngest. As they were crossing the lake the prince who was rowing the youngest said, "I do not know why it is, but the boat seems very heavy tonight."

On the other side of the lake stood a brightly lighted castle, from which came the sound of merry music. There they all landed and went into the castle. Each prince danced with his princess; and the youth, who was all the time invisible, followed the youngest princess about, for he found her very lovely indeed. They danced on thus till four o'clock in the morning; then all their shoes were worn out, so they were obliged to leave off. The princes rowed them back again over the lake, and once more the youth took his place in the boat, close beside the youngest princess. On the opposite shore the princes took leave of the maidens, the princesses promising to come again the next night.

When they came to the stairs, leading up into their chamber, the youth ran on ahead and laid himself in his bed, so when the twelve sisters came up more slowly, he was already asleep and snoring. "You see he has been sleeping all this time just as the others did, and has seen nothing," they said.

Then they undressed themselves, put away their fine clothes, pulled off their shoes and went to bed. In the morning the youth said nothing about what had happened, but determined to see more of this strange adventure. Again the second and third nights, he followed the maidens. Everything happened just as before; the princesses danced each time till their shoes were all worn to shreds and then returned home.

As soon as the time came when he must either declare the secret, or be beaten out of the kingdom, he was taken before the King. With him he carried the three branches from the trees. When the King asked him, "Where do my twelve daughters dance at night?" he answered, "With twelve princes in a castle underground." Then he told the King all that had happened, and showed him the three branches of silver, gold and diamonds.

The King at once called for the princesses and asked them if what the youth said was true. When they found that their secret had been discovered, they told their father all about it. Then the King said, "My young man it is good to be wide awake and watchful," and he asked the youth, just as he had promised, which of the maidens he would choose for his bride. The youth answered, "I will take the youngest."

So he did, and they lived happily ever after.

PEENY PEN PONE*
LAURA CAMPBELL

Peeny-Pen, Peeny-Pen, Peeny-Pen-Pone
Is a little old woman who lives all alone!
Her little brown house is on Reeny-Ren-Road,
It looks like a little round Tippity Toad!
In the little brown house is a little brown room,
In the room is a chair and a bed and a broom,
And a little brown table; I think that is all,
Except for a cupboard that stands by the wall,
And a little red fire that burns in the grate,
And a little blue clock that ticks early and late.
"Peeny-Pen, what do you do every day,
For you live all alone and are too old to play?"
"I rise in the morning, I rise with the sun,
I poke my red fire and I make Sally Lunn!
And then I go out and I feed my pink pig
On bees and on beetles to make him grow big!

*From *John Martin's Book*, published by John Martin's House, Inc.

182

UP ONE PAIR OF STAIRS

And then I go round to my little front gate,
And pat my dog Pim on his little brown pate!
And then I go gather a hundred green peas,
And cook them for dinner as hot as I please!
And right after dinner I lock up my house,
And walk down the road in my Sunday-best blouse;
Down Reeny-Ren-Road and afar, far off,
To call on my little friend Nimmo, the Dwarf.
And Nimmo and I, whatever the weather,
Go faring in Weeny-Wen-Woodland together.
And the rest I can't tell—it's a Secret, you see,
'Tween the Weeny-Wen-Fairies, and Nimmo and me!
And at eight by the clock I am back in my room,
A-sweeping it out with my little brown broom!
Then I sit by the fire to warm my old head,
And at ten by the clock I jump right into bed!"
Thus spoke the old woman that lives all alone,
Peeny-Pen, Peeny-Pen, Peeny-Pen-Pone!

The Boy Hero of Harlem

A LEGEND OF HOLLAND

Little Hans, in his wooden shoes, ran clattering along on the brick pavement beside a canal in the old Dutch city of Harlem. He was on his way to carry some beautiful gingerbread cakes, all decorated with colored seeds, to a very dear friend of his, an old man who lived some five miles away by the sea. Swinging his basket and whistling a merry tune, he hurried along, through the quaint old market place, down the shady streets, and out into the country. Soon he overtook a little girl who was driving a flock of geese.

"Look, boy!" cried the girl. "See how swollen with water the canal is! It is almost overflowing."

"Yes," answered Hans, "it is the spring rains that have done it. My father keeps the sluice-gates. I'm glad his gates are big and strong, so he can shut out the sea, and keep the water from flooding all the land."

The girl with the geese shivered.

"Just suppose," she said, "the sea should once get through the gates or through the dikes! Where would Harlem be then?"

Neither child spoke for a moment. Each was thinking how the mossy old windmills round about, and the black and white cows that grazed peacefully on the rich green meadows, and the neat little farm houses, and the trim shade trees by the canal, and the people, and the whole city of Harlem behind them, would all be swept away, if once the water got through the sluice-gates, or through the great thick embankments called dikes. For Holland lies much lower than the level of the ocean and it is only by building these walls, that the people keep out the sea.

At last Hans drew a deep breath and began to whistle again; he was a brave little fellow and seldom afraid of anything.

"Don't be thinking of that, girl," he said. "The dikes and the sluice-gates are watched so carefully, they could never give way, so Harlem is safe enough after all."

The children trudged on together. Sometimes a little sail boat seemed to fly right over the green meadows before them, so hidden from sight was the tiny thread of canal on which it traveled; sometimes they passed by field after field of the flaming, vari-colored tulips for which Harlem is so famous; often they crossed little bridges over the canals.

At last Hans bade the goose-girl good-bye and went on his way alone. Soon he saw looming up ahead of him the grassy wall of the great sea-dike, with the little house of his friend nestled down beneath it. Above, on a level with the roof of the house—just think, on a level with the roof—he saw the shining sea and the ships afloat on the water.

For a moment, he thought once more how quickly the countryside would be overflowed, if once that sea could find a way to rush through the dikes and down, down over the land. But the sun was shining peacefully and calmly overhead, and all about the world was merry and secure, so he put the thought aside and went on into the house. His old friend was delighted with the beautiful gingerbread cakes, and Hans sat out in front of the house with him all through the afternoon, while he mended his nets and told tales of the sea.

When Hans started out for home once more the sun was setting. It was much later than he had intended staying. He must hurry now. Supper would be ready and mother waiting. In order to return by the shortest way, he took the road along the top of the dike. The soft blue-purple of twilight was settling over the earth, and a star had appeared in the sky, when, as he hurried on, he suddenly heard the faint trickle or gurgle of water. On the instant he stopped; a gurgle meant water running through some small hole. Carefully he leaned down and peered over the embankment on the opposite side from the sea. Sure enough! There in the dike, was a chink, through which a tiny stream was flowing.

A leak in the dike! *A leak in the dike*! All the meaning of those words flashed over the boy in a moment. Bit by bit, the water, running through that small opening, would wash away the earth and rocks of which the embankment was made. So it would make the hole larger till it swept through the dike altogether, and rolled down over the meadows, down over the farm houses, down, down, down, over Harlem and the little brick home where mother and father and brother——

Hans hesitated not an instant. He slid to the bottom of the dike, and thrust his arm into the chink to fill it.

"Not while I can help it, shall Harlem be washed away," he said to himself. Then he shouted loudly for help, but the place was lonely and no one heard him. He looked about to find something with which to stop up the hole while he went for aid. There was

HILDA HANWAY

no material near that was strong enough to hold back the water. His arm alone could keep out the rush of the waves. He held it there bravely.

Loud boomed the sea on the other side of the dike; the night darkened; the moon came out, and still there were no answers to his calls, save the swish and roar of the ocean.

"I am the great, great sea," the waters seemed to say. "I can overwhelm all with my power. What can one small boy do against me?"

But the boy's heart grew strong within him. God would give him the strength to save Harlem. That certainty made him stronger than the sea.

"You cannot make me afraid, great ocean," he cried, "you cannot drive me away."

His hand grew cold and numb; his arm up to the shoulder grew stiff, but he did not falter. He thought of mother and father and little brother; he thought of his cozy home; he thought of the people so peacefully asleep in their beds in Harlem; he thought of the very geese! And the safety of these—of all these—depended on the faithfulness with which he kept that arm fixed fast in the chink until help should come. Ah! then nothing should make him forsake his post.

All night long he listened for sounds, straining his ears to hear. The stillness was unbroken except for the boom of the sea. The boy scarcely moved save now and again to change the arm that he held in the hole.

Then—it seemed as though an age had passed—the first faint streaks of dawn appeared in the sky. Dim lilac faded into rose, the gray sea sparkled into blue, and now at last, at last he heard a faint noise in the distance. Nearer it grew and nearer, till he saw coming toward him a man and a boy with a dog cart. A milkman off for town and his morning rounds!

"Help! Here, help!" cried Hans faintly.

"Who cries help?" the man shouted.

"Here! Here!" answered Hans.

The milkman spied him and hurried down to his side.

"In the name of all that is good, boy, what are you doing?" he cried.

"There's a leak in the dike. I'm keeping the water from running in," the boy answered simply as though he had done but an every day deed. "Go and bring help as soon as you can!"

In another moment, the lad with the dog cart was going at full speed toward the town, to report what had happened, while the man gently helped Hans to stand on his feet and stretch his stiffened limbs. Then he put his own arm into the hole to stop the leak until help should come.

Soon a crowd of men appeared, hurrying out from the city. And when they had mended the dike, they bore brave little Hans back to town on their shoulders.

"Make way for the hero of Harlem!" they cried, so that all who heard stood still to listen. "Make way for the boy who has saved the city!"

And to this very day, there lives in the heart of the Dutch people no finer picture of a noble boy, than that of the little hero, who stuck so faithfully at his post and saved the city of Harlem.

HE prayeth best, who loveth best
  All things, both great and small;
For the dear Lord who loveth us,
  He made and loveth all.
                    —*Samuel T. Coleridge.*

The Fisherman and His Wife
ADAPTED FROM WILHELM AND JACOB GRIMM

There was once upon a time a fisherman who lived with his wife in a wretched little hovel close by the sea, and every day he went out fishing. Once, as he was sitting with his rod, looking at the clear water, his line suddenly went far down below and when he drew it out, up came a big flounder.

Then the flounder said to him, "Hark, you, fisherman, I pray you put me back in the water. I am no common fish; I am a fish who can grant people their wishes."

"Come," said the fisherman, "deliver me from a fish that talks!" With that he put the flounder back into the water, and down went the flounder to the bottom of the sea. Then the fisherman went home to his wife.

"Husband," said the woman, "have you caught nothing today?"

"No," said the fisherman, "I did draw up a flounder, but he said he was no common fish—he was a fish who granted people their wishes, so I put him back again into the water."

"Well, and what did you wish for?" asked the woman.

"Oh!" said the man, "What should I wish for? I wished for nothing. I am quite content with what I have."

"Ah! you stupid good-for-nothing," said the woman, "it is surely hard to have to live always in such a wretched hovel; you might have wished for a pretty cottage for us. Go back and call the fish. Tell him we want to have a pretty cottage; he will surely give us that."

The man did not quite like to go, as he could see no reason why he should trouble the fish again. But his wife insisted, so at last he went. When he reached the sea, the water was all green and yellow and no longer so smooth as it had been before, but the fisherman stood there and said:

> "O Fish of the Sea, come, listen to me,
> For Alice, my wife, the plague of my life,
> Has sent me to beg a boon of thee."

Up came the fish. "What does she want, then?" he said.

"Ah!" said the man, "She says I really ought to have asked you to grant us a wish. She does not like to live in a wretched hovel any longer. She would like to have a little cottage."

"Go then," said the fish, "she has it already."

When the man reached home, his wife was no longer in the hovel, but in its place there stood a pretty cottage, and she was sitting on a bench before the door. She took him by the hand and said, "Just come inside. Look! Now isn't this a great deal better than living as we did before?"

So they went in and there was a pretty little parlor and bed room, and a kitchen and a pantry, all fitted up with the prettiest things. Behind the house was a small yard, with hens and ducks, and a little garden, with flowers and fruit.

"Look!" said the wife, "Is not that nice?"

"Yes," said the husband, "and so we must always think it,—now we shall live quite content."

"Oh, I don't know about that!" said the wife. With that they had a nice little supper and went to bed.

Everything went well for a week or a fortnight, and then the woman said:

"Hark you, husband, this cottage and garden are far too small for us; the Fish might just as well have given us a larger house. I should like to live in a great stone mansion. Go to the Fish and tell him to give us a stone mansion."

"Ah, wife," said the man, "this cottage is quite good enough. Why should we live in a grand house?"

"What," said the woman, "don't you see we would be far happier in a great house than in this little cottage? Go at once."

"No, wife," said the man, "the Fish has just given us this cottage. I do not like to bother him again."

"It will be no bother to him at all," said she, "he will be glad to do it."

The man's heart grew heavy, and he said to himself, "It is not right," and yet he went.

When he came to the sea, the water was purple and blue and beginning to darken; he stood there and said;

"O Fish of the Sea, come, listen to me,
For Alice, my wife, the plague of my life,
Has sent me to beg a boon of thee."

Up came the Fish. "Well, what does she want now?" he said.

"Alas!" said the man, shamefaced. "She wants to live in a great stone mansion."

"Go home," said the Fish. "She has a mansion to live in already."

Then the man went away and when he got home he found a great stone house and his wife was just standing on the steps. She took him by the hand and said, "Come in." Inside the house was a great hall, paved with marble, and many servants who flung wide the doors; the walls were all bright with beautiful hangings, and in the rooms were chairs and tables of gold; crystal chandeliers hung from the ceiling, and food of the very best kind was standing on all the tables. Behind the mansion, too, there was a great courtyard, with stables for horses and the very best of carriages. There was a magnificent large park, quite half a mile long, in which were stags, deer and hares, and everything that could be desired. "Come," said the woman, "isn't this beautiful?"

"Yes, indeed," said the man, "and now we will live in this beautiful house and be content."

"Nay, husband," said the woman, "but I am already beginning to feel that it is not large enough. We need a palace. Go to the Fish. We must have a palace!"

"Ah, wife," said the man, "why do we want a palace? I do not want a palace."

"Well, I do!" said the wife. "Go to the Fish!"

"But," said the man, "I do not like to ask him for anything more."

"Husband," she said, "stop talking! Go!"

So the man went.

"It is not right! It is not right!" thought he, yet he went.

The sea now was quite dark gray and the waves were swelling and heaving. As he stood beside it he called:

> "O Fish of the Sea, come, listen to me,
> For Alice, my wife, the plague of my life,
> Has sent me to beg a boon of thee."

"What does she want now?" said the Fish.

"Alas!" said the man. "She wants a palace."

"Go home to her; she is in the palace," said the Fish.

So the man went and when he came to the palace, the mansion had become much larger; it had a great tower and magnificent ornaments; a sentinel was standing before the door, and there were numbers of soldiers about, with kettle-drums and trumpets. When he went inside, everything was of real marble and gold, with velvet covers and great golden tassels. Then the doors of the hall were opened, and there sat his wife in all this splendor, with rings on her fingers and jewels in her hair. On either side of her stood her maids-in-waiting in a row, each a head taller than the last. Then he went and stood before her and said:

"It is very grand, wife; we can wish for nothing more."

"We will see about that," said the woman. Next morning she awoke first. It was just daybreak and from her bed she saw the beautiful country stretching out before her.

"Husband," she said, "just look out over that land. Think you! Couldn't you be King and rule over all that? Go to the Fish. You must be King."

"Ah, wife," said the man, "he can't make me King. Why should I be King? I do not want to be King."

"Well," said the wife, "if you won't be King, I will; go to the Fish, for I will be King."

"Ah, wife," said the man, "I do not like to say

that to him. Why should you want to be King?"

"Ask no more questions about it! I will be King. Go!"

So off he went but he muttered to himself, "It will not end well! King! It is too shameless that she is not even yet content."

The water rose and roared as though it were boiling, and splashed upon the shore, while a high wind blew over the land, and the clouds flew and the leaves fell from the trees.

Very sorrowfully, the man stood by the shore and called:

> "O Fish of the Sea, come, listen to me,
> For Alice, my wife, the plague of my life,
> Has sent me to ask a boon of thee."

"*What does* she want now?" said the Fish.

"Alas," said the man, "she wants to be King."

"Go home!" said the Fish. "She is King."

So the man went, and when he got there, the whole palace was made of polished marble, soldiers were marching before the door, blowing trumpets and beating cymbals and drums, and in the house barons and dukes and princes were going about as servants. And when he entered, there sat his wife on a great golden throne; she wore on her head a great golden crown set with diamonds; in one hand she had the sceptre of gold, in the other the orb of gold, and on either side of her stood the yeomen of the guard.

"Well, wife, are you King now?" said he.

"Yes," said she, "now I am King."

"Ah, wife," said the man, "and now that you are King, do be satisfied and let well enough alone." But she looked as stiff as a post and all she said was, "I will see about that."

Thereupon she went to bed, but she was not satisfied, and greediness let her have no sleep, for she was continually thinking what there was left for her to be that would make her greater still. At length the sun began to rise, and when the woman saw the red of dawn, she sat up in bed and looked at it.

"Ah," she cried, "I know what there is still left for me to have. I must have power over the sun and the moon. They must only be able to rise at my command."

"Husband," said she, poking him with her elbow, "wake up! Go to the Fish, for I must be ruler over the sun and the moon."

The man was still half asleep, but he was so startled at her words that he rolled out of bed. He thought he must have heard amiss, and rubbed his eyes and said, "Alas, wife, what are you saying?"

"Husband!" she said, "If I can't order the sun and moon to rise, but have to look on and see them rise without my leave, I can't bear it. I shall not know what it is to have another happy hour unless I myself can make them rise."

"Alas! wife," said the man, falling on his knees before her, "the Fish cannot do that. He has made you King. I beseech you do not ask that! Be content."

Then the woman grew angry.

"Go, at once," said she. "I am King—I command you!"

So the man went.　　But outside, a great storm was raging; it was blowing so hard, he could scarcely keep his feet.　The sky was black, and the sea came in with black waves all crested with black foam.　The whole earth seemed to shake, and trees came falling round about.　Then the man cried, but could hardly hear his own words for the noise of the storm:

> "O Fish of the Sea, come, listen to me,
> For Alice, my wife, the plague of my life,
> Has sent me to ask a boon of thee."

"What does she want now?" said the Fish, and his voice was strange and threatening.

"She wants to be Lord of the sun and the moon, so they dare not rise save at her command!"

"Go!" said the Fish.　"She is back in the hovel."

And there they live to this very day.

The Sandy Road*
A Jataka Tale
Ellen C. Babbitt

Once upon a time a merchant, with his goods packed in many carts, came to a desert. He was on his way to the country on the other side of the desert.

The sun shone on the fine sand, making it as hot as the top of a stove. No man could walk on it in the sunlight. But at night, after the sun went down, the sand cooled, and then men could travel upon it.

So the merchant waited until after dark, and then set out. Besides the goods that he was going to sell he took jars of water and of rice, and firewood, so that the rice could be cooked.

All night long he and his men rode on and on. One man was the pilot. He rode first for he knew the stars, and by them he guided the drivers.

At daybreak they stopped and camped. They unyoked the oxen, and fed them. They built fires and cooked rice. Then they spread a great awning

*Taken from *Jataka Tales* by the permission of The Century Co.

over all the carts and the oxen, and the men lay down under it to rest until sunset.

In the early evening, they again built fires and cooked rice. After supper, they folded the awning and put it away. They yoked the oxen and as soon as the sand was cool, they started again on their journey across the desert.

Night after night they traveled in this way, resting during the heat of the day. At last one morning the pilot said: "In one more night we shall get out of the sand." The men were glad to hear this, for they were tired.

After supper that night the merchant said: "You may as well throw away nearly all the water and the firewood. By to-morrow we shall be in the city. Yoke the oxen and start on."

Then the pilot took his place at the head of the line. But instead of sitting up and guiding the drivers, he lay down in the wagon on the cushions. Soon he was fast asleep, because he had not slept for many nights, and the light had been so strong in the day-time that he had not slept well then.

All night long the oxen went on. Near daybreak, the pilot awoke and looked at the last stars fading in the light. "Halt!" he cried to the drivers. "We are in the same place where we were yesterday. The oxen must have turned about while I slept."

They unyoked the oxen, but there was no water for

them to drink. They had thrown away the water that was left the night before. So the men spread the awning over the carts, and the oxen lay down tired and thirsty. The men, too, lay down saying, "The wood and water are gone—we are lost."

But the merchant said to himself, "This is no time for me to sleep. I must find water. The oxen cannot go on if they do not have water to drink. The men must have water. They cannot cook the rice unless they have water. If I give up, we shall all be lost."

On and on he walked, keeping close watch of the ground. At last he saw a tuft of grass. "There must be water somewhere below, or that grass would not be there," he said.

He ran back, shouting to the men, "Bring the spade and the hammer!"

They jumped up and ran with him to the spot where the grass grew. They began to dig and by and by they struck a rock and could dig no further. Then the merchant jumped down into the hole they had dug, and put his ear to the rock. "I hear water running under this rock," he called to them. "We must not give up!" Then the merchant came up out of the hole and said to a serving lad: "My boy, if you give up we are lost! You go down and try!"

The boy stood up straight and raised the hammer high above his head and hit the rock as hard as ever he could. He would not give in. They must be saved.

Down came the hammer. This time the rock broke. And the boy had hardly time to get out of the well before it was full of cool water. The men drank as if they could never get enough, and then they watered the oxen, and bathed.

Then they split up their extra yokes and axles and built a fire, and cooked their rice. Feeling better, they rested through the day. They set up a flag on the well for travelers to see.

At sundown, they started on again, and the next morning reached the city, where they sold the goods, and then returned home.

THE EVENING SKY
Dante Alighieri

When that great sun who gives his light to all the world,
Sinks down so low beneath the earth's far rim,
That on all sides the daylight fades away;
The skies, that once by him alone were lit,
Do now all suddenly shine forth again
With many lights, and one more glorious than the rest.
—*Paradiso, Canto XX.*

The Story of Christopher Columbus*

ELIZABETH HARRISON

Once upon a time, far across the great ocean, there lived a little boy named Christopher. The city in which he lived was called Genoa. It was on the coast of the great sea, and from the time that little Christopher could first remember he had seen boats come and go across the water. I doubt not that he had little boats of his own which he tried to sail, or paddle about on the small pools near his home.

Soon after he was old enough to read books, which in those days were very scarce and very much valued, he got hold of an account of the wonderful travels of a man named Marco Polo. Over and over again little Christopher read the marvelous stories told by this old traveler, of the strange cities which he had seen and of the dark-colored people whom he had met; of the queer houses; of the wild and beautiful animals he had encountered; of the jewels and perfumes and

*From *In Story Land*. Used by special arrangement with the author.

flowers which he had come across during his journeys.

All day long the thoughts of little Christopher were busy with this strange far-away land which Marco Polo described. All night long he dreamed of the marvelous sights to be seen on those distant shores. Many a time he went down to the water's edge to watch the queer ships as they slowly disappeared in the dim distance, where the sea and sky seemed to meet. He listened eagerly to everything about the sea and the voyages of adventure or of trade, which were told by the sailors near.

When he was fourteen years old he went to sea with an uncle, who was commander of one of the vessels that came and went from the port of Genoa. For a number of years he thus lived on a vessel, learning everything that he could about the sea. At one time the ship on which he was sailing had a desperate fight with another ship; both took fire and were burned to the water's edge. Christopher Columbus, for that was his full name, only escaped, as did the other sailors, by jumping into the sea and swimming to shore. Still this did not cure him of his love for the ocean life.

We find after a time that he left Italy, his native country, and went to live in Portugal, a land near the great sea, whose people were far more venturesome than had been those of Genoa. Here he married a beautiful maiden, whose father had collected a rich store of maps and charts, which showed what was then supposed to be the shape of the earth, and told of strange and wonderful voyages which brave sailors had from time to time dared to make out into the then unknown sea. Most people in those days thought it was certain death to any one who ventured very far out on the ocean.

There were all sorts of queer and absurd ideas afloat as to the shape of the earth. Some people thought it was round and flat like a pancake and that the waters which surrounded the land gradually changed into mist and vapor, and that he who ventured out into these vapors fell through the mist and clouds down into — they knew not where. Others believed that there were huge monsters living in the distant waters, ready to swallow any sailor who was foolish enough to venture near them.

But Christopher Columbus had grown to be a very wise and thoughtful man and from all he could learn from the maps of his father-in-law and the books which he read, and from the long talks which he had with some other learned men, he grew more and more certain that the world was round like an orange, and that by sailing westward from the coast of Portugal one could gradually go around the world and find at last the wonderful land of Cathay, the strange country which lay far beyond the sea, the accounts of which had so thrilled him as a boy.

We, of course, know that he was right in his belief

concerning the shape of the earth, but people in those days laughed him to scorn, when he spoke of making a voyage out on the vast and fearful ocean. In vain he talked and reasoned and argued, and drew maps to explain matters. The more he proved to his own satisfaction that this must be the shape of the world, the more people shook their heads and called him crazy.

He remembered in his readings of the book of Marco Polo's travels, that the people whom he had met were heathen, who knew little about the dear God who had made the world, and nothing at all about His son, Christ Jesus, and as Christopher Columbus loved very dearly the Christian religion, his mind became filled with a longing to carry it across the great seas to this far-away country. The more he thought about it the more he wanted to go, until his whole life was filled with the one thought of how to get hold of some ships to prove that the earth was round, and that these far-away heathens could be reached.

Through some friends he obtained admission to the court of the King of Portugal. Eagerly he told the rich monarch of the great enterprise which filled his heart. It was of little or no use, the King was busy with other affairs, and only listened to the words of Columbus as one might listen to the wind. Year after year passed by; Columbus' wife had died, and their one little son, Diego, had grown to be quite a boy. Finally Columbus decided he would leave Portugal and would go over to Spain, a rich country near by, and see if the Spanish monarchs would not give him boats in which to make his longed-for voyage.

II

The Spanish King was named Ferdinand, and the Spanish Queen was a beautiful woman named Isabella. When Columbus told them of his belief that the world was round, and of his desire to help the heathen who lived in this far-off country, they listened attentively to him, for both King Ferdinand and Queen Isabella were very earnest people and very desirous that all the world should become Christian, but their ministers and officers of state persuaded them that the whole thing was a foolish dream; and again Columbus was disappointed in his hope of getting help.

Still he did not give up in despair. *The thought was too great for that.* He sent his brother over to England to see if the English King would not listen to him and give the necessary help, but again he was doomed to disappointment. Only here and there could he find any one who believed that it was possible for him to sail round the earth and reach the land on the other side. Long years passed by. Columbus grew pale and thin with waiting and hoping, with planning and longing.

Sometimes as he walked along the streets of the Spanish capital people would point their fingers at him and say: "There goes the crazy old man who thinks the world is round." Again and again Columbus tried to persuade the Spanish King and Queen that if they would aid him, his discoveries would bring great honor and riches to their kingdom, and that they would also help the world by spreading the knowledge of Christ and His religion. Nobody believed in him. Nobody was interested in his plan. He grew poorer and poorer.

At last he turned his back on the great Spanish court, and in silent despair, he took his little son by the hand and walked a long way to a small seaport called Palos, where there was a queer old convent, in which strangers were often entertained by the kind monks. Weary and footsore he reached the gate of the convent. Knocking upon it, he asked the porter, who answered the summons, if he would give little Diego a bit of bread and a drink of water. While the two tired travelers were resting, as the little boy ate his dry crust of bread, the prior of the convent, a man of thought and learning, whose name was Juan Perez, came by, and at once saw that these two were no common beggars. He invited them in and questioned Columbus closely about his past life. He listened quietly and thoughtfully to Columbus and his plan of crossing the ocean and converting the heathen to Christianity.

Juan Perez had at one time been a very intimate friend of Queen Isabella; in fact, the priest to whom she told all her sorrows and troubles. After a long talk with Columbus, in which he was convinced that Columbus was right, he borrowed a mule and, getting on his back, rode for many miles across the open country to the palace in which the Queen was then staying. I do not know how he convinced her of the truth of Columbus' plan, when all the ministers and courtiers and statesmen about her considered it the foolish and silly dream of an old man; but, somehow, he did it.

He then returned on his mule to the old convent at Palos, and told Columbus to go back once more to the court of Spain and again petition the Queen to give him money with which to make his voyage of discovery. The State Treasurer said the Queen had no money to spare, but this noble-hearted woman, who now, for the first time, realized that it was a grand and glorious thing Columbus wished to do, said she would give her crown jewels for money with which to start Columbus on his dangerous journey.

This meant much in those days, as queens were scarcely considered dignified if they did not wear crowns of gold, inlaid with bright jewels, on all public occasions, but Queen Isabella cared far more to send the gospel of Christ over to the heathen than how she might look, or what other people might say about her. With a glad heart Columbus hastened back to the little town of Palos where he had left his young son.

III

But now a new difficulty arose. Enough sailors could not be found who would venture their lives by going out on this unknown voyage with a crazy man such as Columbus was thought to be. At last the convicts from the prisons were given liberty by the Queen, on condition that they would go with the sailors and Columbus. So, you see, it was not altogether a very nice crew! Still it was the best he could get, and Columbus' heart was so filled with the great work that he was willing to undertake the voyage, no matter how great or how many the difficulties might be. The ships were filled with food and other provisions for a long, long voyage.

Nobody knew how long it would be before the land on the other side could be reached, and many people thought there was no possible hope of its ever being found.

Early one summer morning, even before the sun had risen, Columbus bade farewell to the few friends who had gathered at the little seaport of Palos to say good-bye to him. The ships spread their sails and started on the great untried voyage. There were three boats, none of which we would think, nowadays, was large enough or strong enough to dare venture out of sight and help of land and run the risk of encountering the storms of mid-ocean.

The names of the boats were the Santa Maria, which was the one that Columbus himself commanded, and two smaller boats, one named the Pinta and the other the Nina.

Strange, indeed must the sailors have felt, as hour after hour they drifted out into the great unknown waters, which no man ever ventured into before. Soon all land faded from their sight, and on, and on, and on they went, not knowing where or how the voyage would end. Columbus alone was filled with hope, feeling quite sure that in time he would reach the never before visited shores of a New World. On and on they sailed, day after day—far beyond the utmost point which sailors had ever before reached.

Many of the men were filled with a strange dread and begged and pleaded to return home. Still on and on they went, each day taking them further and further from all they had ever known or loved before. Day after day passed, and week after week until two months had elapsed.

The provisions which they had brought with them were getting scarce. The men grew angry with Columbus, and threatened to take his life if he did not command the ships to be turned back towards Spain, but his patience did not give out, nor was his faith one whit less. He cheered the hearts of the men as best he could.

He promised a rich reward to the first man who should discover land. This somewhat renewed their courage; day and night watches were set and the western horizon before them was scanned at all hours. Time and again they thought they saw land ahead, only to find they had mistaken a cloud upon the horizon for the longed-for shore. Flocks of birds flying westward began to be seen. This gave some ground for hope. For surely the birds must be flying toward some land where they could find food, and trees in which to build their nests. Still fear was great in the hearts of all, and Columbus knew that if land did not appear soon, his men would compel him to turn around whether he wished to or not.

Then he thought of all the heathen who had never heard of God's message of love to man through Christ, and he prayed almost incessantly that courage might be given him to go on. Hour after hour he looked across the blue water, day and night, longing for the sight of land.

At last one night, as he sat upon the deck of the ship, he was quite sure that a faint light glimmered for a few moments in the distant darkness ahead. Where there is a light there must be land, he thought. Still he was not sure. So he called one of the more faithful sailors to him and asked him what he saw. The sailor exclaimed:

"A light, a light!"

Another sailor was called, but by this time the light had disappeared, so the sailor saw nothing, and Columbus' hopes again sank. About two o'clock that night the commander of one of the other boats started the cry:

"Land, land ahead!"

You can well imagine how the shout was taken up, and how the sailors, one and all, rushed to the edge of their ships, leaning far over and straining their eyes for the almost unhoped-for sight.

Early the next morning some one of the sailors picked up a branch of a strange tree, lodged in the midst of which was a tiny bird's nest. This was sure evidence that they were indeed near land, for branches of trees do not grow in water.

Little by little the land came in sight. First it looked like a dim ghost of a shore, but gradually it grew distinct and clear. About noon the next day, the keel of Columbus' boat ground upon the sand of the newly discovered country. No white man had ever before set eyes upon it. No ship had ever before touched this coast.

At last after a long life of working and studying, of hoping and planning, of trying and failing, and trying yet again, he had realized his dream.

The great mystery of the ocean was revealed, and Columbus had achieved a glory which would last as long as the world lasted. *He had given a new world to mankind!* He had reached the far distant country across the ocean, which scarcely any of his countrymen had even believed to have any existence. He now

knew that the whole round world could in time have the Christian religion.

He sprang upon the shore, and dropping on his knees, he first stooped and kissed the ground, and then he offered a fervent prayer of thanks to God.

A learned man who had come with him across the water next planted the flag of Spain upon the unknown land, and claimed the newly discovered country in the name of King Ferdinand and Queen Isabella.

Wonderful, wonderful indeed were the things which Columbus and the sailors now saw! Strange, naked men and women of a copper, or bronze color; strange, new birds with gorgeous tails that glittered like gems such as they had never seen before; beautiful and unknown fruits and flowers met their gaze on every side.

The savages were kind and gentle and brought them food and water. Do you know, my dear children, that this strange, wild, savage country which Columbus had traveled so far and so long to discover was *our country, America?*

IN COLUMBUS' TIME*
ANNETTE WYNNE

Suppose you lived then, do you think that you
Would believe what Columbus said was true,
Or would you be like the wise men who
Laughed in his face and said, "Pooh, pooh?"

*Taken from *For Days and Days*, by the kind permission of Frederick A. Stokes Company.

FAREWELL TO THE FARM
ROBERT LOUIS STEVENSON

The coach is at the door at last;
The eager children, mounting fast
And kissing hands, in chorus sing:
Good-bye, good-bye, to everything!

To house and garden, field and lawn,
The meadow gates we swang upon,
To pump and stable, tree and swing,
Good-bye, good-bye, to everything!

And fare you well for evermore,
O ladder at the hayloft door,
O hayloft where the cobwebs cling,
Good-bye, good-bye, to everything!

Crack goes the whip, and off we go;
The trees and houses smaller grow;
Last, round the woody turn we swing;
Good-bye, good-bye, to everything!

Christening the Baby in Russia*

ARTHUR RANSOME

Somewhere in the forest of great trees—a forest so big that the forests of England are little woods beside it — is the hut where old Peter lives.

The hut was made of pine logs cut from the forest. You could see the marks of the axe. Old Peter was the grandfather of Maroosia and Vanya. He lived alone with them in the hut in the forest, and they were happy with old Peter, who was very kind to them and did all he could to keep them warm and well fed.

Besides old Peter and Maroosia and Vanya there were Vladimir and Bayan. Vladimir was a cat, a big black cat, as stately as an emperor, and just now he was lying in Vanya's arms fast asleep. Bayan was a dog, a tall gray wolf-dog. He could jump over the table with a single bound. When he was in the hut he usually lay underneath the table, because that was the only place where he could lie without being in the way. And, of course, at meal times he was in the way even there. Just now he was out with old Peter.

Vladimir stirred suddenly in Vanya's lap, and a minute later they heard the scrunch of boots. Then the

*From *Old Peter's Russian Tales*. Used by the courteous permission of Frederick A. Stoker Company door opened, and Bayan pushed his way in and shook himself, and licked Maroosia and Vanya and startled Vladimir, and lay down under the table and came out again, because he was so pleased to be home. And old Peter came in after him.

"You are snug in here, little pigeons," he said.

Vanya and Maroosia had jumped up to welcome him, and when he opened his big sheepskin coat, they tumbled into it together and clung to his belt. Then he closed the big woolly coat over the top of them and they squealed; and he opened it a little way and looked down at them over his beard, and then closed it again for a moment before letting them out. He did this every night, and Bayan always barked when they were shut up inside.

Then old Peter took his big coat off and lifted down the samovar from the shelf. The samovar is like a big tea-urn, with a red-hot fire in the middle of it keeping the water boiling. It hums like a bee on the tea-table, and the steam rises in a little jet from a tiny hole in the top. The boiling water comes out of a tap at the bottom. Old Peter threw in the lighted sticks and charcoal, and made a draught to draw the heat, and then set the samovar on the table with the little fire crackling in its inside. Then he cut some big lumps of black bread. Then he took a great saucepan full of soup, that was simmering on the stove, and emptied it into a big wooden bowl. Then he went to the wall where, on three nails, hung three wooden spoons, deep like ladles. There were one big spoon, for old Peter; and two little spoons, one for Vanya and one for Maroosia.

And all the time that old Peter was getting supper ready he was answering questions and making jokes— old ones, of course, that he made every day—about what the Man in the Moon said when he fell out, and what the wolf said who caught his own tail and ate himself up before he found out his mistake.

And Vanya and Maroosia danced about the hut and chuckled. Then they had supper, all three dipping their wooden spoons in the big bowl together, and eating a tremendous lot of black bread. And, of course, there were scraps for Vladimir and a bone for Bayan.

After that they had tea with sugar but no milk, because they were Russians and liked it that way.

Old Peter had a sister who lived in the village not so very far away from the forest. And she had a plump daughter, and the daughter was called Nastasia, and she was married to a handsome peasant called Sergie, who had three cows, a lot of pigs, and a flock of fat geese. And tonight old Peter said to the children, "There's something new in the village."

"What sort of a something?" asked Vanya.

"Alive," said old Peter.

"Is there a lot of it?" asked Vanya.

"No, only one."

"Then it can't be pigs," said Vanya, in a melancholy voice. "I thought it was pigs."

"Perhaps it is a little calf," said Maroosia.

"I know what it is," said Vanya.

"Well?"

"It's a foal. It's brown all over with white on its nose, and a lot of white hairs in its tail."

"No."

"What is it then, grandfather?"

"I'll tell you, little pigeons. It's small and red, and it's got a bumpy head with hair on it like the fluff of a duckling. It has blue eyes, and ten fingers to its fore paws, and ten toes to its hind feet—five to each."

"It's a baby," said Maroosia.

"Yes. Nastasia has got a little son, Aunt Sofia has got a grandson, you have got a new cousin, and I have got a new grand-nephew."

The children had jumped up as soon as they knew it was a baby.

"When is the christening?"

"The day after to-morrow."

"O grandfather!"

"Well?"

"Who is going to the christening?"

"The baby, of course."

"Yes; but other people?"

"All the village."

"And us?"

"I have to go, and I suppose there'll be room in the cart for two little bear cubs like you."

And so it was settled that Vanya and Maroosia were to go to the christening of their new cousin. All the next day they could think of nothing else, and early on the morning of the christening they were up and about, Maroosia seeing that Vanya had on a clean shirt, and herself putting a green ribbon in her hair. The sun shone, and the leaves on the trees were all new and bright, and the sky was pale blue through the flickering green leaves.

Old Peter was up early too, harnessing the little yellow horse into the old cart. The cart was of rough wood, without springs, like a big box fixed on long

UP ONE PAIR OF STAIRS

larch poles between two pairs of wheels. The larch poles did instead of springs, bending and creaking, as the cart moved over the forest track. The shafts came from the front wheels upwards to the horse's shoulders, and between the ends of them there was a tall, strong hoop of wood, called a douga, which rose high over the shoulders of the horse, above his collar, and had two little bells hanging from it at the top. The wooden hoop was painted green with

little red flowers. The harness was mostly ropes, but that did not matter so long as it held together. The horse had a long tail and mane, and looked as untidy as a little boy; but he had a green ribbon in his forelock in honour of the christening, and he could go like anything, and never got tired.

When all was ready, old Peter arranged a lot of soft fresh hay in the cart for the children to sit in. Hay is the best thing in the world to sit in when you drive in a jolting Russian cart. Old Peter put in a tremendous lot, so that the horse could eat some of it while waiting in the village, and yet leave them enough to make them comfortable on the journey back.

Presently Vanya and Maroosia were tucked into the hay, and old Peter climbed in with the plaited reins, and away they went along the narrow forest track, where the wheels followed the ruts and splashed through the deep holes; for the spring was young and the roads had not yet dried. Some of the deepest holes had a few pine branches laid in them, but that was the only road-mending that ever was done. Overhead were the tall firs and silver birches with their little, pale, round leaves; and somewhere, not far away, a cuckoo was calling, while the murmur of the wild pigeons never stopped for a moment.

They drove on and on through the forest, and at last came out from among the trees into the open country, a broad, flat plain stretching to the river.

UP ONE PAIR OF STAIRS

Far away they could see the big, square sail of a boat, swelled out in the light wind, and they knew that there was the river, on the banks of which stood the village. They could see a small clump of trees, and, as they came nearer, the pale green cupolas of the white village church rising above the tops of the birches.

They passed a little girl with a flock of geese, and another little girl lying in the grass holding a long rope which was fastened to the horns of a brown cow. And the little girl lay on her face and slept among the flowers, while the cow walked slowly round her, step by step, chewing the grass and thinking about nothing at all.

And at last they came to the village, where the road was wider; and instead of one pair of ruts there were dozens, and the cart bumped worse than ever. The broad earthy road had no stones in it; and in places where the puddles would have been deeper than the axles of the wheels, it had been mended by laying down fir logs and small branches in the puddles, and putting a few spadefuls of earth on the top of them.

The road ran right through the village. On either side of it were little wooden huts. The ends of the timbers crossed outside at the four corners of the huts. They fitted neatly into each other, and some of them were carved. And there were no slates or tiles on the roofs, but little thin slips of wood overlapping each other. There was not a single stone hut or cottage in the village. Only the church was partly brick, whitewashed, with bright green cupolas up in the air, and thin gold crosses on the tops of the cupolas, shining in the clear sky.

Outside the church were rows of short posts, with long rough fir timbers nailed on the top of them, to which the country people tied their horses when they came to church. There were several carts there already, with bright-coloured rugs lying on the hay in them; and the horses were eating hay or biting the logs. Always, except when the logs are quite new, you can tell the favourite places for tying up horses to them, because the timbers will have deep holes in them, where they have been gnawed away by the horses' teeth. They bite the timbers, while their masters eat sunflower seeds, not for food, but to pass the time.

"Now then," said old Peter, as he got down from the cart, tied the horse, gave him an armful of hay from the cart, and lifted the children out. "Be quick. We shall be late if we don't take care. I believe we are late already."

Old Peter hurried into the church, followed by Vanya and Maroosia. The ceremony was just beginning.

The priest, in his silk robes, was standing before the gold and painted screen at the end of the church, and there were the basin of holy water, and old Peter's sister, and the nurse Babka Tanya, very proud, holding the baby in a roll of white linen, and rocking it to and fro. There were coloured pictures of saints all over the screen, which stretches from one side of the church to the other. Some of the pictures were framed in gilt frames under glass, and were partly painted and partly metal. The faces and hands of the saints were painted, and their clothes were glittering silver or gold. Little lamps were burning in front of them, and candles.

A Russian christening is very different from an English one. For one thing, the baby goes right into the water, not once, but three times. Babka Tanya unrolled the baby, and the priest covered its face with his hand, and down it went under the water, once, twice, and again. Then he took some of the sacred ointment on his finger and anointed the baby's forehead, and feet, and hands, and little round stomach. Then, with a pair of scissors, he cut a little pinch of fluff from the baby's head, and rolled it into a pellet with the ointment, and threw the pellet into the holy water. And after that the baby was carried solemnly three times 'round the holy water.

The priest blessed it and prayed for it; and there it was, a little true Russian, ready to be carried back to its mother, Nastasia, who lay at home in her cottage waiting for it.

When they got outside the church, they all went to Nastasia's cottage to congratulate her on her baby.

Nastasia smiled at Vanya and Maroosia; but they had no eyes except for the baby, and for all that belonged to it, especially its cradle. Now a Russian baby has

a very much finer cradle than an English baby. A
long fir pole is fastened in the middle and at one end
to the beams in the ceiling of the hut, so that the
other end swings free, just below the rafters. From
this end is hung a big basket, and on the ropes by
which the basket hangs are fastened shawls of bright
colours. The baby is tucked in the basket, the shawls
closed round it, and as the mother or the nurse sits

at her spinning, she just kicks the basket gently now and again, and it swings up and down from the end of the pole, as if it were hung from the branch of a tree.

There was a samovar already steaming in the cottage, and a great cake of pastry, and cabbage, and egg, and fish. And there were cabbage soup with sour cream, and black bread and a little white bread, and red kisel jelly and a huge jug of milk.

And everybody ate and drank and talked as if they were never going to stop.

At last, towards evening, old Peter packed what was left of the hay into the cart, and packed Vanya and Maroosia in with the hay. Everybody said good-byes all around, and Peter climbed in and took up the rope reins. Vanya and Maroosia waved their hands, and off they drove, back again to the hut in the forest.

THE BIRCHES*
WALTER PRITCHARD EATON
The little birches, white and slim,
Gleaming in the forest dim,
Must think the day is almost gone,
For each one has her nightie on.

*From *Echoes and Realities*, copyright, 1918.
George H. Doran Company, Publishers

The Little Snow Maiden

A RUSSIAN FOLK TALE

There was once a good man named Peter who lived with his wife Anastasia in a little village on the edge of the forest. Now these two, though there was much merry company in the huts about them, were always sorrowing because they had no children in their home. The woman never had to run to her door and peep out to see that her little one did not wander away, because she had no little one. So Peter and Anastasia would stand at their window and watch the neighbor's children and wish with all their hearts that one of these was their own.

One day they saw the little ones in their sheep-skin coats playing in the snow. They made snow forts and pelted each other with snowballs and laughed and shouted merrily. Then they rolled up the snow into a great snow woman and put an old kerchief on her head and an old shawl about her shoulders.

"Now, there's an idea, wife," said Peter. "Let us go out and make a little snow girl. Who knows?— perhaps she will come alive and be a daughter to us!"

"Good!" says the wife. "It's worth trying at least."

So out went the two in their big coats and their fur hats, and there in the back yard where no one could see them, they set to work. They rolled the snow together and began to fashion it into a little maiden. And so long had they tenderly dreamed of a little girl, that their great love fashioned her now a most beautiful creature—the loveliest ever seen.

Well, towards evening, when the sky was opal and smoke color and the clouds lay purple on the edge of the earth, she was finished. There she stood before them complete.

"Oh, my little white pigeon, speak to us," says Peter.

"Yes, speak, my darling," says Anastasia, "and run and skip and laugh like the other children."

Suddenly, in the twilight glow, the little maid's eyelids began to quiver; a faint flush bloomed on her cheeks; her lips parted in a smile. Then her eyes opened, and lo! they were blue as the sky at noon! All at once, she skipped from her place and began dancing about in the snow, dancing like a little white sprite and laughing softly, dancing like snow flakes whirled in the wind.

"God be thanked," says Peter. "Now we have a little girl to live with us! Run, wife, and fetch a blanket to keep her warm."

So Anastasia ran and got a blanket and wrapped it about the little snow maid, and Peter picked her up and carried her into the house.

"You must not keep me too warm," she said. So

Peter put her gently down on a bench farthest from the stove, and she smiled up at him and blew him a kiss. Then Anastasia got her a little white fur coat, and Peter went to the neighbor's and bought her a white fur cap and a pair of little white boots with white fur around the tops. But when she was dressed, the little snow maiden cried, "It is too hot here in the cottage. I must go out into the cold."

"Nay, nay, little pigeon," says Anastasia, "it is time I tucked you up warm in bed."

"O, ho! No, no!" says the little snow maiden, "I am a little daughter of the Snow. I cannot be tucked up under a blanket. I will play by myself in the yard all night." And out she danced into the cold.

Over the gleaming snow she tripped, down the silver path of the moonlight. Her garments glittered like diamonds, and the frost shone about her head like a little crown of stars.

For a long time the man and his good wife watched her. "Ah, God be thanked for the little girl that has come to us," they said again and again. Then at last they went to bed, but more than once that night they rose to look out of the window and make sure she had not run away. There she was just as before, dancing about in the moonlight and playing all alone.

In the morning she ran into the cottage with shining eyes.

"This is the porridge for me," she cried, and she

showed the good woman how to crush up a little piece of ice in a wooden bowl, for that was all she would eat. After breakfast she ran out into the road and joined the other children at play. How she played and how the children loved her. She could run faster than all the rest. Her little white boots twinkled and gleamed as she ran, and when she laughed, it was like the ringing peals of tiny silver bells.

The man and the woman watched her and were very proud.

"She is all our own," said Anastasia.

"Our little white pigeon," said Peter.

When it was time, she came in for her ice porridge,

but though Anastasia said to her, "To-night you'll surely sleep inside, my darling," she answered just as before, "O, ho! No, no! I am a little daughter of the Snow!"

Thus it went all through the winter. The little snow maiden nade Peter and Anastasia very happy. She was forever singing and laughing and dancing, in and out of the house, in and out of the house. She was very good, too, and she did everything Anastasia told her. Only she would never sleep in doors. She seemed happiest and most at home when the little snow flakes were dancing about in the air, and no storm was ever too severe to seem other than her playfellow.

But when there began to be signs of spring in the air, when the snow melted and one could run down the paths in the forest, when tiny green shoots peeped up here and there, then the little snow girl seemed to be drooping and longing for something. One day she came to Peter and Anastasia and said:

> "Time has come when I must go
> To my friends of Frost and Snow.
> Good-bye, dear ones here, good-bye.
> Back I go across the sky!"

Peter and Anastasia began to weep and lament very loudly. They wished to keep her all to themselves and not to share her with any one.

"Ah, my darling, you must not go!" cried Peter.

"Ah, my darling, you shall not go!" cried Anastasia.

And Peter ran and barred the door while Anastasia put her arms about her darling and held her close beside the stove.

"You shall not leave us! You shall not leave us!" they cried. But even as Anastasia held her tight, she seemed to melt slowly away. At last there was nothing left but a pool of water by the stove with a little fur cap in the midst and a little fur coat and boots. Yet it seemed to Anastasia and Peter as though they saw her still before them with her bright eyes shining, her long hair streaming, and heard her still faintly singing:

> "Time has come when I must go
> To my friends of Frost and Snow.
> Good-bye, dear ones here, good-bye.
> Back I go across the sky!"

"Oh, stay, stay, stay!" they begged, but all at once the very door that Peter had barred burst open. A cold wind swept into the room and when Peter had pushed the door shut again, lo! the little snow maiden had vanished!

Then Peter and Anastasia wept and thought they should never see her again. Anastasia carefully laid away the garments she had left behind and often through the summer she took out the little fur cap, the fur coat and the boots, to kiss them and think of her darling. But when winter had come again it happened one starlit night, that the two heard a silvery peal of laughter just outside the window.

"That sounds like our little snow maid!" cried Peter, and off he hurried to open the door. Sure enough! Into the room she danced again, her eyes as shining as ever, and she sang:

> "By frosty night and frosty day
> Your love calls me here to stay,
> Here till Spring I stay and then
> Back to Frost and Snow again!"

So Peter and Anastasia clasped the little snow maid in their arms; she put on her pretty white clothes again, and soon there she was out on the gleaming snow, tripping down the silver path of the moonlight, her garments glittering like diamonds, and the frost about her head like a crown of shining stars.

Each Springtime off she went northward to play through the summer with her friends on the frozen seas, but every winter, she stayed in Russia with Peter and Anastasia and they came not to mind her going for they knew she would come again.

Boots and His Brothers*
Sir George Webb Dasent

Once on a time there was a man who had three sons, Peter, Paul, and John. John was Boots, of course, because he was the youngest. I can't say the man had anything more than these three sons, for he hadn't one penny to rub against another; and so he told his sons over and over again they must go out into the world and try to earn their bread, for there at home there was nothing to be looked for but starving.

Now, a bit off the man's cottage was the King's palace, and you must know, just against the King's windows a great oak had sprung up, which was so stout and big that it took away all the light from the King's palace. The King had said he would give many, many dollars to the man who could fell the oak, but no one was man enough for that, for as soon as ever one chip of the oak's trunk flew off, two grew in its stead. A well, too, the King would have dug, which was to hold water for the whole year; for all his neighbors had wells, but he hadn't any, and that he thought a shame. So the King said

*From *Popular Tales from the Norse*, published by G. P. Putnam's Sons.

he would give any one who could dig him such a well as would hold water for a whole year round, both money and goods; but no one could do it, for the King's palace lay high, high up on a hill, and they hadn't dug a few inches before they came upon the living rock.

But as the King had set his heart on having these two things done, he had it given out far and wide, in all the churches of his kingdom, that he who could fell the big oak in the King's courtyard, and get him a well that would hold water the whole year round, should have the Princess and half the kingdom. Well, you may easily know there was many a man who came to try his luck; but for all their hacking and hewing, and all their digging and delving, it was no good. The oak got bigger and stouter at every stroke, and the rock didn't get softer either. So one day those three brothers thought they'd set off and try too, and their father hadn't a word against it; for even if they didn't get the Princess and half the kingdom, it might happen they might get a place somewhere with a good master; and that was all he wanted. So when the brothers said they thought of going to the palace, their father said "yes" at once. So Peter, Paul, and Jack went off from their home.

Well, they hadn't gone far before they came to a fir-wood, and up along one side of it rose a steep hillside, and as they went, they heard something hewing and hacking away up on the hill among the trees.

"I wonder now what it is that is hewing away up yonder," said Jack.

"You're always so clever with your wonderings," said Peter and Paul both at once. "What wonder is it, pray, that a woodcutter should stand and hack up on a hill-side?"

"Still, I'd like to see what it is, after all," said Jack; and up he went.

"Oh, if you're such a child, 'twill do you good to go and take a lesson," bawled out his brothers after him.

But Jack didn't care for what they said; he climbed the steep hill-side towards where the noise came, and when he reached the place, what do you think he saw? Why, an axe that stood there hacking and hewing, all of itself, at the trunk of a fir.

"Good day!" said Jack. "So you stand here all alone and hew, do you?"

"Yes; here I've stood and hewed and hacked a long, long time, waiting for you," said the Axe.

"Well, here I am at last," said Jack, as he took the axe, pulled it off its haft, and stuffed both head and haft into his wallet.

So when he got down again to his brothers, they began to jeer and laugh at him.

"And now, what funny thing was it you saw up yonder on the hill-side?" they said.

"Oh, it was only an axe we heard," said Jack.

So when they had gone a bit farther, they came under a steep spur of rock, and up there they heard something digging and shoveling.

"I wonder now," said Jack, "what it is digging and shoveling up yonder at the top of the rock."

"Ah, you're always so clever with your wonderings," said Peter and Paul again, "as if you'd never heard a woodpecker hacking and pecking at a hollow tree."

"Well, well," said Jack, "I think it would be a piece of fun just to see what it really is."

And so off he set to climb the rock, while the others laughed and made game of him. But he didn't care a bit for that; up he clomb, and when he got near the top, what do you think he saw? Why, a spade that stood there digging and delving.

"Good day!" said Jack. "So you stand here all alone, and dig and delve!"

"Yes, that's what I do," said the Spade, "and that's what I've done this many a long day, waiting for you."

"Well, here I am," said Jack again, as he took the spade and knocked it off its handle, and put it into his wallet, and then went down again to his brothers.

"Well, what was it, so rare and strange," said Peter and Paul, "that you saw up there at the top of the rock?"

"Oh," said Jack, "nothing more than a spade; that was what we heard."

So they went on again a good bit, till they came to a brook. They were thirsty, all three, after their long walk, and so they lay down beside the brook to have a drink.

"I wonder now," said Jack, "where all this water comes from."

"I wonder if you're right in your head. Where the brook comes from, indeed!" said Peter and Paul in one breath. "If you're not mad already, you'll go mad very soon, with your wonderings. Have you never heard how water rises from a spring in the earth?"

"Yes; but still I've a great fancy to see where this brook comes from," said Jack.

So up alongside the brook he went, in spite of all that his brothers bawled after him. Nothing could stop

241

him. On he went. So, as he went up and up, the brook got smaller and smaller, and at last, a little way farther on, what do you think he saw? Why, a great walnut, and out of that the water trickled.

"Good-day!" said Jack again. "So you lie here, and trickle and run down all alone?"

"Yes, I do," said the Walnut; "and here have I trickled and run this many a long day, waiting for you."

"Well, here I am," said Jack, as he took up a lump of moss, and plugged up the hole, that the water mightn't run out. Then he put the walnut into his wallet, and ran down to his brothers.

"Well, now," said Peter and Paul, "have you found out where the water comes from? A rare sight it must have been!"

"Oh, after all, it was only a hole it ran out of," said Jack; and so the others laughed and made game of him again, but Jack didn't mind that a bit.

"After all, I had the fun of seeing it," he said.

So when they had gone a bit farther, they came to the King's palace; but as every one in the kingdom had heard how they might win the Princess and half the realm, if they could only fell the big oak and dig the King's well, so many had come to try their luck that the oak was twice as stout and big as it had been at first, for two chips grew for every one they hewed out with their axes, as I daresay you all bear in mind. So the King had now laid it down as a punishment, that if any one tried and couldn't fell the oak, he should be put on a barren island, and both his ears were to be clipped off. But the two brothers didn't let themselves be scared by that; they were quite sure they could fell the oak, and Peter, as he was eldest, was to try his hand first; but it went with him as with all the rest who had hewn at the oak; for every chip he cut out, two grew in its place. So the King's men seized him, and clipped off both his ears, and put him out on the barren island.

Now Paul, he was to try his luck, but he fared just the same; when he had hewn two or three strokes, they began to see the oak grow, and so the King's men seized him too, and clipped his ears, and put him off on the island.

So now Jack was to try.

"If you will look like a marked sheep, we're quite ready to clip your ears at once, and then you'll save yourself some bother," said the King, for he was angry with him for his brothers' sake.

"Well, I'd like just to try first," said Jack, and so he got leave. Then he took his axe out of his wallet and fitted it to its haft.

"Hew away!" said he to his axe; and away it hewed, making the chips fly again, so that it wasn't long before down came the oak.

When that was done, Jack pulled out his spade, and fitted it to its handle.

"Dig away!" said he to the spade; and so the spade began to dig and delve till the earth and rock flew out in splinters, and so he had the well soon dug out, you may think.

And when he had got it as big and deep as he chose, Jack took out his walnut and laid it in one corner of the well, and pulled the plug of moss out.

"Trickle and run," said Jack; and so the nut trickled and ran, till the water gushed out of the hole in a stream and in a short time the well was brimfull.

Then Jack had felled the oak which shaded the King's palace, and dug a well in the palace-yard and so he got the Princess and half the kingdom, as the King had promised. Every one said, "Well, after all, Jack wasn't so much out of his mind when he took to wondering."

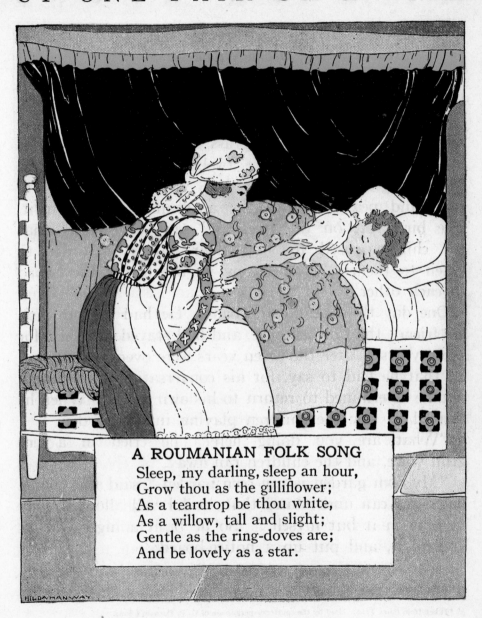

A ROUMANIAN FOLK SONG

Sleep, my darling, sleep an hour,
Grow thou as the gilliflower;
As a teardrop be thou white,
As a willow, tall and slight;
Gentle as the ring-doves are;
And be lovely as a star.

The Selfish Giant*

OSCAR WILDE

Every afternoon, as they were coming from school, the children used to go and play in the Giant's garden.

It was a large, lovely garden, with soft, green grass. Here and there over the grass stood beautiful flowers like stars, and there were twelve peach-trees that in the spring-time broke out into delicate blossoms of pink and pearl, and in the autumn bore rich fruit. The birds sat on the trees and sang so sweetly that the children used to stop their games in order to listen to them. "How happy we are here!" they cried to each other.

One day the Giant came back. He had been to visit his friend, the Cornish ogre, and had stayed with him for seven years. After the seven years were over he had said all that he had to say, for his conversation was limited, and he determined to return to his own castle. When he arrived he saw the children playing in the garden.

"What are you doing here?" he cried in a very gruff voice, and the children ran away.

"My own garden is my own garden," said the Giant; "any one can understand that, and I will allow nobody to play in it but myself." So he built a high wall all around it, and put up a notice-board:

Trespassers Will Be Prosecuted

He was a very selfish Giant.

*Taken from *Fairy Tales*. Used by the courteous permission of G. P. Putnam's Sons.

UP ONE PAIR OF STAIRS

The poor children had now nowhere to play. They tried to play on the road, but the road was very dusty and full of hard stones, and they did not like it. They used to wander round the high wall when their lessons were over, and talk about the beautiful garden inside. "How happy we were there," they said to each other.

Then the Spring came, and all over the country there were little blossoms and little birds. Only in the garden of the Selfish Giant it was still winter. The birds did not care to sing in it as there were no children, and the trees forgot to blossom. Once a beautiful flower put its head out from the grass, but when it saw the notice-board it was so sorry for the children that it slipped back into the ground again, and went off to sleep. The only people who were pleased were the Snow and the Frost. "Spring has forgotten this garden," they cried, "so we will live here all the year round." The Snow covered up the grass with her white cloak, and the Frost painted all the trees silver. Then they invited the North Wind to stay with them, and he came. He was wrapped in furs, and he roared all day about the garden, and blew the chimney-pots down. "This is a delightful spot," he said, "we must ask the Hail on a visit." So the Hail came. Every day for three hours he rattled on the roof of the castle till he broke most of the slates, and then he ran round and round the garden as fast as he could go. He was dressed in grey, and his breath was like ice.

"I cannot understand why the Spring is so late in coming," said the Selfish Giant, as he sat at the window and looked out at his cold, white garden; "I hope there will be a change in the weather."

But the Spring never came, nor the Summer. The Autumn gave golden fruit to every garden, but to the Giant's garden she gave none. "He is too self-ish," she said. So it was always Winter there, and the North Wind, and the Hail, and the Frost, and the Snow danced about through the trees.

One morning the Giant was lying awake in bed when he heard some lovely music. It sounded so sweet to his ears that he thought it must be the King's

musicians passing by. It was really only a little linnet singing outside his window, but it was so long since he had heard a bird sing in his garden that it seemed to him to be the most beautiful music in the world. Then the Hail stopped dancing over his head, and the North Wind ceased roaring, and a delicious perfume came to him through the open casement. "I believe the Spring has come at last," said the Giant; and he jumped out of bed and looked out.

What did he see?

He saw a most wonderful sight. Through a little hole in the wall the children had crept in, and they were sitting in the branches of the trees. In every tree that he could see there was a little child. And the trees were so glad to have the children back again that they had coverd themselves with blossoms, and were waving their arms gently above the children's heads. The birds were flying about and twittering with delight, and the flowers were looking up through the green grass and laughing. It was a lovely scene, only in one corner it was still winter. It was the farthest corner of the garden, and in it was standing a little boy. He was so small that he could not reach up to the branches of the tree, and he was wandering all around it, crying bitterly. The poor tree was still quite covered with frost and snow, and the North Wind was blowing and roaring above it. "Climb up! little boy," said the Tree, and bent its branches down as low as it could; but the boy was too tiny.

And the Giant's heart melted as he looked out. "How selfish I have been!" he said; "now I know why the Spring would not come here. I will put that poor little boy on the top of the tree, and then I will knock down the wall, and my garden shall be the children's playground for ever and ever." He was really very sorry for what he had done.

So he crept downstairs and opened the front door quite softly, and went out into the garden. But when the children saw him they were so frightened that they all ran away, and the garden became winter again. Only the little boy did not run, for his eyes were so full of tears that he did not see the Giant coming. And the Giant stole up behind him and took him gently in his hand, and put him up into the tree. And the tree broke at once into blossom, and the birds came and sang on it, and the little boy stretched out his two arms and flung them round the Giant's neck and kissed him. And the other children when they saw that the Giant was not wicked any longer, came running back, and with them came the Spring. "It is your garden now, little children," said the Giant, and he took a great axe and knocked down the wall. And when the people were going to market at twelve o'clock they found the Giant playing with the children in the most beautiful garden they had ever seen.

Elsa and the Ten Elves

A SWEDISH FAIRY TALE

Once upon a time there was a pretty, sweet-tempered little girl named Elsa. She lived on a farm, but her father, who was very proud of her, sent her to school in the city. There she learned reading, writing, singing, dancing, and a number of other pretty accomplishments, but she did not learn how to cook, sew, or care for a house. The truth of the matter was, that Elsa was lazy and did not like anything that she called work.

When she grew older, many young men wished her for a wife, but among them all she chose her neighbour, Gunner, a handsome, industrious young farmer. So the two were married, and went to live on Gunner's farm.

At first they were very happy, but as the days passed, and Elsa did not direct the servants in their work or see that the house was kept in order, everything went wrong. The provisions in the storerooms were tumbled about, food was found missing, and the house was dirty. Poor Gunner was miserable, but he loved Elsa too much to say a word to her about it.

The day before Christmas came; the sun had been up and people bustling about the house for hours. Still Elsa lay fast asleep in her bed. At last a servant came into her room.

"O mistress," she said, "the master and his men

are ready to set off for the woods. They are waiting for us to make ready their luncheon. What shall we pack in their lunch bags?"

"Don't talk to me," said Elsa sleepily. "Leave the room!"

Soon another servant came in. "Dear mistress," she cried, "the bread dough has risen soft and light. If you come and knead it at once, the bread will be better than usual."

"Go away!" answered Elsa.

"I want candlewicks, dear mistress," called a third.

"Go away!" answered Elsa.

"What food shall we prepare for dinner to-morrow?" shouted a fourth.

"Go away!" answered Elsa.

And so it went; servant after servant came running into the room asking for orders, but Elsa would only answer, "Go away!" and she would not get up.

At last Gunner could stand it no longer. There were he and his men long delayed in their start for the woods because no one knew what to pack for their luncheon. So off he went to Elsa's room.

"Dear Elsa," he said gently, "my mother used to prepare things the night before, so that the servants might begin work early in the morning. She did not lie in bed when the sun was up. My men and I are off now with I know not what in our lunch bags. Surely you are ready by this time to rise. Remember there are a few yards of cloth on the loom waiting to be woven." Then Gunner went away.

As soon as he was gone, Elsa got up grumbling and yawning. After she had dressed herself, she slowly ate her breakfast, and then went, loitering, off through the kitchen to the little house where the

loom was kept. But when she got there, she slammed the door behind her, and threw herself down on a couch.

"No!" she cried, half sobbing, "I won't do this weaving!—I won't toil and drudge! Who would have thought that Gunner would make me work like a servant? Oh, me! Oh, me! Is there no one to help me?"

"I can help you," said a deep voice.

Then Elsa, raising her head in astonishment, saw an old man in a blue cloak and a broad-brimmed hat, standing close by her side.

"I am Old Man Hoberg," he said, "and have served your family for many years. You, my child, are unhappy because you are idle. To be idle makes any man miserable. I will give you ten obedient servants who shall do all your tasks for you."

At that he shook his long, blue cloak, and out of its folds tumbled ten queer little men. For a moment they capered and pranced about. Then they swiftly put the room in order and finished weaving the cloth on the loom. When their work was done, they came running up and stood in a row before Elsa, as though awaiting her orders.

"Dear child, reach hither your hands," said the old man.

Trembling and uncertain, Elsa held out the tips of her fingers.

Then he cried:

"Hop-o'-My-Thumb,
Lick-the-Pot,
Long-Pole,
Heart-in-Hand,
Little-Peter-Funny-Man,
Away all of you to your places!"

In the twinkling of an eye the little men popped into Elsa's fingers, and the old man vanished from sight.

For a moment Elsa sat staring at her hands. Then suddenly a great desire to work came over her. Up she jumped.

"Why am I idling here?" she cried. "It is late in the morning and nothing done in the house!" And she hastened off to the kitchen. Soon she was giving orders to the servants, setting things to rights everywhere and singing while she prepared the dinner.

When Gunner came home that night, all was clean and bright to welcome him, and Elsa's face shone brighter than all the rest. "O ho!" he cried heartily, "some good fairy has been here!"

Elsa smiled and held up her ten rosy fingers.

"Ten good fairies," she said.

After that Elsa rose early each morning, and went about her work sweet-tempered and happy. The farmhouse prospered under her hands, and health, wealth, and happiness came to stay when she learned how to manage those ten little elves.

A PSALM OF DAVID

THE Lord is my Shepherd;
   I shall not want.
He maketh me to lie down in green pastures:
   He leadeth me beside the still waters.
   He restoreth my soul:
   He leadeth me in the paths of righteousness
   For His name's sake.

Yea, though I walk through the valley
   Of the shadow of death, I will fear no evil:
      For Thou art with me;
         Thy rod and Thy staff they comfort me.

Thou preparest a table before me
   In the presence of mine enemies;
      Thou anointest my head with oil;
         My cup runneth over.

Surely goodness and mercy shall follow me
   All the days of my life:
      And I will dwell in the
         House of the Lord forever.   *Psalm 23*

The Feast of Tabernacles
(*The First Thanksgiving Festival*)
ADAPTED FROM THE BIBLE

In the autumn, men gather in from orchard, field and vineyard the rich harvest, and when their storehouses are bursting with golden grain and ripened fruit, their hearts go out in rejoicing and thanksgiving to God who made all that was made, and causes it to grow and bring forth fruit abundantly.

In the early days, long, long ago, the whole nation of the Israelites, men, women, and children, wandered for many years through the desert and through the wilderness, fleeing out of Egypt, where they had served hard task masters and built great treasure-cities, toiling as slaves in the burning sun. They had no settled home, but dwelt in tents, or tabernacles, through all their years of wandering, and they had neither field nor orchard because they journeyed from place to place continually. Yet God led them every step of the way through the wilderness and brought them at last into a good land which He had promised unto them. There He caused them to build again their dwelling places, and to plant vineyard, field, and orchard. And when the people saw once more the fruitfulness of God made manifest in a plenteous harvest, they sang in their hearts:

"O come, let us sing unto the Lord.
Let us come before His presence with thanksgiving
And make a joyful noise unto Him with psalms."

And in honor of Him who had saved them from the wilderness and brought forth for them so rich a harvest, they kept year after year a solemn feast unto the Lord their God.

In the fifteenth day of the seventh month when they had gathered in the fruit of the land, they kept a feast unto the Lord seven days. And the people went forth and brought them olive branches, and pine branches, and myrtle branches, and palm branches, and made themselves booths, everyone upon the roof of his house, and in their courts, and in the courts of the house of God, and in the streets.

And they dwelt not in their houses, but in the booths for seven days, that their children might know that the

Lord made the children of Israel to dwell in booths when He brought them out of the land of Egypt.

And they rejoiced in the feast, they and their sons, and their daughters, and their manservants, and their maidservants, and the Levite, the stranger, and the fatherless that were within their gates.

Seven days they kept a solemn feast unto the Lord their God. Because the Lord their God had blessed them in all their increase, and in all the works of their hands, therefore did they surely rejoice!

WE THANK THEE
RALPH WALDO EMERSON

For flowers that bloom about our feet;
For tender grass, so fresh, so sweet;
For song of bird, and hum of bee;
For all things fair we hear or see,
  Father in heaven, we thank Thee!
For blue of stream and blue of sky;
For pleasant shade of branches high;
For fragrant air and cooling breeze;
For beauty of the blooming trees,
  Father in heaven, we thank Thee!

MARJORIE'S ALMANAC*
THOMAS BAILEY ALDRICH

Robins in the tree-top,
  Blossoms in the grass,
Green things a-growing
  Everywhere you pass;
Sudden little breezes,
  Showers of silver dew,
Black bough and bent twig
  Budding out anew;
Pine-tree and willow-tree,
  Fringèd elm and larch,—
Don't you think that May-time's
  Pleasanter than March?

Apples in the orchard
  Mellowing one by one;
Strawberries upturning
  Soft cheeks to the sun;
Roses faint with sweetness,
  Lilies fair of face,
Drowsy scents and murmurs
  Haunting every place;
Lengths of golden sunshine,
  Moonlight bright as day,—
Don't you think that summer's
  Pleasanter than May?

*Used by permission of, and by special arrangement with, Houghton Mifflin Company.

Roger in the corn-patch
  Whistling negro songs;
Pussy by the hearth-side
  Romping with the tongs;
Chestnuts in the ashes
  Bursting through the rind;
Red leaf and gold leaf
  Rustling down the wind;
Mother "doin' peaches"
  All the afternoon,—
Don't you think that autumn's
  Pleasanter than June?

Little fairy snow-flakes
  Dancing in the flue;
Old Mr. Santa Claus,
  What is keeping you?
Twilight and firelight
  Shadows come and go;
Merry chime of sleigh-bells
  Tinkling through the snow;
Mother knitting stockings
  (Pussy's got the ball),—
Don't you think that winter's
  Pleasanter than all?

The Story of Tom Thumb
AN ENGLISH FOLK TALE

Long ago in the days of the great King Arthur, there was an honest plough-man who lived with his wife in a neat, comfortable cottage. They would have been a very happy couple except for the fact that they had no children.

"I should be the happiest woman in the world," said the wife one day, "if only I had a son. Even if he were no bigger than my husband's thumb, still I should be satisfied."

Some time after this it came to pass that the good woman's wish was fulfilled. She did indeed have a son, and, strange to say, he was not one bit bigger than his father's thumb. The Queen of the Fairies, wishing to see the child, flew in at the window, when he was but a few days old, and found his mother feeding him out of the cup of an acorn. As soon as the Queen saw the little fellow, she kissed him and gave him the name of Tom Thumb. Then she sent for some of her fairies to come and dress him according to her orders.

They made him a little hat of an oak leaf; his shirt was of spider's web, his jacket of thistledown, and his trousers of tiny feathers. His stockings they made of apple-rind and his shoes of nicely tanned mouse's skin.

Tom never grew any bigger than his father's thumb, but he was a brave and merry little fellow, so his parents loved him dearly. One day his mother was making a batter pudding and she placed him in an empty egg shell to keep him out of mischief. But Tom, being very anxious to see how she stirred up the batter, climbed out of the egg shell and up the slippery side of the bowl. The next thing he knew, he lost his footing and plumped head over heels into the batter.

His mother never noticed him but stirred him right into the pudding. Then she dumped him into the pudding bag and put him in the kettle to boil. The batter filled Tom's mouth and prevented him from crying out, but he kicked and struggled with all his might to get himself free. His mother, seeing her pudding dance madly round about in the pot as though it were alive, seized it in alarm and threw it out of the window.

Just at that time a tinker was passing by, and as he saw a nice looking pudding coming his way, he picked it up and started to eat it. By that time, Tom had got his mouth free of the batter and he began to cry aloud:

"Let me go! Let me go, Tom the Tinker!"

The Tinker was so startled to hear the pudding

DONN P CRANE

talk, that he flung it over the hedge and ran away
as fast as his legs would carry him. But the fall had
broken the pudding all to bits, so Tom crept out,
all covered with batter, and made his way home.
His mother was very sorry to see her darling in such a
state, but she put him in a teacup and washed him off
clean; then she kissed him and put him to bed.

Soon after this, Tom's mother went one day to milk
her cow in the pasture, and she took him along with
her. It was a very windy day, and, in order to make
sure that he should not blow away, she tied him to a
thistle with a strand of fine thread. The cow was
peacefully eating, but she soon spied Tom's oak leaf
hat and, thinking it a good looking morsel to eat,
she took up the little fellow and the thistle at a
mouthful. When the cow began to chew, Tom had
great difficulty to keep out of the way of her teeth
and her tongue, but he called out boldly, "Mother!
Mother!"

UP ONE PAIR OF STAIRS

"Oh, Tommy, my dear little Tommy, where are you?" cried his mother.

"I'm here in the red cow's mouth!" he answered bravely.

At that, the cow, surprised at the odd tickling as of something moving in her throat, opened her mouth and let Tom drop out. His mother caught him in her apron as he was falling to the ground, and ran off home with him.

Tom often went to the fields with his father, and, as he was anxious to be of use, he one day begged to be allowed to take home the horse and cart. His father laughed at the very idea of little Tom's driving a huge horse.

"You! why you couldn't even reach up to the top of his hoofs!" he cried. "How are you going to hold the reins?"

"Oh," answered Tom, quite confidently, "I don't need to hold the reins. I'll just sit in the horse's ear and call out which way he is to go!"

The father was amazed that his son should think of anything so bold and clever, so he placed little Tom in the horse's ear and let him set out.

"Yeo hup! Yeo hup!" cried Tom and guided the

horse so well, he reached home in a very short time.

Tom's mother was greatly surprised when she saw the horse arrive at the cottage with no one to drive him, but Tom called out, "Mother, mother, take me down! I'm in the horse's ear!"

"Now just to think of a little man like you driving a great big beast like that!" cried his mother, and she was so pleased with what he had done, that she lifted him carefully down and gave him a whole big red currant for his supper.

Seeing how helpful his son could be, the father now made him a little whip of a barley straw, so he could sometimes drive the cattle home. As he was in the field thus at work one day, a raven spied him and picked him up, soaring high in the air and carrying him away. He dropped him at last from his talons into the top of a tree near a giant's castle. Pretty soon, out came the giant for a walk on the terrace. Mistaking Tom for the fruit of the tree, he plucked him off the branch and opened his mouth to swallow him. But just then along through the air came the Queen of the Fairies, in a chariot drawn by flying mice. Snatching Tom from the giant's hand, she placed him beside her and drove off with him to Fairyland.

In that lovely country Tom spent many happy days, being well entertained by the fairies, but, after a time, the Queen dressed him in a new little suit of bright green, and sent him floating on a lively breeze straight to King Arthur's palace.

As Tom was flying over the palace yard, the King's cook passed along below with a great bowl of the King's favorite dish, frumenty. At that moment the breeze dropped Tom and he fell plumb into the middle of the bowl, making the cook drop it with a smash and spill all the King's dainty frumenty.

"Help! help! thieves!" cried the cook who was a red-faced, cross-grained fellow. Swearing that Tom had meant to play this trick on him, he caught him and put him in a mouse trap, there to keep him till he could take him and make complaint of him before the King.

But while Tom was there, the cat, seeing something moving in the cage, thought him a mouse, and so rolled the cage about between her paws till she had broken it and set him loose. Then Tom ran off and hid himself in an empty snail's shell. There he stayed in safety till he grew hungry. Peeping out in search of some means to get food, he saw a great butter-fly alight on a flower near him, so he sprang at once astride the butterfly's back and the little creature flew up with him into the air and flitted from flower to flower. But at last, attracted by a light in the King's dining-room, the butterfly flew in at the open window. King, Queen and nobles tried to catch him, but they could not. What with the darting and dodging,

however, Tom, having neither saddle nor bridle, lost his seat and fell sprawling on the table.

King, Queen and nobles all spied the little man at once and everyone was delighted with him. Far from punishing him for spoiling his frumenty, the King gave him a half blackberry for his supper, and he soon became a great favorite. His tricks and gambols and lively words amused the whole court, and when the King rode out, he often took Tom along, he thought so much of his company. If it happened to rain, Tom would creep in the King's pocket and sleep there quite cozily till the rain was over.

At length King Arthur ordered a little chair to be made, so that Tom might sit before him on the table. And he caused to be built for him also a palace of gold, a span high, with a door just an inch in width, and he gave him a little golden coach with six small white mice to draw it.

But Tom still thought of his mother and father, and one day he asked the King to let him pay them a visit. King Arthur not only consented, but when he heard that Tom's parents were poor, he led him into the treasury where he kept all his gold and told him he might take them as much money as he could carry. Tom, with much difficulty, dragged out a three-penny piece, and loaded it on his back. Then he toiled along the road beneath his mighty burden for two whole days and nights before he reached his father's cottage.

His mother met him at the door and could not thank him enough for taking so much trouble, all for love of them. She placed him in a walnut shell by the fireside, made him comfortable and cozy, and feasted him for three days, till he had consumed the

DONN P CRANE

whole of a hazel-nut which had been prepared for him.

When he had thoroughly rested and enjoyed himself with his family, his duty told him it was time to return to court. So he bade his mother and father good-bye and was off.

As soon as he returned, King Arthur made him a knight. Sir Thomas Thumb he was now called, and the King gave him a needle for a sword and a mouse for a horse. Thus armed and mounted, he rode out with the King and his knights, and all enjoyed a hearty laugh at sight of Sir Thomas and his prancing steed.

One fine day as they passed a farm house, a large black cat jumped out and rushed upon him and his mouse. But Tom drew his needle and boldly defended himself and his steed, till one of the King's knights came to his assistance and carried him safely off.

Thus Sir Thomas Thumb held his own bravely in the world and withal was so merry, lively and bold, that he won the respect and affection of all. In later years he was often heard to sing:

"My name is Tom Thumb;
From the fairies I've come;
When King Arthur shone,
His court was my home.
In me he delighted,
By him I was knighted;
Did you never once hear of Sir Thomas Thumb?"

The Girl Who Used Her Wits
A CHINESE FOLK TALE

There lived once a long time ago in China, a woman named Fow Chow who had two sons. These sons married young girls from a village some distance away, and when the wedding festivities were over, they brought their wives home to live with their mother.

Now Lotus-blossom and Moon-flower, the two daughters-in-law, were good and obedient young women. They were always very respectful to their mother-in-law. They waited upon her, made her tea whenever she wished it, and served her her bowl of rice and stewed meat, or salt fish and vegetables, three times a day on her little carved red lacquer table in the best blue china dishes. But, though they were always thus obedient to the head of the family, they were forever coming to the place where she sat in state in the house, bowing low before her and begging respectfully:

"Honored lady, we pray you, let us go for a few days and pay a visit in the village where we were born."

The mother-in-law grew wearied at last with their always wanting to leave home and go a merry-making, so she thought to herself, "I will find a way to end this once and for all."

The next time they came, bowed low before her, and made their request, she said:

"Yes, little pheasants, you may go and pay the visit in your old village. Go as soon as you like.

271

But remember this—you must bring me back when you come, the only two things for which I have a desire in all the world, or you shall never again return to your husbands and your home!"

"Oh, we will gladly bring you whatever you like, honored lady!" cried the thoughtless young women.

"Very well then," said the mother-in-law, "you, Lotus-blossom, shall bring me back some fire, wrapped in a paper, and you, Moon-flower, shall bring me wind in a paper!"

So anxious were the young girls to be off, that they promised at once to bring back what the honored lady asked, without once stopping to think how they should ever be able to get such remarkable presents.

They took leave of their husbands and started at once, chatting gaily together on the way. Through the crowds of pigs, and fowls, and children in the village street they tripped, past rows of little one-story houses with quaintly carved, gay-colored porches, and out of the gate of the village. They had made their way well along the highway and put many a field of indigo, rice, and sugar-cane behind them, when all of a sudden it came over Lotus-blossom just what her mother-in-law had asked of her. She must bring back some fire wrapped in a paper or she could never again return to her husband and her home.

On the instant, Lotus-blossom stopped short in the road and began to cry. And when Lotus-blossom began

to cry, Moon-flower stopped too and remembered what she had been ordered to bring back—wind in a paper! Who could ever do such a thing?

So Lotus-blossom and Moon-flower both flung themselves down by the roadside and cried together. "Never, never, never," they sobbed, "can we go home again."

As they sat there, along toward them from the fields came a young girl riding on a water-buffalo. She stopped before them and asked, "Why are you crying?"

The only answer was, "Boo hoo! Boo hoo! Boo hoo!"

"Crying will not help matters," said the girl. "It is better to consider and see if you cannot find a way out of your difficulties. Tell me what troubles you."

So at last the young women dried their tears long enough to tell her their trouble.

"Well," said the girl, "it is true you have been

thoughtless and heedless, but if you are ready now to use your wits, we may still find a way out of the matter. Come home with me; we will put our heads together and see if we cannot think how to fulfill your mother-in-law's commands."

Now Lotus-blossom and Moon-flower had never even dreamed of thinking, but seeing that the girl honestly hoped to help them, they got up behind her on the water-buffalo and went off with her. When they reached her father's house, they all sat down on the floor of the porch and began to consider. Soon the girl sprang to her feet and ran into the house.

In a few moments she returned and in her hand she held, lo! a paper lantern as round as the moon, and inside the lantern was a lighted candle!

"Ah," cried Lotus-blossom, raising her hands joyously toward the lantern, "There you have it! The very thing for me to take back to my honored mother-in-law—fire wrapped in a paper."

But Moon-flower was still frowning; she had thought of no way whereby she could fulfill her mother-in-law's command.

So their hostess sat down between them again and thought for a time longer. Then she rose once more, went into the house, and returned with a beautifully painted fan.

"Take this and wave it back and forth!" she cried to Moon-flower. The young wife did as she was told,

and behold! the paper carried wind against her face!

"Wind in a paper!" cried Moon-flower in astonishment. "Now I too may return to my home!"

So the two young women gratefully took leave of the girl who used her wits. They paid the visit to their native village and when they had stayed long enough they set out once more for home.

Their mother-in-law saw them coming and was greatly surprised. She did not even wait for them to

come to her, as she did on most occasions, but went to meet them at the doorway.

"Have there come to this family daughters-in-law who do not obey their mother-in-law?" she cried sternly. "Have you come here without fire wrapped in a paper, and wind in a paper?"

As she spoke, Lotus-blossom held up her paper lantern with fire inside it, and Moon-flower began to send the wind against her mother-in-law's face by gently waving her paper fan.

"Well, someone has done some thinking!" the honored lady cried. "Come into the house and serve me with tea!" As they all sipped their tea from the blue china dishes on the red lacquer table, the lantern swung gaily above their heads and they cooled themselves with the paper fan.

276

Heidi in the Alpine Pasture

JOHANNA SPYRI

Heidi was awakened by a loud whistle; and as she opened her eyes a yellow sunbeam, shining through the opening, fell on her bed, and turned it, and all the hay that was spread about the loft, to glistening gold. She looked about her with astonishment, and could not make out where she was.

Soon she heard her grandfather's deep voice, and it all came back to her; how she came there, and that now she lived with her grandfather up on the Alm. How glad was she to awake in her new home; and to think of all the coming day had in store for her, above all of Schwanli and Barli, the goats!

Springing up, she soon had on all her clothes. Down the ladder she ran, and away out-of-doors. There stood Peter, the goatherd, with his goats; and her grandfather brought out his from the stall, that they might join the flock. Heidi bade both him and the goats a good-morning.

"Would you like to go with Peter to the pasture?" asked the old man.

The child jumped for joy, she was so delighted.

Her grandfather then went into the hut, and soon called out to Peter:

"Come here, goat-general, and bring your knapsack."

Peter obeyed in surprise, and opened his bag, in which was his poor little dinner.

"Wider, wider," said the old man, and put in a big piece of bread and another piece of cheese. Peter opened his eyes as wide as ever he could, for the pieces were each twice as large as his own.

"Now the mug goes in, too, for the little one can't drink as you do from the goats themselves; no, indeed. And you must milk this twice full at noon; for the child will go with you, and stay till you come back in the evening. Now, take care that she does not fall off the cliffs."

Heidi was soon ready, and off they went, climbing joyfully up the Alm. The wind had swept the last trace of cloud from the sky, which was of a wonderful dark blue. The green Alp was covered with blue and yellow flowers, and their wide-open petals seemed laughing back at the sun, while everything shimmered and shone.

Heidi scampered hither and thither, shouting for joy. Now it was a whole group of red primroses; one place was perfectly blue with lovely gentians; and here and everywhere the tender blossoms of the yellow buttercups nodded and laughed in the sunlight. Carried away with delight by all the beckoning,

glistening flowers, the child forgot the goats, and
Peter also, running now forwards, now back again;
first on this side, then on that; for here they were
like red, and there like yellow sparkles, and she was
tempted in every direction. Gathering great handfuls
of flowers, she stuffed them all into her apron; for
she must carry them home with her, and place them
in the hay in her bedroom, to make it look there
as it did on the Alp.

Poor Peter was obliged to keep his eyes about
him to-day; for the goats were like Heidi, they ran
about everywhere, while Peter must whistle and
shout and swing his rod to bring together all the
wanderers.

"Where have you gone to now, Heidi?" he called out. "Here," came back the reply from somewhere. Peter could see no one; for Heidi sat on the ground behind a little mound that was covered with the sweetest smelling prune flowers, and the whole air was perfumed. Heidi had never breathed anything so perfectly delicious.

"Come here now," shouted Peter. "You must not fall over the cliffs, your grandfather has forbidden it."

"Where are the cliffs?" asked the child, but did not stir from her seat; for with every breeze the sweet perfume was wafted to her nostrils.

"Up there, above. We have still a good bit to climb; so come along. Up there, at the very top, sits the old eagle, and screams!"

This stirred the little girl. She jumped up, and ran towards her companion, with her apron full of flowers.

She now kept along with Peter; and the goats, too, went in better order, for they scented the sweet herbs from their pasture on the heights afar, and pushed forward without pausing.

The pasture where Peter usually stopped and made his resting place for the day, lay at the foot of the peak, which rose steep and naked towards the sky, its base clothed with scrub trees and bushes. On one side of the Alp the great rocks were divided by steep clefts and chasms, and the old man was quite right to warn them against falling there.

UP ONE PAIR OF STAIRS

As they now had reached the highest point, Peter took off his knapsack, placing it carefully in a little hollow where it would be sheltered from the wind, which blew often in strong gusts up so high on the mountain. This Peter knew very well, and he did not mean to see his knapsack, with the nice dinner, go rolling down the hillside. Then he stretched himself his full length on the sunny sod, to rest after the steep climb.

Heidi had also tucked her apron into the same hollow with the knapsack, having rolled it up with all the flowers in it; then she seated herself beside Peter, and looked about her on every side. Below lay the valley in the full glow of the morning sun; before her was a huge white snow-field rising towards the dark-blue heaven; to the left, an enormous mass of rocks was piled up, on each side of which stood a pillar of rock, bald and jagged against the blue sky. Heidi thought the pinnacles were looking down at her; and she sat there as still as a little mouse, and looked and looked on every side. All was still; only a light, soft breeze stirred the blue harebells, and the shining yellow buttercups, that grew all about, and stood nodding to her on their slender stalks. Peter had fallen asleep, and the goats climbed here and there, and up into the bushes.

Never was the child so happy in her life. She drank in the golden sunlight, the fresh air, the sweet perfume of the flowers, and longed for nothing but to stay where she was forever.

Thus a long, long time passed; and Heidi gazed at the needles of rock above her so long and steadfastly that they seemed to have gotten faces, and to be returning her gaze like old friends, when suddenly she heard above her a loud, sharp scream. As she looked up, a huge bird circled overhead, such as she had never seen before; with wide-spread wings it soared through the air, and in great sweeps came back again and again, screaming loud and piercingly over Heidi's head.

"Peter, Peter! wake up!" cried Heidi aloud. "See, the eagle is here; look, look!"

Peter roused himself at her cry; and the children gazed at the bird, which rose higher and higher, disappearing at last in the blue ether over the gray rocks.

"Where is he now?" asked Heidi, who had watched the bird with breathless interest.

"In his home up there."

"Oh, how beautiful to live up there! But why does he scream so?"

"Because he must."

"Let us climb up there to see his home," suggested Heidi.

UP ONE PAIR OF STAIRS

"Oh, oh, oh!" cried Peter; and each "oh" was louder than the last. "Even the goats are not able to climb up there, and the Alm uncle said you must not fall over the cliff."

After this Peter began to whistle and call so loudly that Heidi did not know what had happened; but the goats knew well enough, and came running and jumping, and were soon all gathered on the green field. Some nibbled at the sweet grass, others ran here and there, while some stood opposite each other a little way apart, and butted playfully with their horns.

Springing to her feet, Heidi ran in amidst the goats, for she found it a new pleasure to see the dear little

creatures gamboling together so happily; and she, too, jumped from one to another to make herself acquainted with each separately, for each had its own peculiarities, and looked and behaved differently.

While Heidi played with the goats, Peter had fetched the knapsack, and arranged the four parcels of food in a square on the grass, the big ones on Heidi's side, and the little ones on his; then he filled the mug with fresh milk from Schwanli, and placed it in the middle of the square.

Then he called to Heidi to come, but he had to call again and again, longer than to the goats; for the child was so delighted with the thousand movements and pranks of her new playfellows, that she saw and heard nothing further. Peter understood how to make himself heard. He shouted so very loud that he could have been heard up on the rocks, causing Heidi to run as fast as she could; and then the table looked so inviting, that she hopped about it for joy.

"Stop dancing about, it is time to eat," said Peter, seating himself and beginning.

"Is the milk for me?" asked Heidi, as she took her seat.

"Yes," he replied, "and the two biggest packages are yours also; and when you have emptied the mug, you can have another full from Schwanli; and when you have finished 'tis my turn."

"And where do you get your milk?" asked the little girl curiously.

"From my goat, from Snail. Do begin."

Heidi began at last, with the milk; and when she had emptied the mug, Peter rose and filled it again. Heidi broke some of her bread into it, and then handed the rest of it to Peter. It was a big piece, twice as large as his, which he had already eaten, together with the rest of his dinner. She gave him also her big lump of cheese, saying, "You can have it all, I have had enough." Peter stared at Heidi, with his big eyes, in speechless astonishment; for never in his life had he been able to say that he had had enough and could give something away. He hesitated a little, for he could not believe that Heidi was in earnest; but the child held her pieces towards him again, and when he did not take them, she laid them on his knee.

When he saw that she was serious, he took his present, nodded for thanks and pleasure, and made forthwith the heartiest meal that had fallen his share since he first tended the goats. While he ate, Heidi watched the flock.

"What are their names, Peter?" said she.

He knew them all and could remember them easily enough. So he began and named them one after the other without hesitating, and pointed at each with his finger as he spoke. To this lesson Heidi gave all her attention, and soon she, too, could name them all; for each had its peculiarity, which was easily learned with a little pains.

There was the big Turk with his strong horns, who was forever butting the others; so that they generally scampered away when he came towards them, and would have nothing to do with such a rough comrade. Only the bold and slender Thistlebird did not avoid him, but struck out sharply, once, twice, sometimes six times, until the great Turk stood still in astonishment, and did not try again soon.

And the little white Snowball, who was always bleating beseechingly, often Heidi ran to it, taking its head between her hands to comfort it. She put her arm round the little creature's neck, saying sympathizingly, "What ails you, Snowball?"

The animal nestled confidingly against the little girl, and was quiet again; and Peter called out from his seat, explaining Snowball's trouble between each mouthful.

"She does that because her old one does not come with us any more. She has been sold to Mayenfeld, the day before yesterday, and will not come any more to the Alm."

"Who is the old one?" asked Heidi.

"Pooh! its mother," was the reply.

"Where is the grandmother?" asked the child.

"Has none."

"Or the grandfather?"

"Has none."

"Oh, you poor little Snowball!" said Heidi tenderly, pressing the goat softly to her side. "But now don't cry so any more; I will come here every day with you, then you will not be lonely; and if you are feeling very badly, you may come to me."

Snowball rubbed her head trustingly on Heidi's shoulder, and bleated no more.

When Peter had finished his dinner, he came again to look after his flock.

By far the loveliest and cleanest of the goats were Schwanli and Barli. The animals had begun again to climb up towards the bushes, each in its own way; one springing lightly over every obstacle, others carefully searching all along the way for a good mouthful, Turk trying now and then to give some one a blow, Schwanli and Barli climbing prettily and lightly, finding the best bushes, and eating in a delicate and dainty manner. Heidi stood with her hands behind her back, watching all that went on.

DONN P. CRANE

Suddenly Peter sprang to his feet, and was after the goats with great leaps; Heidi followed him, for something must have happened, and she could not stay behind.

Away went Peter through the flock towards the side of the Alp, where the rocks rose up steep and naked, and where a heedless goat might easily fall while climbing. He saw that the giddy Thistlebird had strayed in that direction, and he ran after her only just in time, for she had reached the very edge of the precipice. As he was about to seize her, he tripped and fell, catching her only by the leg as he came down; but he held her fast, though she bleated with surprise and anger to find herself held, while she persisted in pressing forward. Peter called loudly for Heidi; he was unable to rise, and seemed to himself almost pulling the little goat's leg off, she was so determined to go on. In a trice Heidi was there, saw the danger of his situation and of the goat's. Pulling quickly a sweet-smelling herb, she held it under Thistlebird's nose, saying soothingly, "Come, come, little goat; come and be good, Thistlebird. See, now, you might have fallen, and that would have hurt you sadly." The goat turned quickly about to nibble at the herb held out by Heidi, and was quite content. But Peter, having regained his feet, hastened to seize the string that hung from her collar, while Heidi took the collar from the other side; and they led the wanderer between them to rejoin the rest of the flock, which was peaceably feeding below.

Once Peter had his goat in safety again, he raised his rod, and was about to whip her soundly, while Thistlebird drew back in alarm, for she saw what was coming. Heidi, however, screamed out: "No, Peter, no! you must not strike her!"

"She deserves it," said he angrily, and was about to strike; but the child seized him by the arm, calling out, "You must let her alone!"

Her companion stood staring in surprise at her commanding tones and flashing eyes, while he dropped his arm, saying, "So, then, she may go, if you will give me some of your cheese to-morrow." He felt that he must have something for his trouble.

"You may have it all, to-morrow and every day, for I do not care for it," said Heidi, "and a big piece of bread also,'as I gave you to-day; but you must promise me not to strike Thistlebird nor Snowball, nor any of the goats."

"It's all the same to me," said Peter. That was his way of promising, and he let the little goat go. Away she sprang with great leaps, in amongst the others.

Almost unheeded the day had passed, and now the sun was beginning to sink behind the mountain. Heidi sat quietly on the ground, gazing at the hare-bells and bluebells, as they shone in the golden light, watching how the grass took a golden hue, and how the rocks above began to shimmer and flash, when suddenly she started to her feet, shouting, "Peter, Peter! it is burning, it is on fire! All the mountains flame, and the great snow yonder, and the sky. Look, look! the highest peak is glowing. Oh, the beautiful fire! Now look, Peter, it has reached the eagle's nest. See the rock! see the pines! everything burns!"

"It is always like that, but it is no fire," said Peter kindly.

"What is it, then?" cried Heidi, and ran about in every direction to look; for she could not see enough of it standing still, it was so beautiful everywhere. "What is it, Peter? what is it?" she asked again.

"It comes of itself," explained the lad.

"Look, look now!" she screamed, in the wildest excitement, "just this minute it is all as red as roses. Look at the snow and those high, pointed rocks!"

UP ONE PAIR OF STAIRS

"Oh, the lovely, rosy snow! and all over the rocks are roses. Oh, now they are growing gray! It is going! it has all gone, Peter!" and little Heidi threw herself on the ground, looking as unhappy as if there were an end to all beauty in the world.

"It will be just so again to-morrow," said the lad. "Get up, we must go home now." So, he whistled the herd together, and they set out on their homeward track.

Heidi scarcely spoke a word until the Alm hut came in sight, and she saw her grandfather sitting on his bench outside, waiting for the goats.

Then she ran to him quickly, with Schwanli and Barli at her heels.

Peter called out, "Come again to-morrow! goodnight." He was very anxious for Heidi to go again. And the child gave him her hand, promising to go to-morrow, and bidding good-bye to the departing goats. She put her arm about the neck of little Snowball especially, saying, "Good-night, Snowball; sleep well; don't forget that I am going with you again to-morrow, and you must not bleat so sadly again."

The goat looked at her with friendly eyes, and then sprang joyfully after the others.

Then Heidi came back under the pine tree, calling out before she could reach her grandfather: "Oh, it was so beautiful! The fire, and the roses on the rock, the blue and yellow flowers."

So she told him all that had happened during the day; particularly about the fire at sunset, and she begged him to explain it to her, for Peter knew nothing whatever about it.

"Yes," said her grandfather, "the sun does that when he says good-night to the mountains. He casts his most beautiful beams across them, so that they will not forget that he is coming again in the morning."

This pleased the little girl, and she could scarcely wait until the morrow, she was in such haste to go again to see the sun bid good-night to the mountains. But first she must go to sleep; and she did sleep through the whole night soundly in her little hay bed, and dreamed of pink mountains covered with roses, in the midst of which Snowball jumped gayly about.

Betsy Ross and the First American Flag

Many, many years ago there was no United States at all, but just thirteen little colonies along the Atlantic Ocean, ruled over by a King who lived across the sea in England. In those days there lived in Philadelphia a good woman named Betsy Ross. Betsy had a little, old-fashioned, red brick house, with tiny window panes and a great front door with a shiny brass knocker. The prim, quaint, little Quaker ladies of Philadelphia often came and rapped with that knocker. For Betsy was a dressmaker and she made these ladies their trim gray gowns. "The finest needle-woman in all America," she had been called.

One fine June day, Betsy sat by her window in a high back chair with her feet on a footstool. She was sewing busily and her big black cat, Powder, was beside her, playing with a spool on the floor. All at once she heard the sound of fifes and drums.

"Troops coming, Powder!" she cried, and, laying her work aside, she hurried to the front door. There, on her doorstep, she stood, waving her handkerchief while a regiment of soldiers marched by. Awkward enough were the men, as though they had had little training; many were not even in uniform; yet all Betsy's neighbors stood on their doorsteps, just as she did, and cheered them. For at that time, the thirteen little American colonies had suffered great wrong from the King of England and those who helped him govern. "Be a King, George!" the King's mother had taught him when he was a boy, and he had grown to believe that the only way to be a King was to make others do whatever he willed, whether or not it was right or just. Year after year, the wrong he had done the American colonists had grown greater, till at last there was nothing for brave men to do, but stand with courage and fight for their freedom. So these troops marching past Betsy's house had left their peaceful homes and their dear ones, to help drive out of their country the soldiers of the King.

"Hurrah! Three cheers for the brave men from Virginia!" cried the people. But as Betsy turned to go into the house, a neighbor called to her:

"What a shame that we have no flag for our troops."

"Aye, truly, sir!" answered Betsy. "Since we hauled down the flag of England, we sadly need one of our own."

Scarcely had she settled herself at her work again, when suddenly there came a loud rapping at her door. As she hastened to open it, with Powder close by her side, whom should she see before her but General Washington himself, accompanied by two other men. Betsy hastened to drop a curtsy.

"A fine summer's day, Mistress Ross," said Washington in his pleasant voice. "We come to you on important business."

At once Betsy led the men into her quiet little back

parlor, which looked out on the side yard, and there she begged them to tell her their errand.

"Congress has just accepted a design for the flag we need so sadly," said Washington, "and we have come to you to see if you can make it for us."

Betsy's face lit up with pleasure.

"I shall try my best," she answered.

Then General Washington took from his pocket a paper on which was a drawing.

"See," he said, "there are to be thirteen stripes, seven red ones and six white ones, and in the upper left hand corner there will be a blue field with a circle of thirteen white stars, one star for each of our thirteen good colonies."

Betsy studied the drawing with interest, then she said: "The design is a good one. But why have the stars six points? I see no reason for that."

"Ah," answered General Washington, "the stars we have known so long on shields and coats-of-arms in England, are always made with six points." For Washington did not forget that his fathers had come from England. Though he led the American troops with all his heart against the soldiers of the King, he had not ceased to love the English people, and he liked the star that reminded him of the land across the sea.

"If six-pointed stars are English, all the more reason why ours should be different!" cried Betsy with spirit. "Here in America we start afresh. We look at things

with our own eyes, not with the eyes of our fathers who lived in England. The real stars—the stars in the sky—seem always to have but five points. Is it not better to place on our flag the stars as they really appear in the sky, rather than as men have drawn them for ages on dusty old shields in England?"

General Washington's face was grave. He still did not find it easy to part with the six-pointed star.

"I doubt very much," he said, "if you will be able to cut a perfect five-pointed star."

Betsy hurried into the next room. Soon she returned with her work basket. Taking out a square piece of paper, she folded it quickly and cut it with one snip of her scissors. Then opening it, she held up triumphantly a perfect five-pointed star.

The men with Washington smiled.

"You are defeated, General," they cried, and even Powder jumped up, with his forepaws against his mistress's knees, as though to say she had well done.

Then an answering smile lit up Washington's face.

"So be it!" he agreed, as he rose to go. "Let America's star be hers alone—a shining light for all the world, five-pointed like the stars in the sky."

Thus it was that Betsy Ross made the first flag of our country—the first Stars and Stripes.

As time went by, Americans saw the Stars and Stripes go forth again and again to do battle with wrong, and to uphold the right. So they grew to love it still more dearly and to understand more of its meaning. The stars on the blue field, that have grown far beyond the thirteen of Betsy's day, stand for all the states in this great Union, shining out into the world with the light of freedom and justice. The thirteen stripes stand for the thirteen little colonies that first fought so nobly for freedom. The red says to all, "Be brave!" The white says, "Be pure!" The blue says, "Be true!" So to-day when the flag goes by, it is not the beautiful colors we bare our heads to salute, but the courage, the truth, and purity, the true idea of freedom, for which "Old Glory" stands.

Two Little Birds and A Great Man

Four men once rode along a muddy country highway.
The sun was just coming out after a hard rain storm,
and the trees were glistening with little raindrop
diamonds. As the men passed beneath a great oak tree,
they suddenly saw a couple of robins fluttering
anxiously about, and heard a faint chirping in the
grass near them.

"What is the matter with those robins?" asked one
of the men, reining up his horse.

"It looks as though some little ones had been blown
from their nest by the storm," answered another.
"What a pity! They will starve if they are not put back!"

"What's the difference if they do starve," cried a
third, impatiently. "Who will miss two less robins
in the world? Come along! Here are four good lawyers
dallying on their way to court over some stupid robins.
If we do not hurry, we shall be late for far more important
things."

So the three men chirruped to their horses and went
galloping off.

Now the fourth man had said not a single word. He
had a kindly, tender face, though his figure was as
ungainly as a gaunt, scraggly pine tree. Down from
his horse he sprang as the others rode away. Among
the grasses he searched till he found two little birds.
Gently he picked them up and held them safe in his great
loving hands.

Their nest was high up in the tree, but not for a moment did that stay the man from what he meant to do. He was dressed in his best, all ready to appear in the law court before the judge, but he climbed up that tree just the same. Nor did he rest till he had laid the two little birds gently in their nest. There they cuddled down cozily, while the mother and father hovered above them.

"I could never have slept tonight if I had left them," said the man to himself. Then he slid down the tree, jumped on his horse and was off.

Who do you think he was—that gaunt, awkward, tender-faced man, who climbed the tree like a boy? Abraham Lincoln—that's who he was! After many years he became president of the United States. Today all the world honors and loves him, and dear to every American is he whose heart was so big that he could not leave even two little birds, helpless, to starve by the roadside.

The Babe of Bethlehem
ADAPTED FROM THE BIBLE

And it came to pass in those days, that there went out a decree from Caesar Augustus, that all the world should be taxed. And all went to be taxed, every one unto his own city.

And Joseph also went up from Galilee, out of the city of Nazareth, into Judea, unto the city of David, which is called Bethlehem, to be taxed with Mary his wife.

And so it was that, while they were there, there was born unto Mary a son and they wrapped him in swaddling clothes and laid him in a manger, because there was no room for them in the inn.

And there were in the same country shepherds abiding in the field, keeping watch over their flock by night. And, lo, the angel of the Lord came upon them, and the glory of the Lord shone round about them: and they were sore afraid. And the angel said unto them, "Fear not: for, behold, I bring you good tidings of great joy, which shall be to all people. For unto you is born this day in the city of David a Saviour, which is Christ the Lord. And this shall be a sign unto you; ye shall find the babe wrapped in swaddling clothes, lying in a manger."

And suddenly there was with the angel a multitude of the heavenly host praising God, and saying, "Glory to God in the highest, and on earth peace, good will toward men."

And it came to pass, as the angels were gone away from them into heaven, the shepherds said one to another, "Let us now go even unto Bethlehem, and see this thing which is come to pass, which the Lord hath made known unto us."

And they came with haste, and found Mary and Joseph, and the babe lying in a manger. And when they had seen it, they made known abroad the saying which was told them concerning this child. And all they that heard it wondered at those things which were told them by the shepherds. But Mary kept all these things, and pondered them in her heart.

And the shepherds returned, glorifying and praising God for all the things that they had heard and seen, as it was told unto them.

Now when Jesus was born in Bethlehem of Judea in the days of Herod the king, behold, there came wise men from the east to Jerusalem, saying, "Where is he that is born King of the Jews? For we have seen his star in the east, and are come to worship him."

And lo, the star, which they saw in the east, went before them, till it came and stood over where the young child was. When they saw the star, they rejoiced with exceeding great joy.

And when they were come into the house, they saw the young child with Mary his mother, and fell down, and worshiped him: and when they had opened their treasures, they presented unto him gifts; gold, and frankincense, and myrrh.

A CHILD'S THOUGHT OF GOD

ELIZABETH BARRETT BROWNING

They say that God lives very high!
  But if you look above the pines
You cannot see our God,
  And why?

God is so good, He wears a fold
  Of heaven and earth across His face—
Like secrets kept, for love, untold.

But still I feel that His embrace
  Slides down by thrills, through all things made,
Through sight and sound of every place:

As if my tender mother laid
  On my shut lids, her kisses' pressure,
Half-waking me at night; and said,
  "Who kissed you through the dark, dear guesser?"

Piccola*

Gay was little Piccola! Busy was little Piccola! Her father was often away from home fishing far out at sea. Then she and her mother were left all alone in their little stone cottage, in a small village in France.

Piccola helped keep the cottage clean; she scoured the pots and pans; she tended the geraniums that bloomed in the windows; she dragged in great armfuls of wood for the fire.

"My little Piccola is busy as the bee," said her mother.

"My little Piccola is gay as the lark," said her father.

When her work was done, Piccola raced with the other children through the narrow streets of the village, her little wooden shoes going rat-a-tat-too on the cobble-stones, or she climbed up high on the rocks that rose behind the town and looked far out to sea where the sailboats danced in the breeze.

"A jolly good comrade is Piccola," her playmates said.

But one year, when the yellowed leaves fell from the trees, and the snow began to fall, there came to Piccola's home a time of sadness. Poor had the fishing season been the summer before, and the good father had laid little money by to meet their needs for the winter. He came in from the stormy sea, to go out no more till the spring returned, and he could get no work to earn money through the winter.

"I do not know how we shall ever get on until spring," he mourned.

*Based upon the poem, *Piccola*, by Celia Thaxter. Used by the permission of Houghton Mifflin Company.

But Piccola was none the less happy. "God gives us our daily bread," she said, and her little heart was grateful for each day's simple food.

As the weeks slipped by, and their little store of money grew smaller and smaller, the Christmas-tide drew near.

"What shall we do for Piccola?" said the mother, "we are so poor, we cannot buy her even one small gift."

"No," said her father, "not even one small gift."

Now close by the church, past which Piccola often romped in her play, there stood a mass of old gray stone, carved with quaint figures that told of the life of Jesus. Stiff and queerly fashioned were the figures, but they had been carved by those who loved the story, and Piccola loved it too. As she carefully traced out all the tale, she said to herself with a heart full of reverence:

"It was Jesus who taught men to know the good God as their father, to let His goodness shine in their hearts, and to love one another."

So when the Christ-mass drew near and men made ready to celebrate the coming of Jesus Christ to men, Piccola had no thought but that all the earth must rejoice.

"I love the good Christmas-tide!" she cried.

"But, Piccola," said her mother, "do you not know that no gifts can come to you this year?"

"Good gifts must come to all with Christmas," the child made answer, simply.

"Poor little one," said the mother in a low voice to the father, "if we only had one sou to spare to buy her the least little gift."

So the father and mother were sorrowful, but Piccola was happy.

On the night before Christmas, Piccola sang as she swept up the hearth, and when her share of the evening's work was done, she seized her father and mother each by the hand.

"Let us go out and be merry!" she cried.

So they left their dingy little cottage and went out into the village. All the windows were brightly ablaze

with lights, and hung with festoons and gay Christmas baubles. So close to the street were the little stone houses, that Piccola and her mother and father could see all the happiness and Christmas cheer within.

"Every house but ours is gay," said the father. But Piccola did not even hear him. She was laughing with joy at the joy she saw. Every gay festoon, every gay Christmas bauble, all the happiness and cheer in every house they passed was hers to enjoy! She was richer far than those who had only one cottage with festooned windows!

So they went on to the very last house in the village. There they saw three little children carefully setting their wooden shoes by the fireplace, to be filled with Christmas gifts.

"Tomorrow they will be full of goodies!"

"And full of toys!" rang their shrill little voices.

"I shall set out my shoe too!" cried Piccola with shining eyes.

"Piccola, there can be no Christmas gifts for you!" her mother repeated half sobbing. But still Piccola did not hear. Too firm was her faith that every child shared alike in the love of the good God, and none could be shut out from receiving His good gifts.

By the dim candle light she made ready for bed. In her heart was all the joy of the merriment she had seen in the village. Last of all she set by the hearth, where the fire was dying down, her little wooden shoe.

"Through all the year, I have been as good as I know how," she said, "so I shall find something good here to-morrow."

Then Piccola crept happily into bed, but her mother and father sat long by the embers, and looked sorrowfully at the waiting shoe they had no gifts to fill.

Slowly the night wore away and the gray dawn came. Piccola opened her eyes.

"Christmas is come!" she cried and sprang from her bed. Eagerly, expectantly, she crept to her little shoe.

Her mother and father heard her, and listened with bated breath. "Another minute," they thought, "and she will cry out in disappointment!"

But gay on the air, rang a sound of gladness.

"See! Oh, see! My shoe is full!"

Astonished, father and mother hurried into the room. There stood Piccola with shining face, caressing her shoe, and cozily resting in it, lay—a bright-eyed little bird!

"It fell down the chimney and into her shoe!" her father said; but Piccola did not heed him. The bird had come as her Christmas gift, she knew. And every wish of her heart was satisfied and fulfilled. All day long she warmed the bird, and cuddled it, and fed it, till at last her father and mother, seeing how happy she was, caught her joy and were happy, too. So Christmas came to Piccola rich and full, because Christmas was always in her heart.

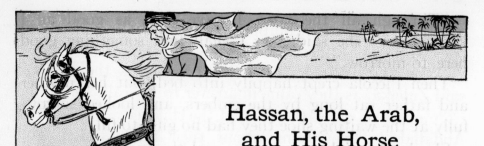

Hassan, the Arab, and His Horse

Hassan, the Arab, went dashing along on his splendid white horse, Abdallah, beneath the tall date palm trees, between the tents of the Arab camp, and up to his very own door.

"Zuleika! Zuleika!" he called to his wife.

Zuleika, in a long blue robe, with strings of glass beads about her neck, was grinding corn between two stones, but she rose at once when Hassan called.

"Zuleika," he said, "I am off with a party for a journey across the desert. It may be weeks before I come back. Call the children to bid me good-bye."

Zuleika turned without a word to obey him, but under her blue robe, her heart beat fast. Hassan was going out into the desert, and there, on those lonely yellow sands, that stretched away for miles and miles, were many fierce bands of Turks. The Turks were enemies of the Arabs, and, if Hassan were to meet them there would be a struggle, Zuleika knew. But no good Arab wife spoke of such things. It was her husband's business to go, and she called the children, obediently.

Ali and his little sister, Fatima, had been playing

among the camels, climbing on their backs, tumbling over and about them.

"Your father is off on a journey across the desert," said Zuleika, as they came in answer to her call.

"Good-bye, our father!" cried the children. "Good-bye, Abdallah!" They hung about their father's neck and then about Abdallah's. For they loved Abdallah almost as much as if he were one of the family. He had been their playfellow always; he was so kind and gentle, and he understood every word they said. They knew very well that all Arab horses are fine, the finest in the world, but they were equally sure that the finest of all Arab horses was Abdallah!

As Hassan turned and rode away, the children ran after him to the center of the camp. There a number of men on horseback had gathered together, each in a long white gown, with a kerchief bound about his head, and a striped mantle floating behind him. In their hands they all carried tall, slender spears. As soon as Hassan arrived, the party made off. Then Ali and Fatima ran on still farther, to the very edge of the little green oasis where their band was encamped, and they stood looking off across the sands, watching the party as it slowly disappeared in the distance.

"Take care of our father, Abdallah!" they called. "Bring him back to us safe!" And then they went back to their mother.

Hassan and his friends flew on across the desert.

Miles and miles of yellow sand the strong, swift horses put behind them. But, just as the sun was sinking low in the western sky, a band of the dreaded Turks came suddenly swarming about them. Down into position went the spears of the Arabs; the enemy rushed upon them. Nobly the Arabs defended themselves and fierce was the struggle, but the Turks were far greater in numbers; they soon overwhelmed the Arabs and took them all prisoners. Hands and feet they bound them, with tough leather straps, and they tied their horses with ropes.

"Tomorrow we will carry these men off to the slave-market and sell them," they said, as they squatted about on the sand and ate their evening meal. "The horses, too, will bring us a wonderful price. It is not so often one finds for sale a real Arabian horse."

During the night, while the Turks slept, Hassan lay awake, looking up at the quiet stars, and thinking of Zuleika, Ali, and little Fatima.

"Shall I never see them again? Shall I never again go home?" he murmured, and his heart was too full for words. "Shall I spend all my days far, far away, at the hardest labor for some cruel Turk?"

Just then he heard a gentle neighing.

"That is Abdallah calling me," he said, and he managed to pull himself, bound hand and foot though he was, across to the spot where Abdallah was tied. Abdallah put down his nose and sorrowfully rubbed his master's face. "I am sad for you, so sad," he seemed to say.

"My poor horse," cried Hassan, "you shall not go off with these Turks! You at least shall not be their slave!" With his teeth he began to gnaw the rope that bound Abdallah. At last he cut it quite in two.

"There, now you are free, my beauty!" he half sobbed. "Run! Save yourself! Carry home my love to Zuleika and the little ones. I — alas! I shall never see them again."

But for once, Abdallah did not obey. He did not dash away to save himself the moment he knew he was free. No! too often when they had been out together in the desert, far, far from home and far away from any well of water, had Hassan shared the half of his dates, and the last of the precious water in his water-skin with Abdallah. Abdallah would not leave him now— alone and in trouble. Instead, he stood where he was, and still caressed his master with his nose. Suddenly, he jerked his head decisively up and down as though to say, "That's it! That's what I will do." Firmly he caught Hassan by his belt; quietly he dragged him between the rows of sleeping Turks. In a moment more, they were out in the desert.

"My good Abdallah! Abdallah, my beloved! You would not forsake me!" cried Hassan.

Over the soft sands the faithful horse gently dragged him—on, steadily on! All through the night, on and

on! When the first faint glow of dawn began to shimmer over the desert, there before them rose the tall palms of the oasis, and the tents of Hassan's tribe. Never once did Abdallah stop till he had laid his master before his own tent. Then he whinnied faintly for help and sank down on the grass.

Zuleika heard him. "Abdallah!" she cried, and hastened out of the tent. "Hassan! O Hassan!"

"The Turks! We met the Turks!" murmured Hassan, as Zuleika helped him into the tent. "It was Abdallah who saved me!"

Ali and Fatima sat up and rubbed their eyes to see their father thus come home, and, while Zuleika made him comfortable on the rude mat that formed the floor of their tent, they rushed out to the aid of the noble horse.

"O Abdallah! Abdallah!" they cried as they stroked and petted him. "You brought our father home safe in spite of the Turks! We knew you would! O Abdallah, our dearly beloved!"

THE ARAB TO HIS HORSE
BAYARD TAYLOR

Come, my beauty! come, my desert darling!
　On my shoulder lay thy glossy head!
Fear not, though the barley-sack be empty,
　Here's half of Hassan's scanty bread.

Thou shalt have thy share of dates, my beauty!
　And thou know'st my water-skin is free:
Drink and welcome, for the wells are distant,
　And my strength and safety lie in thee.

Bend thy forehead now, to take my kisses!
　Lift in love thy dark and splendid eye:
Thou art glad when Hassan mounts his saddle,—
　Thou art proud he owns thee: so am I.

Let the Sultan bring his boasted horses,
　Prancing with their diamond-studded reins;
They, my darling, shall not match thy fleetness
　When they course with thee the desert plains!

We have seen Damascus, O my beauty!
　And the splendor of the Pashas there;
What's their pomp and riches? why, I would not
　Take them for a handful of thy hair!

313

Blunder

LOUISE E. CHOLLET

Blunder was going to the Wishing-Gate to wish for a pair of Shetland Ponies and a little coach, like Tom Thumb's. And of course you may have your wish if you once get there. But the thing is to find it; for it is not, as you imagine, a great gate with a tall marble pillar on each side and a sign over the top, like this, WISHING-GATE—but just an old stile, made of three sticks. Put up two fingers, cross them on the top with another finger, and you have it exactly,—the way it looks, I mean,—a worm-eaten stile in a meadow; and as there are plenty of old stiles in meadows, how are you to know which is the one?

Blunder's fairy godmother knew, but then she could not tell him, for that was not according to fairy rules and regulations. She could only direct him to follow the road, and ask the way of the first owl he met; and over and over she charged him, for Blunder was a very careless little boy, and seldom found anything: "Be sure you don't miss him,—be sure you don't pass him by." And so far Blunder had come on very well for the road was straight; but at the turn it forked.

UP ONE PAIR OF STAIRS

Should he go through the wood or turn to the right? There was an owl nodding in a tall oak-tree, the first owl Blunder had seen; but he was a little afraid to wake him up, for Blunder's fairy godmother told him that this was a great philosopher, who sat up all night to study the habits of frogs and mice, and knew everything but what went on in the daylight, under his nose; and he could think of nothing better to say to this great philosopher than, "Good Mr. Owl, will you please show me the way to the Wishing-Gate?"

"Eh! what's that?" cried the owl, starting out of his nap. "Have you brought me a frog?"

"No," said Blunder, "I did not know that you would like one. Can you tell me the way to Wishing-Gate?"

"Wishing-Gate! Wishing-Gate!" hooted the owl, very angry. "Winks and naps! how dare you disturb me for such a thing as that? Do you take me for a mile-stone? Follow your nose, sir, follow your nose!"—and, ruffling up his feathers, the owl was asleep again in a moment.

But how could Blunder follow his nose? His nose would turn to the right, or take him through the woods, whichever way his legs went, and "what was the use of asking the owl," thought Blunder, "if this was all?" While he hesitated, a chipmunk came scurrying down the path, and, seeing Blunder, stopped short with a little squeak.

"Good Mrs. Chipmunk," said Blunder, "can you, without

too much trouble, tell me the way to the Wishing-Gate?"

"I can't, indeed," answered the chipmunk, politely. "What with getting in nuts, and the care of a young family, I have so little time to visit anything! But if you will follow the brook, you will find an old water-sprite under a slanting stone, over which the water pours all day with a noise like wabble! wabble! who, I have no doubt, can tell you all about it."

So Blunder went on up the brook, and, seeing nothing of the water-sprite, or the slanting stone, was just saying to himself, "I am sure I don't know where he is,—I can't find it," when he spied a frog sitting on a wet stone.

"Mr. Frog," asked Blunder, "can you tell me the way to the Wishing-Gate?"

"I cannot," said the frog. "I am very sorry, but the fact is, I am an artist. Young as I am, my voice is already remarked at our concerts, and I devote myself so entirely to my profession of music that I have no time for general information. But in a pine-tree beyond, you will find an old crow, who, I am quite sure, can show you the way, as he is a traveler, and a bird of an inquiring turn of mind."

"I don't know where the pine is,—I am sure I can never find him," answered Blunder, discontentedly; but still he went on up the brook, till, hot and tired, and out of patience at seeing neither crow nor pine, he sat down under a great tree to rest. There he heard tiny voices squabbling. And looking about him, Blunder spied a bee, quarreling with a morning-glory elf, who was shutting up the morning-glory in his face.

"Elf, do you know which is the way to the Wishing-Gate?" asked Blunder.

"No," said the elf, "I don't know anything about geography. But if you will keep on in this path, you will find a Dream-man, coming down from fairyland, with his bags of dreams on his shoulder; and if anybody can tell you about the Wishing-Gate, he can."

"But how can I find him?" asked Blunder more and more impatient.

"I don't know, I am sure," answered the elf, "unless you look for him."

GENEVIEVE STUMP

So there was no help for it but to go on; and presently Blunder passed the Dream-man, asleep under a witch-hazel, with his bags of good and bad dreams laid over him to keep him from fluttering away. But Blunder had a habit of not using his eyes, for at home, when told to find anything, he always said, "I don't know where it is," or, "I can't find it," and then his mother or sister went straight and found it for him. So he passed the Dream-man without seeing him, and went on till he stumbled on Jack-o'-Lantern.

"Can you show me the way to the Wishing-Gate?" said Blunder.

"Certainly, with pleasure," answered Jack, and, catching up his lantern, set out at once.

Blunder followed close, but, in watching the lantern, he forgot to look to his feet, and fell into a hole filled with black mud.

"I say! the Wishing-Gate is not down there," called out Jack, whisking off among the treetops.

"But I can't come up there," whimpered Blunder.

"That is not my fault, then," answered Jack, merrily, dancing out of sight.

Oh, a very angry little boy was Blunder when he clambered out of the hole. "I don't know where it is," he said, crying; "I can't find it, and I'll go straight home."

Just then he stepped on an old, moss-grown, rotten stump; and it happening, unluckily, that this rotten stump was a wood-goblin's chimney, Blunder fell through, headlong, in among the pots and pans in which the goblin's cook was cooking the goblin's supper. The old goblin, who was asleep upstairs, started up in a fright at the tremendous clash and clatter, and, finding that his house was tumbling about his ears, as he thought at first, stumped down to the kitchen to see what was the matter. The cook heard him coming, and looked about her to hide Blunder.

"Quick!" cried she. "If my master catches you, he will have you in a pie. In the next room stands a pair of shoes. Jump into them, and they will take you up the chimney."

Off flew Blunder, burst open the door, and tore frantically about the room, in one corner of which stood the shoes; but of course he could not see them, because he was not in the habit of using his eyes. "I can't find them! Oh, I can't find them!" sobbed poor little Blunder, running back to the cook.

"Run into the closet," said the cook.

Blunder made a dash at the window, but—"I don't know where it is," he called out.

Clump! clump! That was the goblin, halfway down the stairs.

"Mercy me!" exclaimed cook. "He is coming. Jump into the meal-chest."

"I don't see it," squeaked Blunder, rushing towards the fireplace. "Where is it?"

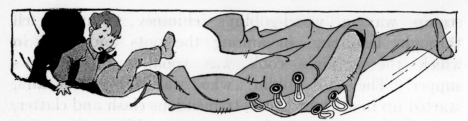

Clump! clump! That was the goblin at the foot of the stairs, and coming towards the kitchen door.

"There is an invisible cloak hanging on that peg. Get into that," cried cook, quite beside herself.

But Blunder could no more see the cloak than he could see the shoes, the closet, and the meal-chest; and no doubt the goblin, whose hand was on the latch, would have found him prancing around the kitchen, and crying out, "I can't find it," but, fortunately for himself, Blunder caught his foot in the invisible cloak, and tumbled down, pulling the cloak over him. There he lay, hardly daring to breathe.

"What was all that noise about?" asked the goblin gruffly, coming into the kitchen.

But as he could see nothing amiss, he went grumbling upstairs again, while the shoes took Blunder up the chimney, and landed him in a meadow, safe enough, but so miserable! He was cross, he was disappointed, he was hungry. It was dark, he did not know the way home, and, seeing an old stile, he climbed up, and sat down on the top of it, for he was too tired to stir. Just then came along the South Wind, with his pockets crammed full of showers, and, as he happened

to be going Blunder's way, he took Blunder home.
The boy was glad enough of this, only he would have
liked it better if the Wind had not laughed all the
way. For what would you think, if you were walking
along a road with a fat old gentlemen, who went
chuckling to himself, and slapping his knees, and
poking himself, till he was purple in the face, when
he would burst out in a great windy roar of laughter
every other minute?

"What are you laughing at?" asked Blunder, at last.

"At a little boy who sat on the top of the Wishing-
Gate, and came home because he could not find it."

"What? what's that?" cried Blunder; but just then
he found himself at home. There sat his godmother

by the fire, her mouse-skin cloak hung up on a peg, and toeing off a spider's silk stocking an eighth of an inch long. And though everybody cried, "What luck?" and, "Where is the Wishing-Gate?" she sat mum.

"I don't know where it is," answered Blunder. "I couldn't find it;" and thereon told the story of his troubles.

"Poor boy!" said his mother, kissing him, while his sister ran to bring him some bread and milk.

"Yes, that is all very fine," cried his godmother, pulling out her needles, and rolling up her ball of silk; "but now hear my story! There was once a little boy who must needs go to the Wishing-Gate, and his godmother showed him the road as far as the turn, and told him to ask the first owl he met what to do then; but this little boy seldom used his eyes, so he passed the first owl, and waked up the wrong owl; so he passed the water-sprite, and found only a frog; so he sat down under the pine-tree, and never saw the crow, so he passed the Dream-man, and ran after Jack-o'-Lantern, so he tumbled into the goblin's chimney, and couldn't find the shoes and the closet and the chest and the cloak; and so he sat on the top of the Wishing-Gate till the South Wind brought him home, and never knew it. Ugh! Bah!" And away went the fairy godmother up the chimney in such deep disgust that she did not even stop for her mouse-skin cloak.

Toads and Diamonds
ADAPTED FROM PERRAULT

Once upon a time a woodcutter found a little baby girl in the forest. At night he took her home to live with his wife and his own little daughter who was a year or so older than the foster child.

As the little one grew up, the mother and her own daughter were both so continually thinking of themselves, so continually wanting to be served with the best of everything and to do no work at all, that they made it hard indeed for anyone to live with them. The younger girl, however, was good and sweet of temper, and one of the most beautiful creatures ever seen. No matter how hard the Mother and older daughter made her work, nor how little they gave her in return, she was always kind, patient, and obedient.

Among other things, it was her duty to go twice every day to draw water more than a mile and a half from the house, and bring home a pitcher full of it. One morning as she stood by the fountain, there came to her a poor woman, who begged her for a drink.

"Oh, yes, I will give you a drink with all my heart, Goody," said the pretty child. Rinsing the pitcher at once, she took some of the clearest water from the fountain, and gave it to the stranger, holding up the pitcher all the while, that she might drink the more easily.

Then the good woman said to her:

"You are so good and courteous, that I cannot help

giving you a gift." For this was a fairy who had
taken the form of a poor country-woman in order to
learn just how good and kind the young girl really was.
"I will give you for a gift," continued the fairy, "that
at every word you speak, there shall come out of your
mouth either a flower or a jewel."

When the pretty girl returned home, the mother
began to scold her for staying so long at the fountain.

"I beg your pardon, mamma," she answered, "but
I could not make more haste."

As she spoke these words, there came out of her
mouth two roses, two pearls, and two large diamonds.

"What is this I see?" cried the woman in great
astonishment. "Pearls and diamonds drop out of the
girl's mouth! How happened this, my child?"

The girl told her the whole story frankly, not without dropping great numbers of diamonds.

"Truly," cried the mother, "I must send my own dear child thither. Fanny, look at what comes out of your sister's mouth when she speaks. Would you not be glad, dear, to have the same gift? You have only to go and draw water out of the fountain, and when a poor woman asks you for a drink, to give it to her very politely."

"I would like to see myself going to the fountain to draw water," said this proud, ill-natured creature, for she thought herself too fine to do work of that sort.

"I insist you shall go," said the mother, who was very fond of her own daughter and wanted her to have the best of everything. "Go instantly."

So the girl was obliged to do as she was bid, but she grumbled all the way, and she took with her the

best silver tankard in the house, instead of the plainer one her sister was accustomed to use.

No sooner had she reached the fountain than she saw coming out of the wood a magnificently dressed lady who came to her and asked for a drink. This was the same fairy who had appeared to her sister, but she had purposely taken upon herself another form, so the older girl should not know her. Never dreaming that this very fine lady was the same poor woman who had in her power the wonderful gift, the girl answered rudely

"Oho! I suppose you think I came hither just to serve you with water! I suppose I carried this silver tankard all along the way through the forest purely to please your ladyship! If you want a drink, get it yourself."

"You are scarcely polite," answered the fairy very calmly. "Well then, since you answer me in such a way, I give you for a gift that at every word you speak there shall come out of your mouth either a toad or a snake."

The girl's mother had been watching eagerly for her return, and as soon as she saw her coming through the woods, she called out, "Well, my daughter?"

"Well, mother!" answered the girl, but at the first words she spoke, out of her mouth fell a toad and a snake.

"Oh, mercy!" cried the mother. "What is this I see? No jewels, but toads and snakes!"

Yet so foolish was she in her fondness for her own child,

that she never dreamed of questioning whether the girl had been at fault for what had happened to her. Indeed she began at once to think who else could have been to blame.

"I know," she cried, running toward the kitchen where her foster daughter was at work. "It is you who are to blame for this—you who brought all this misery on your sister. But you shall pay for it. Out of this house you go. At once and forever."

Then she drove the young girl out of the house and into the forest. But as the pretty creature sat on a fallen log alone and weeping, who should come by but a King's son. Seeing her so sad and beautiful, he asked her what she did there alone.

"Alas, sir," she cried, "my mother has turned me out of doors."

The King's son who saw five or six pearls and as many diamonds drop out of her mouth as she spoke, was astounded and desired her to tell him all that had happened. Perceiving as she told her story that she was as beautiful in heart as in face, the King's son fell in love with her on the spot. Asking her leave, he conducted her to the palace of the King, his father, and there married her.

As for the sister, snakes and toads kept falling from her mouth, till she became so hateful to all that her own mother turned her out of doors. She wandered off into the forest and was never heard of again.

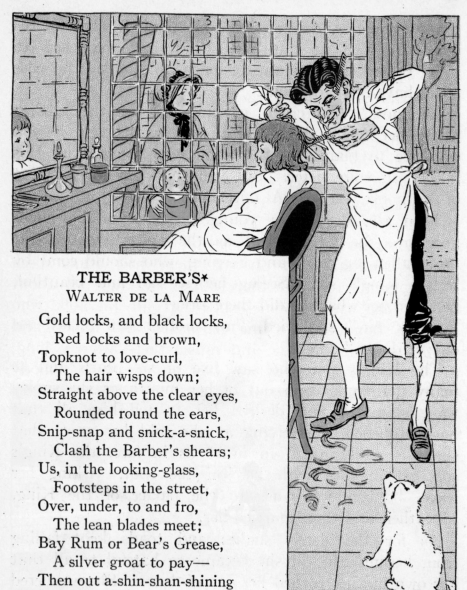

THE BARBER'S*
WALTER DE LA MARE

Gold locks, and black locks,
  Red locks and brown,
Topknot to love-curl,
  The hair wisps down;
Straight above the clear eyes,
  Rounded round the ears,
Snip-snap and snick-a-snick,
  Clash the Barber's shears;
Us, in the looking-glass,
  Footsteps in the street,
Over, under, to and fro,
  The lean blades meet;
Bay Rum or Bear's Grease,
  A silver groat to pay—
Then out a-shin-shan-shining
  In the bright, blue day.

*From *Peacock Pie.* Quoted by permission of Henry Holt & Company.

Dick Whittington and His Cat

A long time ago, in the reign of King Edward III, there lived a boy called Dick Whittington. Dick had no father or mother and, as he was not old enough to work for his living, he had a hard time getting on in the world. Sometimes he had no breakfast; sometimes he had no dinner; and he was happy indeed when the poor people in the village where he lived could spare him a crust of bread or a few potatoes to eat.

Now, these good country-people were forever talking about London. Not one of them had really been to the great city, but they seemed to know all about it just the same. Some said that all the folk who lived in London were fine gentlemen and ladies, and that there was singing and music there all day long; others said that nobody was ever hungry there, nobody

had to work, and the streets were all paved with gold.

Dick listened eagerly to these stories, and began to wish with all his heart that he could visit that wonderful place.

One day as he was leaning against the sign post, there came dashing up to the village inn a great wagon drawn by eight horses, all with bells on their heads. Dick said to himself at once that this wagon must be going to the fine city of London.

When the driver was ready to start off again, the lad ran up to him and asked if he might not walk by the side of the wagon Thinking that such a ragged boy could not be worse off than he now appeared to be, and learning that he had neither father nor mother to keep him in the village, the driver told him that he might do as he liked. And off they started.

It was a long walk for Dick, but he trudged sturdily on, and so he did indeed come at last to the city of London. In such a hurry was he to see the wonderful sights of the place, that he ran off at once even forgetting altogether to thank the good natured driver. Up one street and down another he went, trying to find those that were paved with gold, for he had once seen a beautiful piece of money called a guinea that was gold, and he knew how many fine things it would buy.

"Now," he thought to himself, "if I could only find those golden streets, I could break a little bit off the pavement, and buy everything I need." Ah! he did not yet know that fortune is not so easily won!

He ran and ran and ran till he was so tired he could go no farther, but in all the streets there was only dirt and not a sign of gold. At last, as night was falling, he sat down in a dark corner, and cried himself to sleep.

When he awoke, it was morning, and he was very hungry. Having nothing whatever to eat and no money with which to buy food, he walked about from one street to another, asking those whom he met to give him a penny.

"Go to work, you idle fellow," said some of these; and the rest passed him by without even looking at him.

By and by, having grown so hungry and tired that he could go no farther, he laid himself down by the door of a very fine house. "If only I knew how to find work!" he sobbed. Here he was soon seen by the cook, who called out to him in a temper:

"What are you doing there, you little beggar? If you don't get away quick, I'll throw a panful of dish-water over you! I've some here hot enough to make you jump!"

Just at that moment, Mr. Fitzwarren, who was the master of the house, happened to be coming home to dinner. When he saw the ragged little fellow at his door, he said to him:

"Well, well, my lad! Why are you lying there? You seem old enough to work. Can it be that you are lazy?"

"No, indeed, sir!" said Dick. "I would work with all my heart, if I could find anything to do. But I do not know a single soul in London, and I have not had anything to eat for a long time."

"Poor little fellow!" said Mr. Fitzwarren. "Come in, and I will see what I can do for you." So the kind merchant ordered his cook to give the lad a good dinner, and then to find some sort of work for him.

Thus Dick was settled in the Fitzwarren house and would have lived there very happily if it had not been for the ill-natured cook. She would often say:

"You are under my orders now! Do as I tell you! Stand around there! Clean the spit and the dripping pan! Make the fires! Wash these dishes! Sweep the floor! Bring in the wood! And do it all quickly or——" And she would shake her ladle, box his ears, or flourish her broomstick over his shoulders.

At last, little Mistress Alice Fitzwarren, daughter of the kind merchant, chanced to see how the lad was treated, and she told the cook she should be turned away at once if she did not use him more kindly. After that, Dick had an easier time of it; but there was still something else that troubled him.

UP ONE PAIR OF STAIRS

His bed was in a garret at the top of the house, and there were so many holes in the floor and walls, that every night a great number of rats and mice came in. They raced back and forth over Dick, and made his room so unpleasant that he did not know what to do.

One day he earned a penny from a gentleman for cleaning his shoes, and he said to himself that the best use he could make of the money would be to buy a cat with it. The very next morning he met a girl with a cat in her arms.

"I'll give you a penny for that cat," he said.

"Well and good!" the girl answered. "You may have her, and you will find that the mice don't stay long about where she is."

So Dick hid his cat in the garret, and every day he was careful to save a part of his dinner and carry it up to her. Soon she had driven all the rats and mice away; and then Dick could sleep soundly every night.

Not long after this, a ship that belonged to Mr. Fitzwarren was loaded and made ready to start on a voyage to a far-off land across the sea. Now, Mr. Fitzwarren always gave his servants the chance to send out in his ships something of their own, in the hopes of making a good trade for them, so he called them all together, and asked what each would like to venture.

Everyone had something to send,—every one but Dick; and as he had neither money nor goods, he did not go with the rest into the parlor. Little Mistress Alice guessed at once why he did not come, and she said:

"Dear father, surely Dick should have a chance too. Here is some money from my own purse that you may take for him."

But Mr. Fitzwarren answered, "No, my child! He must send something of his own." Then he called Dick to him and said, "What are you going to venture on the ship, my lad?"

"I have nothing in the world to send," answered Dick, "nothing but a cat which I bought some time ago for a penny."

"Fetch your cat, then," said Mr. Fitzwarren, "and let her go. Who knows but that she may be traded for some good profit?"

So Dick brought down poor Puss with tears in his eyes, carried her to the ship, and gave her with many sad farewell squeezes, to the captain. Everybody laughed at the thought of making a fortune by trading a cat—everybody, that is, except Mistress Alice, and she was sorry for Dick and tried to comfort him.

After that, though Dick worked as faithfully as ever, the cook gave way more and more to ill-temper. She made fun of him, too, for sending his cat to sea.

"Do you think," she used often to say, "that your puss will sell for as much money as would buy a stick to beat you?"

At last Dick thought he could bear the hard work and harsh treatment no longer, so he made up his mind to leave the place. He packed up his few poor things and very early on All-hallows Day, he started. He walked as far as the place called Holloway, and there he sat down on a stone to rest.

As he sat there, thinking sadly, and wondering which road he should take, he heard the six great bells on Bow Church, ringing out a merry chime in the distance. He listened. They seemed to say something, and this was what they said:

"Turn again, Whittington,
Thrice Lord Mayor of London!
Turn again, Whittington,
Thrice Lord Mayor of London!"

"Lord Mayor of London!" he said to himself.

"Well, if I thought I could become Lord Mayor at last, and make London a better city, that would be worth working for! I think I will go back and get straight to work again! Let the old cook cuff and scold as she pleases!"

Straightway Dick did go back, and it fell out very happily that he got into the kitchen and at work, before the cook even came down-stairs. And the stone on which he sat and made that important decision is to this day called "Whittington's Stone."

Meantime Mistress Puss was journeying in Mr. Fitzwarren's ship over the seas. The ship made a long voyage, and at last was driven by the winds on to the coast of Africa. The Moors who lived there had never seen any white men before, and they came in great crowds to look at their pale faces which they thought very strange. Soon they began to buy the fine things with which the ship was loaded. Seeing this, the captain sent samples of the best wares he had to the King of the country, which was Barbary; and it was not long before the King sent for him to come to the palace.

When the captain arrived, he was shown into a splendid chamber and invited to seat himself on a rich carpet all flowered with silver and gold. The

UP ONE PAIR OF STAIRS

King and Queen were seated in very grand state at the upper end of the room, and no sooner was all in readiness than a number of steaming dishes were brought in for dinner.

Hardly had the dishes been set down before them, however, when an army of rats and mice rushed in, and devoured all the food in a twinkling. The captain wondered greatly at this. "Is it not most unpleasant to have so many rats and mice about?" he asked. "And do you do nothing to drive them away from the palace?"

"Oh, alas!" was the answer. "It is indeed most unpleasant; but we have tried in vain to drive them away. The King would give half his treasure if he could get rid of them."

At that an idea flashed into the captain's mind! Dick Whittington's cat! Dick Whittington's cat! He cried out to the King that he had a little creature on board his ship which would make short work of the pests.

The King was overjoyed. "Bring her here to me," he said. "If she will indeed do what you say, I will load your ship with gold in exchange for her!"

"It is not very convenient to part with her," said the captain, "but to oblige your majesty, I will fetch her."

"Do! Ah, do!" said the Queen. "I do so wish to see the dear creature!"

So the captain went down to the ship, while another dinner was being made ready.

He took puss in his arms and returned to the palace just in time to see a second army of rats rush out on the newly brought food. The cat was out of his arms in a moment and in among the troublesome creatures. Oh! how they scampered and scurried! Hither and yon! Hither and yon! Soon there was not one of them left on the table.

The King cried out in his joy at this feat, and the Queen desired that the little creature which had served them so well, should be brought for her to look at. Upon this, the captain called, "Pussy, pussy, pussy!" and Mistress Puss came bounding to him. He lifted her up, and offered to put her on the Queen's lap, but the Queen drew back at first and would not touch her. However, when she saw how the captain stroked the little creature, and called "Pussy, pussy, pussy!" she ventured to touch her. "Putty, putty, putty!" was all she could say, for she had not learned to speak English. When once she had the cat curled up snug on her lap and gently purring, she would not for worlds have parted with her.

So the King at once made a bargain with the captain to buy all the goods on board the ship; but he gave him ten times as much for the cat as for all the goods put together.

The captain then took leave of the King and Queen

of Barbary, and the very next day set sail for England.

One morning, some months after this, Mr. Fitzwarren. was in his counting-house, counting out his money, when he heard some one tap at his door.

"Who's there?" said he.

"A friend," was the answer. "A friend with news of your good ship 'Unicorn.' "

Mr. Fitzwarren hastened to open the door and whom should he see before him but the captain himself, with a bill of lading in one hand, and a box of jewels in the other. So full of joy was the good merchant then, that he lifted his eyes and thanked Heaven for sending him such good fortune.

The first story the captain told was about Mistress Puss; and he showed the rich payment which the King and Queen had made to poor Dick in exchange for her. As soon as the good gentleman heard this, he called out loudly to his servants:

"Go send him in, and tell him of his fame;
Pray call him Mr. Whittington by name!"

Dick was diligently scouring pots for the cook when word was brought to him that he was called to the counting-house.

"To the counting-house! I cannot go! I am too dirty!" he cried. But he was bidden to go just the same.

No sooner had he appeared in the room than Mr. Fitzwarren addressed him as Mr. Whittington and ordered a chair to be set for him. Then the lad thought surely his master and the men about must be poking fun at him.

"Do not poke fun at a simple lad like me," he said. "Let me go back, if you please, to my work."

"Mr. Whittington," said Mr. Fitzwarren, "no one is poking fun at you. This is what has happened. The captain has sold your cat to the King of Barbary and has brought you, in return for her, more riches than all I have put together."

Then he bade his men open the chest of treasure and show it to Dick.

The poor boy could scarcely believe his eyes. He begged his master to take a part of the treasure, but Mr. Fitzwarren said, "No, it is all your own; and I feel sure you will use it well."

Dick next asked Mistress Alice to take some of the jewels, but she too thanked him and refused. "Your good fortune makes me happy," she said, "and you have deserved it all!"

But Dick was too big-hearted to keep all the treasure himself. He made presents to the captain, the

sailors, the servants in Mr. Fitzwarren's household, and even to the ill-natured old cook.

When Whittington's face was washed, and his hair curled, and he was dressed in a nice suit of clothes he appeared as handsome a young man as one could wish to see.

Some years after this, there was a fine wedding at one of the great churches in London. Mistress Alice became the wife of Mr. Richard Whittington. And the lord mayor was there, and the great judges, and the sheriffs, and many more besides.

But Richard Whittington, in spite of his great fortune, worked on as diligently and faithfully as ever. He was first a great merchant, then sheriff of the city, and thrice lord mayor; King Henry V bestowed upon him the honor of knighthood and he became Sir Richard Whittington.

As Lord Mayor, he did many fine things for the city of London and left it much better than he found it. So for three hundred years after his time, there have been pointed out to all visitors the figures of Dick and his cat carved in stone on the archway of one of the great buildings he caused to be erected. Thus it came to pass that by going back to his place and keeping faithfully at his work, no matter how hard he found it, he proved the words of the great bells of Bow to be true when they called him "Whittington, thrice Lord Mayor of London."

The Pony Engine and the Pacific Express*
WILLIAM DEAN HOWELLS

Christmas Eve, after the children had hung up their stockings and got all ready for St. Nic, they climbed up on the papa's lap to kiss him good-night, and when they both got their arms round his neck, they said they were not going to bed till he told them a Christmas story. Then he saw that he would have to mind, for they were awfully severe with him, and always made him do exactly what they told him; it was the way they had brought him up. He tried his best to get out of it for a while, but after they had shaken him first this side, and then that side, and pulled him backward and forward till he did not know where he was, he began to think perhaps he had better begin. The first thing he said, after he opened his eyes, and made believe he had been asleep, or something, was, "Well, what did I leave off at?" and that made them just perfectly boiling, for they understood his tricks, and they knew he was trying to pre-

*From *Christmas Every Day and Other Stories*. Copyright, by Harper & Brothers.

tend that he had told part of the story already; and they said he had not left off anywhere because he had not commenced, and he saw it was no use. So he commenced.

"Once there was a little Pony Engine that used to play round the Fitchburg Depot on the side tracks, and sleep in among the big locomotives in the car-house—"

The little girl lifted her head from the papa's shoulder, where she had dropped it. "Is it a sad story, Papa?"

"How is it going to end?" asked the boy.

"Well, it's got a moral," said the papa.

"Oh, all right, if it's got a moral," said the children; they had a good deal of fun with morals the papa put to his stories. The boy added, "Go on," and the little girl prompted, "Car-house."

The papa said, "Now every time you stop me I shall have to begin all over again." But he saw that this was not going to spite them any, so he went on: "One of the locomotives was its mother, and she had got hurt once in a big smash-up, so that she couldn't run long trips any more. But she could work round the depot, and pull empty cars in and out, and shunt them off on the side tracks, and she was so anxious to be useful that all the other engines respected her, and they were very kind to the little Pony Engine on her account, though it was always getting in the way, and under their wheels, and everything. They all knew it was an orphan, for before its mother got hurt its father went through a bridge one dark night into an arm of the sea, and was never heard of again; he was supposed to have been drowned. The old mother locomotive used to say that it would never have happened if she had been there; but poor dear No. 236 was always so venturesome, and she had warned him against that very bridge time and again. Then she would whistle so dolefully, and sigh with her air-brakes enough to make anybody cry. You see they used to be a very happy family when they were all together, before the papa locomotive got drowned. He was very fond of the little Pony Engine, and told it stories at night after they got into the car-house, at the end of some of his long runs. It would get up on his cow-catcher, and lean its chimney up against his, and listen till it fell asleep. Then he would put it softly down, and be off again in the morning before it was awake. I tell you, those were happy days for poor No. 236. The little Pony Engine could just remember him; it was awfully proud of its papa."

The boy lifted his head and looked at the little girl, who suddenly hid her face in the papa's other shoulder. "Well, I declare, Papa, she was putting up her lip."

"I wasn't any such thing!" said the little girl. "And I don't care! So!" and then she sobbed.

"Now, never you mind," said the papa to the boy. "You'll be putting up *your* lip before I'm through. Well, and then she used to caution the little Pony Engine against getting in the way of the big locomotives, and told it to keep close round after her, and try to do all it could to learn about shifting empty cars. You see, she knew how ambitious the little Pony Engine was, and how it wasn't contented a bit just to grow up in the pony-engine business, and be tied down to the depot all its days. Once she happened to tell it that if it was good and always did what it was bid, perhaps a cow-catcher would grow on it some day, and then it could be a passenger locomotive."

"I don't think she ought to have deceived it, Papa," said the boy. "But it ought to have known that if it was a Pony Engine to begin with, it never could have a cow-catcher."

"Couldn't it?" asked the little girl, gently.

"No; they're kind of mooley."

The little girl asked the papa. "What makes Pony Engines mooley?" for she did not choose to be told by her brother; he was only two years older than she was, anyway.

"Well, it's pretty hard to say. You see, when a locomotive is first hatched—"

"Oh, are they hatched, Papa?" asked the boy.

"Well, we'll call it hatched," said the papa; but they knew he was just funning. "They're about the size of tea-kettles at first; and it's a chance whether they will have cow-catchers or not!

"The thing that the little Pony Engine wanted to be,

the most in this world, was the locomotive of the Pacific Express, that starts out every afternoon at three, you know. It intended to apply for the place as soon as its cow-catcher was grown, and it was always trying to attract the locomotive's attention, backing and filling on the track alongside of the train; and once it raced it a little piece, and beat it, before the Express locomotive was under way, and almost got in front of it on a switch. My, but its mother was scared! She just yelled to it with her whistle; and that night she sent it to sleep without a particle of coal or water in its tender.

"But the little Pony Engine didn't care. It had beaten the Pacific Express in a hundred yards, and what was to hinder it from beating it as long as it chose? The little Pony Engine could not get it out of its head.

"Well, one dark, snowy, blowy afternoon, when his mother was off pushing some empty coal cars up past the Know-Nothing crossing beyond Charlestown, he got on the track in front of the Express, and when he heard the conductor say 'All aboard,' and the starting gong struck, and the brakeman leaned out and waved to the engineer, he darted off like lightning. He had his steam up, and he just scuttled.

"Well, he was so excited for a while that he couldn't tell whether the Express was gaining on him or not; but after twenty or thirty miles, he thought he heard it pretty near. Of course the Express locomotive was drawing a heavy train of cars, and it had to make a stop or two—at Charlestown, and at Concord Junction, and at Ayer—so the Pony Engine did really gain on it a little; and when it began to be scared it gained a good deal. But the first place where it began to feel sorry, and to want its mother, was in Hoosac Tunnel. It never was in a tunnel before, and it seemed as if it would never get out. It kept thinking, What if the Pacific Express was to run over it there in the dark, and its mother off there at the Fitchburg Depot, in Boston, looking for it among the side-tracks? It gave a perfect shriek; and just then it shot out of the tunnel. There were a lot of locomotives loafing around there at North Adams, and one of them shouted out to it as it flew by, 'What's your hurry, little one?' and it just screamed back, 'Pacific Express!' and never stopped to explain. They talked in locomotive language—"

"Oh, what did it sound like?" the boy asked.

"Well, pretty queer; I'll tell you some day. It knew it had no time to fool away, and all through the long, dark night, whenever a locomotive hailed it, it just screamed, 'Pacific Express!' and kept on. And the Express kept gaining on it. Some of the locomotives wanted to stop it, but they decided they had better not get in its way, and so it whizzed along across New York State and Ohio and Indiana, till it got to Chicago. And the Express kept gaining on it. By that time it was so hoarse it could hardly whisper, but it kept saying, 'Pacific Express! Pacific Express!' and it kept right on till it reached the Mississippi River. There it found a long train of freight cars before it on the bridge. It couldn't wait, so it slipped down the track to the edge of the river, jumped across, and then scrambled up the embankment to the track again."

"Papa!" said the little girl, warningly.

"Truly it did," said the papa.

"Ho, that's nothing," said the boy. "A whole train of cars did it in that Jules Verne book."

"Well," the papa went on, "after that it had a little rest, for the Express had to wait for the freight train to get off the bridge, and the Pony Engine stopped at the first station for a drink of water and a mouthful of coal, and then it flew ahead. There was a kind old locomotive at Omaha that tried to find out where it belonged, and what its mother's name was, but the Pony Engine was so bewildered it couldn't tell. And the Express kept gaining on it. On the plains it was

chased by a pack of prairie wolves, but it left them far behind; and the antelopes were scared half to death. But the worst of it was when the nightmare got after it."

"The nightmare? Goodness!" said the boy.

"I've had the nightmare," said the little girl.

"Oh yes, a mere human nightmare," said the papa. "But a locomotive nightmare is a very different thing."

"Why, what's it like?" asked the boy. The little girl was almost afraid to ask.

"Well, it has only one leg, to begin with."

"Pshaw!"

"Wheel, I mean. And it has four cow-catchers, and four head-lights, and two boilers, and eight whistles, and it just goes whirling and screaming along. Of course it wobbles awfully; and as it's only got one wheel, it has to keep skipping from one track to the other."

"I should think it would run on the cross-ties," said the boy.

"Oh, very well, then!" said the papa. "If you know so much more about it than I do! Who's telling this story, anyway? Now I shall have to go back to the beginning. Once there was a little Pony En—"

They both put their hands over his mouth, and just fairly begged him to go on, and at last he did. "Well, it got away from the nightmare about morning, but not till the nightmare had bitten a large piece out of its tender, and then it braced up for the home-stretch. It thought that if it could once beat the Express to

the Sierras, it could keep the start the rest of the way, for it could get over the mountains quicker than the Express could, and it might be in San Francisco before the Express got to Sacramento. The Express kept gaining on it. But it just zipped along the upper edge of Kansas and the lower edge of Nebraska, and on through Colorado and Utah and Nevada, and when it got to the Sierras it just stooped a little, and went over them like a goat; it did, truly; just doubled up its fore wheels under it, and jumped. And the Express kept gaining on it. By this time it couldn't say 'Pacific Express' any more, and it didn't try. It just said 'Express! Express!' and then ''Press! 'Press!' and then ''Ess! 'Ess!' and pretty soon only ''Ss! 'Ss!' And the Express kept gaining on it. Before they reached

UP ONE PAIR OF STAIRS

San Francisco, the Express locomotive's cow-catcher was almost touching the Pony Engine's tender; it gave one howl of anguish as it felt the Express locomotive's hot breath on the place where the nightmare had bitten the piece out, and tore through the end of the San Francisco depot, and plunged into the Pacific Ocean, and was never seen again. "There, now," said the papa, trying to make the children get down, "that's all. Go to bed." The little girl was crying and so he tried to comfort her by keeping her on his lap.

The boy cleared his throat. "What is the moral, Papa?" he asked, huskily.

"Children, obey your parents," said the papa.

The boy thought awhile. "Well, I don't see what it had to do with Christmas, anyway."

"Why, it was Christmas Eve when the Pony Engine started from Boston, and Christmas afternoon when it reached San Francisco."

"Ho!" said the boy. "No locomotive could get across the continent in a day and a night, let alone a little Pony Engine."

"Well, perhaps it was a year. Maybe it was the *next* Christmas after that when it got to San Francisco."

The papa set the little girl down, and started to run out of the room, and both of the children ran after him, to pound him.

When they were in bed the boy called down-stairs to the papa, "Well, anyway, I didn't put up my lip."

—Abridged.

Old Johnny Appleseed

A long time ago, when the early settlers of Ohio still lived in little log cabins in the midst of a lonely wilderness, there wandered from farm to farm a queer, but lovable old man. Johnny Appleseed he was called, though his real name was John Chapman, and he brought the little girls ribbons and small gay pieces of calico, and all the children loved him. Years ago, Johnny Appleseed had given away to a poor woman with a large and needy family, his home at Pittsburgh Landing, and he had lashed two Indian canoes together and packed them to the rim with deer-skin bags full of apple seeds. Then he had drifted off with the current down the Ohio River, having only one wish in his heart, to make people happier, more at home in the wilderness by planting apple trees.

Now farms were far apart in those days, with long, lonely stretches between, billowy, treeless prairies, or shadowy old forests, where bears, deer, wolves, and Indians wandered about. Men, women and children toiled hard to raise the simplest food, and for fruit they had only berries and sour wild plums or crabs. They had no friendly apple trees to comfort them of an evening with juicy, round, red apples, munched by all the family about the open fire. Often the hearts of those pioneers were heavy with homesick longing, as they thought of the low rambling farmhouses left far away in the east, so cozy and so peaceful beneath the pink and white glory of blossoming apple trees.

UP ONE PAIR OF STAIRS

Old Johnny knew how they felt. Old Johnny knew what they wanted. The greatest adventure in life to him was to wander off in the wilderness and plant his precious seeds. Every year he gathered the seeds that were thrown away from the cider-presses in Western Pennsylvania. Then he tramped back with his load all the way to Ohio.

Along the road he trudged, merrily whistling a tune, but dressed in nothing whatever except a coffee sack with holes for his arms and head. As a hat, he wore an old tin pan wherein he had cooked his mush, or a home-made pasteboard contraption, with a peak, like a roof, extending far out in front to protect his eyes from the sun. Usually he was barefooted. Only when snow lay deep on the ground was he sometimes to be seen with a cast-off boot on one foot and a moccasin on the other. Aye, he was queer, was Old Johnny; yet no one ever laughed at him. They loved him far too dearly.

Sometimes the pioneers paid Johnny small sums for his seeds or the tiny slips of trees which he grew in his different nurseries, but he never thought of spending his money on buying clothes for himself. No, he gave it away to some unfortunate family, and every fall he gathered together the poor, old, worn-out horses turned adrift by the settlers, buying food for them until Spring, when he led them away to pasture.

Often people asked Johnny if he was not afraid to wander about barefooted. In that land other men wrapped up their legs in bandages of dried grass. They

thought even buckskin leggings not tough enough to protect them from the sting of snakes that abounded in the tall, strong, prairie grass. But Johnny only replied that he was afraid of nothing. He loved every creature that God had made and so he tramped through the forest, fearless, safe and free. Mother bears let him play with their cubs and even the Indians loved him. He would not carry a gun and yet they never harmed him. Too many times had he done them some little kindness.

In the war of 1812, when the red-men broke out savagely against the lone white settlers along the frontiers of the West, they still let Johnny go free, safe and unmolested through the narrow trails of the woods. And, though he did not fight, he often wandered for days, sleepless and taking no food, but giving alarm of attacks intended by the red-men, and warning the pioneers to flee to the nearest blockhouse.

UP ONE PAIR OF STAIRS

One brilliant moonlight night he thrilled the heart of a farmer by thundering forth his message as though he had been a prophet out of the Bible that he loved:

"The spirit of the Lord is upon me and He hath anointed me to sound an alarm in the forest; for behold the tribes of the heathen are round about your doors!"

With all his heart Johnny believed that God had sent him forth to preach the gospel of love and to plant his apple seeds. When he came to a cabin at nightfall and the family sat about the fire, he would stretch himself out on the floor and ask the little group if they wished to hear "some news right fresh from heaven." Then he would take

out his Bible and read the words of Jesus, his voice now strong and loud as the roar of the wind and waves, and now sinking soft and low and soothing as summer breezes.

Once a wandering preacher, talking under the treetops and scolding his listeners roundly, cried aloud with importance: "Where now is a man who, like the early Christians, is traveling to heaven barefoot and clothed in coarsest raiment?"

Suddenly Johnny rose from the log on which he sat.

"Here is your early Christian," he pointed to his coffee-sack, and the preacher hung his head. He himself was not ready to lead such a simple life of quiet, unselfish deeds, and so he dismissed his hearers and quickly slunk away.

Slowly many people came pressing into the wilderness. Towns and churches appeared and stage coaches broke, with the blare of their horns, the ancient, peaceful stillness of prairies and age-old forests. So in 1858 Johnny said farewell to his friends and turned his face farther westward, to spend his last nine years still in advance of settlement, far on the western frontiers, even pressing as far as Casey, Illinois. And when, after forty years, his long unselfish labors came to an end, how richly they had borne fruit! One hundred thousand square miles in Ohio and Indiana bore witness to the labors of one stout-hearted old hero, who had no thought for himself, but planted his little brown seeds in order that men and women, youths and maids and children, whom he had never seen, should some day eat rosy apples around their glowing hearths, and wander in the Springtime beneath the fragrant branches of blossoming apple trees.

THE PLANTING OF THE APPLE TREE
WILLIAM CULLEN BRYANT

What plant we in this apple tree?
Buds, which the breath of summer days
Shall lengthen into leafy sprays;
Boughs where the thrush, with crimson breast,
Shall haunt and sing and hide her nest;
We plant, upon the sunny lea,
A shadow for the noontide hour,
A shelter from the summer shower,
   When we plant the apple tree.

What plant we in this apple tree?
Fruits that shall swell in sunny June,
And redden in the August noon,
And drop, when gentle airs come by,
That fan the blue September sky,
   While children come, with cries of glee,
And seek them where the fragrant grass
Betrays their bed to those who pass,
   At the foot of the apple tree.

357

The Fairy Who Judged Her Neighbors

JEAN INGELOW

There was once a Fairy, who was a good Fairy on the whole, but she had one very bad habit; she was too fond of finding fault with other people, and of taking for granted that everything must be wrong if it did not appear right to her.

One day, when she had been talking very unkindly of some friends of hers, her mother said to her, "My child, I think if you knew a little more of the world you would become more charitable. I would therefore advise you to set out on your travels; you will find plenty of food, for the cowslips are now in bloom, and they contain excellent honey. I need not be anxious about your lodging, for there is no place more delightful for sleeping in than an empty robin's nest when the young have flown. And if you want a new gown, you can sew two tulip-leaves together which will make you a very becoming dress, and one that I should be proud to see you in."

UP ONE PAIR OF STAIRS

The young Fairy was pleased at this permission to set out on her travels; so she kissed her mother, and bade good-bye to her nurse, who gave her a little ball of spider's threads to sew with, and a beautiful little box, made of the egg-shell of a wren, to keep her best thimble in, and took leave of her, wishing her safe home again.

The young Fairy then flew away till she came to a large meadow, with a clear river flowing on one side of it, and some tall oak-trees on the other. She sat down on a high branch in one of these oaks, and, after her long flight, was thinking of a nap, when, happening to look down at her little feet, she observed that her shoes were growing shabby and faded. "Quite a disgrace, I declare," said she. "I must look for another pair. Perhaps two of the smallest flowers of that snapdragon which I see growing in the hedge would fit me. I think I should like a pair of yellow slippers." So she flew down, and, after a little trouble, she found two flowers which fitted her very neatly, and she was just going to return to the oak-tree, when she heard a deep sigh beneath her, and peeping out from her place among the hawthorn blossoms, she saw a fine young

Lark sitting in the long grass, and looking the picture of misery.

"What is the matter with you, cousin?" asked the Fairy.

"Oh, I am so unhappy," replied the poor Lark; "I want to build a nest, and I have got no wife."

"Why don't you look for a wife, then?" said the Fairy, laughing at him. "Do you expect one to come and look for you? Fly up, and sing a beautiful song in the sky, and then perhaps some pretty hen will hear you; and perhaps, if you tell her that you will help her to build a capital nest, and that you will sing to her all day long, she will consent to be your wife."

"Oh, I don't like to," said the Lark, "I don't like to fly up, I am so ugly. If I were a goldfinch, and had yellow bars on my wings, or a robin, and had red feathers on my breast, I should not mind the defect which now I am afraid to show. But I am only a poor brown Lark, and I know I shall never get a wife."

"I never heard of such an unreasonable bird," said the Fairy. "You cannot expect to have everything."

"Oh, but you don't know," proceeded the Lark, "that if I fly up my feet will be seen; and no other bird has feet like mine. My claws are enough to frighten any one, they are so long; and yet I assure you, Fairy, I am not a cruel bird."

"Let me look at your claws," said the Fairy.

So the Lark lifted up one of his feet, which he had

kept hidden in the long grass, lest any one should see it.

"It certainly looks very fierce," said the Fairy. "Your hind claw is at least an inch long, and all your toes have very dangerous-looking points. Are you sure you never use them to fight with?"

"No, never!" said the Lark earnestly. "I never fought a battle in my life; but yet these claws grow longer and longer, and I am so ashamed of their being seen, that I very often lie in the grass instead of going up to sing, as I could wish."

"I think, if I were you, I would pull them off," said the Fairy.

"That is easier said than done," answered the poor Lark, "I have often got them entangled in the grass, and I scrape them against the hard clods; but it is of no use. You cannot think how fast they stick on."

"Well, I am sorry for you," observed the Fairy; "but at the same time I cannot but see that, in spite of what you say, you must be a quarrelsome bird, or you would not have such long spurs."

"That is just what I am always afraid people should say," sighed the Lark.

"For," proceeded the Fairy, "nothing is given us to be of no use. You would not have wings unless you were to fly, nor a voice unless you were to sing; and so you would not have those dreadful spurs unless you were going to fight. If your spurs are not to fight with," continued the unkind Fairy, "I should like to know what they are for."

"I am sure I don't know," said the Lark, lifting up his foot and looking at it. "Then you are not inclined to help me at all, Fairy? I thought you might be willing to mention among my friends that I am not a quarrelsome bird, and that I should always take care not to hurt my wife and nestlings with my spurs."

"Appearances are very much against you," answered the Fairy; "and it is quite plain to me that those spurs are meant to scratch with. No, I cannot help you. Good morning."

So the Fairy withdrew to her oak-bough, and the poor Lark sat moping in the grass while the Fairy watched him. "After all," she thought, "I am sorry he is such a quarrelsome fellow; for that he is such is fully proved by those long spurs."

While she was so thinking the Grasshopper came chirping up to the Lark, and tried to comfort him.

"I have heard all that the Fairy said to you," he observed, "and I really do not see that it need make you unhappy. I have known you some time, and have never seen you fight or look out of temper; therefore I will spread a report that you are a very good-tempered bird, and that you are looking out for a wife."

The Lark upon this thanked the Grasshopper warmly.

"At the same time," remarked the Grasshopper, "I should be glad if you could tell me what is the use of those claws, because the question might be asked me, and I should not know what to answer."

"Grasshopper," replied the Lark, "I cannot imagine what they are for—that is the real truth."

"Well," said the kind Grasshopper, "perhaps time will show."

So he went away, and the Lark, delighted with his promise to speak well of him, flew up into the air, and the higher he went the sweeter and the louder he sang. He was so happy, and he poured forth such delightful notes, so clear and thrilling, that the little ants who were carrying grains to their burrows stopped and put down their burdens to listen; and the doves ceased cooing, and the little field-mice came and sat in the openings of their holes; and the Fairy, who had just begun to doze, woke up delighted; and a pretty brown Lark, who had been sitting under some great foxglove leaves, peeped out and exclaimed, "I never heard such a beautiful song in my life—never!"

"It was sung by my friend, the Skylark," said the Grasshopper, who just then happened to be on a leaf near her. "He is a very good-tempered bird, and he wants a wife."

"Hush!" said the pretty brown Lark. "I want to hear the end of that wonderful song, if I may."

For just then the Skylark, far up in the heaven, burst forth again, and sang better than ever—so well, indeed, that every creature in the field sat still to listen; and the little brown Lark under the foxglove leaves held her breath, for she was afraid of losing a single note.

"Well done, my friend!" exclaimed the Grasshopper, when at length he came down panting, and with tired wings; and then he told him how much his friend the brown Lark, who lived by the foxglove, had been pleased with his song, and he took the poor Skylark to see her.

He walked as carefully as he could, that she might not see his feet; and he thought he had never seen such a pretty bird in his life. But when she told him how much she loved music, he sprang up again into the blue sky as if he was not at all tired, and sang anew, clearer and sweeter than before. He was so glad to think that he could please her. He sang several songs, and the Grasshopper did not fail to praise him, and say what a cheerful, kind bird he was. The consequence was, that when he asked her to overlook his spurs and be his wife, she said she would see about it.

"I don't mind your spurs particularly," she observed.

"I am very glad of that," said the Skylark. "I was afraid you would disapprove of them."

"Not at all," she replied. "On the contrary, now I think of it, I should not have liked you to have short claws like other birds; but I cannot exactly say why, as such birds seem to be of no use in particular."

This was very good news for the Skylark, and he sang such delightful songs in consequence, that he very soon won his wife; and they built a delightful little nest in the grass, which made him so happy, that he almost forgot to be sorry about his long spurs.

The Fairy, meanwhile, flew about from field to field, and I am sorry to say that she seldom went anywhere without saying something unkind or ill-natured; for, as I told you before, she was very hasty, and had a sad habit of judging her neighbors.

She had been several days wandering about in search of adventures, when one afternoon she came back to the old oak-tree, because she wanted a new pair of shoes, and there were none to be had so pretty as those made of the yellow snapdragon flowers in the hedge hard by. While she was fitting on her shoes, she saw the Lark's friend.

"How do you do, Grasshopper?" asked the Fairy.

"Thank you, I am very well and very happy," said the Grasshopper. "People are always so kind to me."

"Indeed!" replied the Fairy. "I wish I could say that they were always kind to me. How is that quarrelsome Lark, who found such a pretty brown mate the other day?"

"He is not a quarrelsome bird indeed," replied the Grasshopper. "I wish you would not say that he is."

"Oh, well, we need not quarrel about that," said

the Fairy, laughing; "I have seen the world, Grasshopper, and I know a few things, depend upon it. Your friend the Lark does not wear those long spurs for nothing."

The Grasshopper did not choose to contend with the Fairy, who all this time was busily fitting yellow slippers to her tiny feet. When, however, she had found a pair to her mind—

"Suppose you come and see the eggs that our pretty friend the Lark has got in her nest," asked the Grasshopper. "Three pink eggs spotted with brown."

Off they set together; but what was their surprise to find the poor little brown Lark sitting on them with rumpled feathers, drooping head, and trembling limbs.

"Ah, my pretty eggs!" said the Lark, as soon as she could speak, "I am so miserable about them—they must be trodden on, they will certainly be found."

"What is the matter?" asked the Grasshopper. "Perhaps we can help you."

"Dear Grasshopper," said the Lark, "I have just heard the farmer and his son talking on the other side of the hedge, and the farmer said that tomorrow morning he should begin to cut this meadow."

"That is a great pity," said the Grasshopper. "What a sad thing it was that you laid your eggs on the ground!"

"Larks always do," said the poor little brown bird; "and I did not know how to make a fine nest such as those in the hedges. Oh, my pretty eggs!—my heart aches for them! I shall never hear my little nestlings chirp."

So the poor Lark lamented, and neither the Grasshopper nor the Fairy could do anything to help her. At last her mate dropped down from the white cloud

where he had been singing, and when he saw her drooping, and the Grasshopper and the Fairy sitting silently before her, he inquired in a great fright what the matter was.

So they told him, and at first he was very much shocked; but presently he lifted first one and then the other of his feet, and examined his long spurs.

"He does not sympathize much with his poor mate," whispered the Fairy; but the Grasshopper took no notice of the speech.

Still the Lark looked at his spurs, and seemed to be very deep in thought.

"If I had only laid my eggs on the other side of the hedge," sighed the poor mother. "Among the corn, there would have been plenty of time to rear my birds before harvest time."

"My dear," answered her mate, "don't be unhappy." And so saying, he hopped up to the eggs, and laying one foot upon the prettiest, he clasped it with his long spurs. Strange to say, it exactly fitted them.

"To be sure I can," replied the Lark, beginning slowly and carefully to hop on with the egg in his right foot; "nothing more easy. I have often thought it was likely that our eggs would be disturbed in this meadow; but it never occurred to me till this moment that I could provide against the misfortune. I have often wondered what my spurs could be for, and now I see." So saying, he hopped gently on till he came to the hedge, and then got through it, still holding the egg, till he found a nice little hollow place in among the corn, and there he laid it, and came back for the others.

"Hurrah!" cried the Grasshopper. "Larkspurs forever!"

The Fairy said nothing, but she felt heartily ashamed of herself. She sat looking on till the happy Lark had carried the last of his eggs to a safe place, and had called his mate to come and sit on them. Then, when he sprang up into the sky again, exulting, and rejoicing, and singing to his mate, that now he was quite happy, because he knew what his long spurs were for, she stole gently away, saying to herself, "Well, I could not have believed such a thing. I thought he must be a quarrelsome bird as his spurs were so long; but it appears that I was wrong, after all."

ARIEL'S SONG
William Shakespeare

Where the bee sucks, there suck I;
In a cowslip's bell I lie;
There I couch when owls do cry—
On the bat's back I do fly
After summer merrily.
Merrily, merrily shall I live now
    Under the blossom that hangs on the bough.

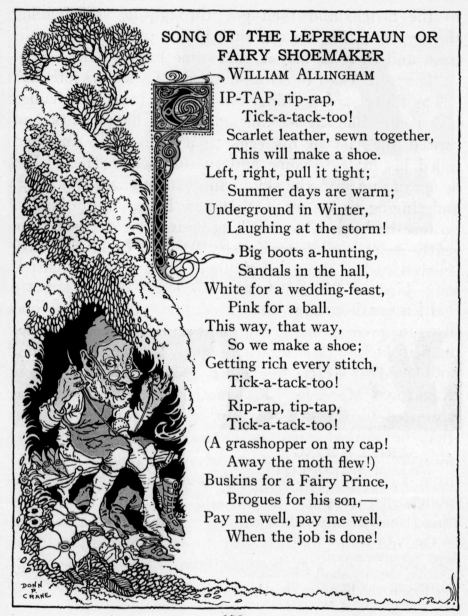

SONG OF THE LEPRECHAUN OR FAIRY SHOEMAKER
William Allingham

IP-TAP, rip-rap,
  Tick-a-tack-too!
Scarlet leather, sewn together,
  This will make a shoe.
Left, right, pull it tight;
  Summer days are warm;
Underground in Winter,
  Laughing at the storm!

Big boots a-hunting,
  Sandals in the hall,
White for a wedding-feast,
  Pink for a ball.
This way, that way,
  So we make a shoe;
Getting rich every stitch,
  Tick-a-tack-too!

Rip-rap, tip-tap,
  Tick-a-tack-too!
(A grasshopper on my cap!
  Away the moth flew!)
Buskins for a Fairy Prince,
  Brogues for his son,—
Pay me well, pay me well,
  When the job is done!

370

Jack and the Beanstalk*

In a small cottage near a country village, there once lived a poor woman who had only one child, a lad named Jack. Jack was a heedless young fellow, sound and good at heart, but much given to acting without thinking. Moreover, his mother had almost never corrected him as he grew up, so the consequence was that he worked when he chose, and followed his own pleasure when he chose. As Jack's mother was far from rich, and the lad worked so irregularly, she was obliged to support herself and him by selling everything she had. At last nothing remained except one cow.

One day the mother said to her son with tears in her eyes, "Oh, you heedless boy, while you were idly amusing yourself in the village, we have eaten up

*Freely adapted from the English Folk Tale.

everything we had. I have not money enough left to buy even a bit of bread for today. Nothing remains but my poor cow, and that must be sold or we will go hungry."

Jack was much ashamed of himself for a few moments, but, as he grew hungrier and hungrier, he teased his mother to let him sell the cow. Knowing nothing else to do, the mother sadly consented, bidding her son use good judgment and get a fair price in exchange. So Jack started out for market, but on his journey he met a butcher, who asked why he was driving the cow from home. Jack replied he was going to sell it. Now the butcher had in a bag some wonderful beans of different colours, which caught Jack's fancy. This the butcher saw, and knowing Jack's easy temper, he made up his mind to take advantage of it, so he offered the beans for the cow. The foolish boy forgot all about their great need at home, and thought only what pleasure it would give him to have the beans. So the bargain was struck on the moment, and the butcher went off with the cow. Then Jack hastened home in great excitement and told his mother what he had done, but the poor woman burst at once into tears. "Foolish boy," she cried, "now we have nothing at all to eat. You have sold my good cow for a few paltry beans that happened to tickle your fancy. Go play with your childish playthings, but we shall have no supper tonight." And she tossed the beans out the back door with all her strength, scattering them everywhere, while she continued to weep hot tears for her son's folly.

For the first time in his life, Jack was thoroughly sorry for what he had done; he now saw the beans for the useless things they were, and his mother's grief moved him deeply. He had no further wish to amuse himself. Instead, he went to his room and fell a-thinking. He remembered how good his mother had always been to him, and how he had repaid her only with thoughtless idleness. Tonight, through his fault, she was going hungry. He sat a long, long time in sorrow and resolved the very next day to set himself earnestly to work.

Early in the morning, he arose from his bed, but he saw that in the night something strange and green had grown up past his window. Hurrying to the lattice he opened it, and there he saw a great vine growing up from the ground. Some of his beans had taken root and sprung up wonderfully. The stalks grew of an immense thickness, and had so entwined that they formed a ladder. Looking upwards, he could not even see the top; it seemed to be lost in the clouds. He tried it, found it firm and not to be shaken. Then a new idea struck him. This ladder, grown up past his window so strangely, from the beans he had taken, must be meant for him to climb. Since he was now thoroughly sorry for his faults, he told himself that this chance was given him to make amends and climb up to some new opportunity. Doubtless that ladder would lead him to the very spot where those tasks or adventures awaited him that should prove his new-found manliness.

Full of this idea, Jack hastened to tell his mother. She would gladly have held him back, but she saw at last that the time had come when she must let him go forth to make his way in the world. At once he set out. He climbed and he climbed and he climbed. He began to grow weary, but still he climbed and he climbed. He grew very weary indeed, but still he climbed. So at last he reached the top and stepped off into a strange country. It seemed to be a rocky, barren place; not a tree, shrub, house or living creature, was to be seen anywhere about. Jack sat himself down thoughtfully on a block of stone to rest. He was very, very hungry, for he had had nothing to eat since noon of the day before, but still he thought most of the hope that now at last he had reached the place where he should find his task. Suddenly, as he was thinking, lo and behold! there appeared before him a queer little old lady. She wore a pointed cap of quilted red satin, turned up with ermine; her hair streamed loose over her shoulders, and in her hand she carried a wand. "Jack," she said as she drew near him, "I am a Fairy. Your sorrow for your folly and idleness and your wish at last to perform some worthy task made your beans sprout and formed the ladder that brought you to me. Had you only looked at the gigantic beanstalk and stupidly wondered about it, you would never have found me. But you showed an inquiring

mind, great courage and enterprise, therefore you deserve to rise. It is my business to tell you what great things you have to do here. The story I am about to relate, your mother has never dared tell you. Lad though you are, the chance lies before you to do the deeds of a man."

Jack held his breath with interest and astonishment while the Fairy continued:

"Your father was a rich man with a greatly generous nature. It was his practice to be kind to everyone about him, and to help not only those who asked his aid, but all beside who needed anything. So good a man was he that he roused the anger of a huge giant who lived nearby. This creature was the embodiment of cruelty and wickedness, so of course he could not bear to hear others talked of for their goodness. Hearing that your parents were about to pass a few days with a friend at some distance from home, he caused them to be waylaid, seized and bound hand and foot. Then he went forward, drove out your father's servants, and took possession of your castle. At the time all this happened, you were but a few months old, and, with your mother and father, you were cast by the giant into the deepest dungeon of the castle. There you all three lay for months, but at last the giant offered to restore you and your mother to liberty on condition that she would solemnly swear never to tell anyone the story of her wrongs.

"To put it out of her power to do him any harm, the giant had her placed on shipboard with you in her arms, and taken to a distant country. There she was left with no more money for her support than what she got by selling a few jewels she had hidden in her dress. Now the giant lives in this country, and still keeps your father prisoner in the castle. You are the person who must set him free and restore to him his goods. All that the giant has is yours. Regain what you can. You will meet with dangers and difficulties, but you must have courage and stick to your task. Moreover, you must do nothing rashly, but use wisdom at all times. Remember Right and Justice are with you and before these, Wickedness cannot stand. If you go forward fearlessly, sure in this knowledge, then you will be one of those who conquer giants."

As soon as she had made an end the Fairy dis-

appeared, leaving Jack greatly aroused by what she
had said, to follow his journey. It was no easy task
that lay before him. He walked on and on and on and
still he came to no dwelling. At length as night came
on, he lay down beneath the shelter of a rock and fell
asleep. In the morning to his great joy, he saw not
far away the large house for which he was looking.
Now very greatly in need of food, he made his way
slowly to the door, lifted the knocker and rapped. A
very large woman opened the door for him, with a face
that seemed none too kindly, and she stood listening
in great astonishment while he begged her for a bite
to eat. It was most uncommon, she said roughly, to
see any strange creature near their house, for it was
well known that her husband was a cruel and ugly
giant who bullied all who came near him. "If you
know what is good for you," she went on, "you will
run away at once as fast as your legs will carry you."

In spite of his hunger and need, Jack's first thought
was to act at once on her words, and run away as
fast as he could. Then he remembered what the Fairy
had said, and the reason for his being there. So he
bravely stood his ground, and asked again for food,
offering in return to do any kind of work. At this
the woman considered a moment. She herself drudged,
toiled and labored from morning till night and she was
greatly in need of someone to help her. So at last she let
herself be persuaded and led Master Jack inside the house.

First they passed an elegant hall, finely furnished; then they went through several spacious rooms, all in the same style of grandeur, but lonely-looking and dreary. A long gallery came next; it was very dark, just light enough to show that, instead of a wall on either side, there was a grating of iron which parted off a dismal dungeon, whence Jack could hear sighs and the clanking of chains. His heart beat fast as he thought that here perhaps his father was confined and he grew more than ever determined to stick to his task until he set him free.

The woman took Jack into a large kitchen where a great fire was kept. There she bade him sit down and gave him plenty to eat and drink. Now he saw that after all she was a kindly woman, only much overworked and worried by the bullying of the giant. When he had done his meal, she set him to work scrubbing and burnishing. All day long he worked harder and more steadily than he had ever done in all his life before and she fed him well. At length evening came, then there was suddenly a great knocking at the gate that caused the whole house to shake. "Let me in! Let me in!" roared a blustering voice. The giant's wife hid Jack in the oven, then she ran to let her husband in.

Soon he came striding into the room, an ugly creature enough, with little pig eyes and the face of a bully. The moment he crossed the threshold, he began to sniff about and shout:

"Fee Fi Fo Fum,
I smell the blood of an Englishman!"

Jack crouched further down in a corner of the oven,
but he called to mind that the Fairy had said Right
was with him, and if he stood fearlessly by that fact,
he should be one of those who conquered giants. So
he found his courage again and quietly waited. The
woman meantime had answered her husband gruffly,
"You'll go on smelling Englishmen as long as you
keep them in the dungeon."

"Humph!" grunted the giant and seated himself

by the fire while the wife prepared supper for him.

Through a crevice in the oven Jack continued to look on. He was much surprised to see what an amazing quantity the giant devoured, and supposed he would never have done eating and drinking. After his supper was ended, a very curious hen was brought and placed on the table before him. Jack's curiosity was great to see what would happen. He saw that the hen stood quiet before the giant, and every time he said "Lay!" she laid an egg of solid gold. The giant amused himself with her for a long time, while his wife went to bed. But at length he fell asleep in his chair and snored like the roaring of a cannon. Knowing it was his business to recover the hen, Jack crept softly from his hiding place, seized her and ran off with her as fast as his legs would carry him. The hen began to cackle which woke the giant, and just as Jack got out of the house he heard him calling:

"Wife, wife, what have you done with my golden hen?"

But that was all Jack heard, for he hurried back to the beanstalk and climbed down like a streak of lightning. His mother was overjoyed to see him. "Now mother," said Jack, "I have brought you home that which will meet all our needs." The hen laid as many golden eggs as he desired. Jack sold them and soon had as much money as they two needed.

For a short time, Jack and his mother lived very happily, but the lad never left off thinking of his father. So early one morning he again climbed the beanstalk, and reached the giant's mansion in the evening. The woman came and answered his knock as before. Jack at once begged her to give him a night's lodging. At first she began to scold him roundly for having taken her husband's hen on his previous visit, but by this time Jack felt assured that she was a kindly woman and he had no need to fear her. Moreover, in her heart she knew the giant had no right to the treasures he had stolen, so at last she admitted the lad and gave him some supper. After his meal, Jack repaid her by working faithfully till they heard the giant's knock at the gate. This time the woman hid the boy in the lumber closet. Soon after the giant came blustering in and began to sniff, sniff, sniff about.

"Fee Fi Fo Fum,
I smell the blood of an Englishman!"
he roared, but his wife once more reminded him that he had an Englishman in his dungeon, so the giant sat down and ate his supper. Then he ordered his wife to bring down his bags of gold and silver. Jack peeped out from his hiding place and watched him count over the treasure, which he had stolen from the lad's father. At last the giant put everything back in the bags again, dropped his chin on his chest and fell asleep. Jack crept very, very quietly from the closet and approached the table. All at once

a little dog under the giant's chair began to bark furiously. The giant sleepily opened one eye; Jack seized the bags and ran! So he reached the beanstalk in safety and was soon back again in his own room.

If his mother was glad to see him before, she was twice glad to have him safe returned this time, and they found themselves now very well off indeed. Still all this wealth and comfort at home did not make Jack wish to remain there at ease and leave his father shut up in the dungeon.

On the longest day of the year he arose as soon as it was light and climbed the beanstalk. He arrived at the giant's house in the evening and found his wife standing at the door. This time her manner was rougher than ever, for her husband had been very hard on her after the disappearance of the treasure. It was difficult indeed to persuade her to admit him. But at last he prevailed and was allowed to go in to work and eat his supper as usual. When the giant came home, Jack was hidden in the copper kettle.

The great bully was as ugly as ever, and began once more to roar:

> *"Fee Fi Fo Fum,*
> *I smell the blood of an Englishman!"*

Then, notwithstanding all his wife could say, he searched in every nook and corner of the room. Whilst this was going on, Jack held his breath. The giant approached the copper kettle and put his hand squarely on the lid. Jack thought he must surely be discovered, but no! the search ended here and the bully sat quietly down by the fireside.

When supper was over, the giant commanded his wife to fetch him his harp. Jack peeped from under the copper lid, and soon saw the giantess bring in the instrument. It was carved of gold and on the front was the figure of a beautiful woman with wings. Her robes flowed to the floor and ended in the form of a stand like a common harp. The harp was put by the giant on the table and when he said "Play!" it instantly played of its own accord. The music was

so soft and melodious that Jack was filled with delight and felt very anxious to recover so great a treasure. But the giant's soul could find no pleasure in such harmony, so instead of listening to the music, he soon fell soundly asleep. Jack at once climbed out of the copper kettle and seized the harp. He had no sooner done so, however, than it began to cry out, "Master! Master!" Jack thought this must surely awaken the giant, so he started to run away as before. "Master! Master!" still cried the Harp. "Master! Master!" The lad was almost ready to drop it, when he suddenly felt that it was turning in his arms as if alive, directing itself by its wings, and pulling him along with it. Not toward the outer door did it go, but back, back into the house, toward the dungeons. "Master! Master!" it kept repeating, and soon it dragged Jack to the very spot where he knew his father must be imprisoned. "Master! Master!" it twanged louder than ever, and lo there came to the grating of one of the dungeons a white haired old man in chains.

"My harp! My harp!" he cried. "Who bears you hither?"

Jack answered at once, "Thy son!"

"My son!" repeated the man with tears of joy. "My son!"

As he spoke, he stretched his arms through the grating and the Harp flew immediately into them.

"Harp! Harp! Play off my chains!" he commanded.

Such music as the Harp then played! The chains fell away from the old man's feet.

"Harp! Harp! Play open my dungeon door!" The Harp played again. Then the heavy door swung open, Jack's father passed through, and the two hurried down the gallery.

But by this time there was a great commotion from the kitchen. The giant was now thoroughly awake and roaring for his harp. As Jack and his father ran out the great gate of the Castle, the giant was hot on their heels. They ran and they ran! Behind them the giant roared in a voice of thunder. Often he almost had them, but they clung to the Harp and it helped them on with its wings. At last they came to the beanstalk. Jack and his father climbed quickly down. No sooner had they reached the bottom, than the giant appeared, shaking his fists at the top of the ladder above. Down, down he came, snorting and raging, but Jack called loudly for a hatchet and when he was almost upon them, he laid his hatchet to the root of the beanstalk. No sooner had he done so, than of a sudden, the whole beanstalk shriveled up and the giant burst like a monstrous bubble. Then Jack and his mother and father fell into each other's arms and rejoiced to be once more together. As for the giant's wife in the land beyond the beanstalk, she without doubt was glad to be freed from such wickedness and cruelty.

THE CIRCUS PARADE

OLIVE BEAUPRÉ MILLER

Tomorrow, tomorrow's the circus parade!
  Just think what I shall see!
What crowds of people in gay-colored clothes
  All lined up the street there will be.

And some of the children will have red balloons,
  As up by the curbing they stand,
Then off in the distance we'll suddenly hear
  The circus's big brass band!

Behind the crash bang! of the music they play,
  Come riders in red velvet gowns,
And after them doing the funniest things,
  A silly procession of clowns.

386

UP ONE PAIR OF STAIRS

Then lions and tigers that pace up and down,
  In wagons all painted with gold,
And monkeys a-playing just all kinds of tricks,
  As they grimace and chatter and scold.

O, next there come camels and elephants, too,
  With men on their backs astride,
And queer little ponies, no bigger than dogs,
  And a donkey perhaps beside!

And then there come chariots rumbling by
  With horses all four in a row;
And the wheezing, old, piping calliope is
  The very tail end of the show!

BERT R. ELLIOTT

387

Ikwa and Annowee*

ELIZABETH E. FOULKE

They lived in the frozen North,—these little Eskimo children. They had been alone for several days. Most of the villagers had gone away to fish. It was nearly time for them to return, and Ikwa was hitching the dogs to the sledge that he and Annowee might go to meet them.

Kookoo, the leader of the team, had given him a playful chase all around the village; but he had harnessed him at last, and he was now ready for work.

Ikwa had never had the sole care of the dogs before, and he was very much pleased about it. He had not wished to stay at home with Annowee. He had watched the boys starting off with their fishing-spears, and he had longed to go with them.

"Never mind, Ikwa," his mother had said as she started off; "you may fish awhile when you bring the sledge." So Ikwa was comforted.

When the rest were gone, the children tried all the sports that they knew. The snow still clung to the hillsides; and Annowee had learned to make a ball of her little body, and roll down a slope almost as fast as Ikwa could. They had played "Sand Bag" until they were tired, but at last it was time to start.

*Taken from *Braided Straws* by the permission of Silver, Burdett & Company.

UP ONE PAIR OF STAIRS

Annowee sat upon the sledge, while her brother ran along by the side of the dogs. They were pulling finely. Kookoo seemed the more ready for work after his frolic.

"Let us go across the ice-fields, it is nearer that way," said the boy.

They were facing the bay. Far beyond the great sheet of ice, the waves danced and lifted their white arms in the sunlight. Farther still, the stately bergs drifted out to sea. The wind was rising, and the air was very cold.

"Look, Ikwa!" cried Annowee pointing off to landward. There was a roaring noise as the ice on the mountain-side let go its hold, and went crashing into the bay. How it bowed, and plunged, and splashed! The whales moved off to make room. But Ikwa was not watching. He was thinking of the ice beneath his feet. He had felt it tremble.

"We must go back," he said.

He turned as he spoke, and looked along the path they had taken. Then he gave a low cry. There was a narrow strip of water flowing between them and the shore. He knew at once that the ice upon which they were standing had broken away from land.

"Back! Back!" he cried to the dogs, who were trotting ahead.

They turned at the sound of his voice, and ran toward the shore at his bidding, but the narrow path of water had grown too wide, and they could not cross it, try as they might. No help was near. Must they drift out to sea among the bergs? What if the ice where they stood should part, and let them down into the foaming water beneath! Already the edges began to crack and float off. And how it rocked,— the great floe!

"We must go over toward the middle again," said Ikwa, to his sister. The girl did not understand. Ikwa turned, and looked earnestly in her face.

"See, Annowee," he said, "we are on an ice-floe. We cannot get off."

She looked at him in a puzzled way.

"Don't you see?" he asked, pointing to the water that rolled and dashed between them and the shore, "we are afloat upon the bay."

A look of terror came into his sister's face as she cried, "Annowee is afraid!"

How helpless Ikwa felt! The gale was blowing fierce and bleak. The waves dashed rough and wild, around, beneath. The children could only crouch down with the dogs and wait. What would become of them?

Annowee began to cry. "I'm cold!" she sobbed.

Ikwa looked around. All about them the snow lay deep as it did on the land.

"I'll make an igloo, Annowee," the boy cried.

He rose at once, and began to cut the blocks. He had often done this work for his father at home.

Annowee forgot her fear in watching him. He made the dogs lie down at her feet to keep her warm. The wall was in the form of a half igloo around the group. Soon it was so high that Annowee could not see him at his work.

"It is so much warmer here, Ikwa," she called; "come in and try it."

But Ikwa worked on. He was glad to have something to do.

Presently he heard her voice again. "See, Ikwa!" she called.

The boy hurried around, and saw a walrus lying on the floe at one side. It had climbed up there to rest.

A vast sheet of water now lay before them, and they had drifted far from land; but the wind was changing, and the tide, too, was beginning to wash them toward the shore.

There was a long strip of land reaching outward near the mouth of the bay. The floe was approaching this opening. Ikwa was watching. He walked over to the side of the floe.

"Annowee," he called, "when we float near that point, we must try to gain the land."

His sister came across to look.

"Unless we go ashore there," said he, "we shall never reach home again."

He went over, and brought the dogs to the same side with them.

"Now, Annowee," he said, "sit down upon the sledge and cling to it. Don't let go your hold whatever happens."

"But what shall you do?" she asked.

"I'll spring on behind when the time comes," he said.

The little girl sat as Ikwa had directed, and just as the floe swept into the narrow channel, the boy gave the dogs the signal. Annowee heard the ringing of his voice, the cracking of his whip, as the dogs sprang forward.

There was a swaying of the ice, the cold salt water

dashed over them, and then the little dogs drew them out upon the shore. What a drenching they had had! The dogs were shaking the water from their coats, while Ikwa and Annowee were catching their breath after their plunge.

Ikwa turned to see if Annowee was safe. She was brushing the water from her furs.

"I was afraid the waves would carry you away," said he.

"If it hadn't been for Kookoo we should have gone down; he led the other dogs straight ahead."

Annowee ran and gave the dog a hug, even though his shaggy hair was wet.

"You dear, good Kookoo," she cried, "you are the very best dog I know!" Kookoo pranced and frisked before her as if he understood.

They were now out of danger, but they were no nearer their friends than before.

"Shall we go on to the river?" asked the girl.

Ikwa, who had not thought of turning back, answered, "Yes; climb upon the sledge, and let us be off. We are losing time from the fishing."

In a moment they were speeding away over the snow again.

When the Eskimos heard the story of the children's escape, they called Ikwa a brave lad. "His father," they said, "could have done no more had he been with them upon the floe."

Bikku Matti*

FROM THE SWEDISH OF ZACHARIAS TOPELIUS
BY GUDRUN THORNE-THOMSEN

On a wooded hillside stood a little cabin. It had but one window and this was so small that, when the round, fair, curly head of a little boy appeared in it, the whole window was filled. Some years ago there had been a brick chimney and the walls had been painted red. At that time the cabin and the little potato field were fenced in neatly. But now it all looked poor, very poor. The smoke escaped through a hole in the turf and the fence had fallen to pieces long ago. In this place lived an old blind soldier and his wife. They could not work in the field to make their living; but the old man earned a little money by tying nets; and the old woman made a few brooms; the church gave them each year three barrels of rye for bread, and thus they managed to live.

So the old couple remained there with a little grandchild, whose name was Matti. Because he was so little they called him Bikku Matti. Those who don't under-

*From *The Birch and the Star*. Used by special arrangement with the author and the publishers, Row, Peterson & Co.

stand Finnish will have to guess what the name means.

Bikku had cheeks as red and as round as an apple, clear, blue eyes and hair as yellow as gold, the only gold to be found in the cabin. It was Bikku's round face which often filled the cottage window when anything passed on the road.

If you happen to come that way in summer, you will see a gate across the road close to the cottage. You will have to stop your carriage, unless some one comes to open the gate.

But just wait a little, Bikku Matti will soon be there. There he is in the cabin door. How he runs to reach the gate in time, with his golden hair streaming in the wind. Now he is at the gate. If you have a penny, throw it to him; he rather expects it; but let

it be a shiny one—he does not know the value of
money and a penny, if bright and new, gives him as
much pleasure as a silver coin. But take care not to
throw your coin on the road before the horse and
carriage have passed the gate; Bikku Matti has but
little sense yet, and if he sees the bright penny in the
road, he is likely to throw himself over it, allowing the
gate to shut in front of your horse.

On week-days Bikku Matti had only coarse bread
and herring to eat, but on Sundays he had potatoes
and sour milk. Still on such food he throve and
grew rounder and rounder as the years went by. He
could not read much—some prayers and the ten com-
mandments were about all.

But then Matti could do other things. He could
stand on his head and turn somersaults where the
grass was soft. He could skip stones over the smooth
lake, while his grandmother was washing his shirt.
He could drive a horse on the main road and ride the
neighbor's horse to the watering trough, if someone
walked beside him. He could tell the tracks of the
blue-jay from those of the crow on the new-fallen snow,
and wolf tracks he knew well. He could carve a boat
or a sled out of chips of wood and could make horses
and cows of pine cones with small twigs for legs. But,
although Bikku possessed all these powers (and they
were many for a small boy like Bikku), there were
some necessary things he did not possess—he had no

trousers. This may seem very strange to you, but it was after all not so strange. His grandparents were very poor, and then it was customary in that neighborhood for little boys to go about in plain cotton slips as Bikku did. But this was only on week days; on Sundays the other boys were dressed in blouses and trousers. It was only Bikku who neither Sunday nor Monday wore anything but the little slip. But for a long time he did not know that trousers were a necessary garment for a little boy. But see what happened.

One Sunday morning when the whole parish were to meet at the beach to go to church, Bikku declared that he was going too. "That will never do, dear child," said Grandmother.

"Why not?" asked Bikku Matti.

"You have no trousers." Bikku became very serious.

"I might have an old skirt to lend you," said Grandmother, "but then everybody would take you for a girl."

"But I am not a girl, I am a man," said Bikku.

"Of course you are," said Grandmother. "A man is a man, be he no larger than a thumb. Stay nicely at home, Bikku dear." And Bikku remained at home that time.

But soon after that there was to be a fair in the valley, a Horse Fair, and Bikku loved horses better than anything else in the world. He knew they would be there—black, white and brown ones. And there would be a Punch and Judy Show, a merry-go-round, and many more wonderful things. Bikku Matti had heard the boys tell great tales about all these things, and now Bikku said that he must go to the Fair.

"It won't do, dear child," said Grandmother again.

"Why not?" asked Bikku Matti.

"There will be many people there, my dear, and you cannot go without trousers."

Bikku Matti struggled with himself a while, and Punch and Judy danced before his eyes. At last he said, "If Grandmother would lend me her skirt?"

"Here it is," said Grandmother, and laughed to herself when the little boy stumbled on the kitchen floor in the skirt. "But you look like a girl," she said.

"If I look like a girl, I won't go," said Bikku Matti. "I am no girl, I am a man."

"Well, you look like a girl," said Grandmother, "but you might tell everybody whom you meet that you are a man."

"That's what I will do," thought Bikku Matti, and so he started off.

On the road he met a gentleman who stopped and said, "Little girl, can you tell me the way to the Fair?"

"I am no girl, I am a man," said Bikku Matti.

"You don't look like a man," said the stranger.

Bikku made no answer, but when he reached the Fair he called out so that all could hear him, "I only look like a girl, but I am a man."

Men and women laughed out loud. Boys and girls gathered about Bikku Matti, clapped their hands and cried, "Oh, look at little Mary, where did you get your pretty clothes?"

"It's Grandmother's skirt, and not mine," said Bikku Matti. "I am no Mary, I am Matti, don't you see?"

Then the largest and naughtiest of the boys took Bikku Matti on his back, carried him to the Punch and Judy show and cried out, "Come and see a penny-lad! Come and see my man in a petticoat."

Bikku Matti grew angry and pulled the boy's hair with all his might. "It is not my skirt, it is Grandmother's skirt!" he cried, and began to weep.

But the naughty boys kept on. "Come and see this man in a skirt."

And in this way he ran around the whole Fairgrounds, the boy calling, Bikku pulling his hair and crying. Never had Bikku had such a ride. He cried, he screamed, he scratched, and when at last he got loose, he ran as fast as he could, but he stumbled in the skirt, crawled up again, stumbled, got up again, and ran on until he reached Grandmother's cabin all out of breath and sobbing.

"Take off the skirt," he cried. "I won't have any skirt, I am a man."

"Don't cry, Bikku dear," said his Grandmother, trying to comfort him. "When you grow old, you will show them that you are a man as good as any."

"Yes," said Grandfather, "and next time I will lend you my trousers."

They loved Bikku more than anything else in the world, those old grandparents; they would have given him gold embroidered velvet trousers, if it had been in their power. Now Grandmother gave him a large piece of bread and butter, and Bikku Matti sat in the corner eating it while the tears dried on his cheek.

Some time after this there was great excitement in the valley. The road was one cloud of dust, from all the driving and running. A gentleman of much importance was expected to come through the valley. It was even said that the gentleman was next to the King himself. All the people came to see him and strange things were told about him. "He drives in a golden carriage," said some, "with twelve horses before it." "He is dressed from top to toe in silver and velvet," said others. But the children had their own thoughts about him. They imagined that the high gentleman carried a big sack on his back filled with silver coins and candy sticks, which he threw out among them.

Bikku Matti also heard about it and this time he had to be by the roadside with the other children; there was no help for that.

"But what about your clothes?" said Grand-father, smiling. "Perhaps you are to borrow Grand-mother's skirt?"

"I won't have any skirt," cried Bikku Matti, and turned red to the roots of his hair when he remembered all that he had suffered because of that skirt. "No, never in the world will I wear a skirt again. I want Grandfather's trousers. I want to wear them."

"Well, little one, come with me to the garret and we will see how well the trousers fit you," said Grandfather. And now Bikku Matti was happy. He climbed up the garret ladder like a cat, so fast that Grandfather could not keep up with him. Then they came to the big painted chest farthest off in the corner.

Of this chest Bikku stood in great awe, but he had only had glimpses into it once or twice. Now it was opened and the first thing that lay there glittering before him was a large sword in its gleaming sheath. "Oh, Grandfather, I want that," he cried.

"Oh, you do?" said Grandfather. "Hold the sword till I get the uniform out of the chest."

Bikku Matti took the sword; it was so heavy that he could hardly lift it. Old Grandfather stroked his cheek. "When you become a man," he said, "perhaps you may carry a sword too, and be allowed to fight for your country. Here are the trousers. You need the coat too, I suppose."

"Yes, Grandfather, and the sword, and the cap too."

"Here you have it all, Bikku, but you must promise not to go further than the gate." And Bikku promised.

Just as they came down from the garret they heard the sheriff driving on the road calling and shouting to the people to get out of the road, that the high gentleman was coming soon. There was a great deal of hurry and flurry on the road as well as in the kitchen.

Grandfather's trousers were put on Bikku Matti. They were gray with light blue stripes along the sides and so wide and long that Bikku could easily have hidden himself in one of the trouser legs. It looked very discouraging but on they must go. From below about half the length of the trousers was rolled up and fastened with pins, and from above they were hitched up and tied with a kerchief under Bikku's arms.

There was just as much difficulty with the coat. When it was on the little fellow, the sleeves and coat tails swept the floor.

"No, this will not do," said Grandmother, and she rolled up the sleeves and coat tails and fastened them with pins. Bikku was waiting patiently.

The tall soldier cap was then placed on his head, but it would have fallen down over his little head and neck clear to his shoulders, if it had not been filled with hay. At last they tied the heavy sword on Bikku's back and the little knight was ready.

There never was a hero returning from victory half as proud as was Bikku in his first pair of trousers. The little body was lost in the big uniform, only the blue, honest eyes, the red cheeks and the important little pug-nose could be seen between the collar and the cap. The brave knight started off with the sword scraping the ground. But soon the pins began to fall out, the cap nearly upset, and it looked as if our soldier would surely fall at each step he took. The old people had not laughed so heartily for a long time.

Grandfather, who could hear but could not see the outfit, swung the little boy about, kissed the little nose that stuck out and said, "God bless you little Bikku, may no lad worse than you wear our country's uniform. Now take care to salute when the great gentleman comes—so." And then he taught Bikku to stand straight as a stick with a serious face, left arm stretched straight down, right hand at the fore-head.

"Yes, Grandfather," said Bikku, who was always willing to learn. Bikku had just arrived at the gate when a dust cloud was seen on the road and the great gentleman came driving. Now he was quite near, oh, how fast he came! Suddenly the driver called, "Whoa!" and again, "Open the gate."

Now this was what happened. The sheriff himself was standing at the gate to see that everything should go off right. He was to give the command and his assistant was to open it. But when the carriage approached with lightning speed, the sheriff wanted to make a deep bow. In doing so he fell, and there he lay sprawling in the ditch by the road. His assistant waited for the word of command, and when he saw his superior officer fall, he became so confused that he could not think of opening the gate. Therefore the gate remained shut right before the nose of the high gentleman. The carriage had stopped and now the gentleman looked out surprised to see what was the matter, while the driver kept on calling, "Open the gate."

Then Bikku Matti stepped up, though with much difficulty, opened the gate and saluted exactly as Grandfather had taught him. The driver whipped up the horses, the carriage started, but the gentleman called, "Stop!" and the carriage stopped a second time.

"Who are you, little one, in my regiment's uniform?" called out the high gentleman and laughed so heartily that the carriage shook.

Bikku did not understand anything of this and did only what Grandfather had told him to, saluted again as straight and serious as could be. This amused the high gentleman still more, and he asked the people who stood near about the parents of the little boy.

The sheriff, who by this time had crept out of the ditch, came hurriedly forward to tell that the little boy was an orphan and lived with his Grandfather, an old soldier named Hugh.

What was the surprise of all, when the gentleman stepped out of his carriage, took Bikku by the hand and walked with him straight to the little cabin, and what excitement in the little hut! Grandmother could say nothing when the stranger entered, but stood there open-mouthed. Grandfather, because he saw nothing, had more courage and pointed politely in the direction where he knew the bench was.

"God's blessings on you, my friends," said the stranger and shook hands with the old people. "It seems to me I recognize you, old comrade," he continued, while he looked searchingly at Grandfather. "Are you not Hugh No. 39 of my old regiment?"

"Yes, Captain," answered Grandfather in great surprise, for he recognized the voice of the man.

"God be praised, that at last I have found you. Do you think I could forget you, who saved my life? You, who carried me on your back across the stream while the bullets ran about your ears, and the enemies were all about? After you have forgotten it, do you think I ever should forget it? After the war was over, I looked for you and inquired for you everywhere, but without success. But now I have found you, and now I may repay you a little by looking after you and yours in your old age. And what a fine boy you have!"

The gentleman caught Bikku Matti in his arms, lifted him high up and kissed him so heartily that the hat fell off, the sword rattled and the rest of Grandmother's pins fell out of the coat and the trousers.

"No, no, let me alone," said Bikku. "Now you have made me drop the cap, and Grandfather will be angry."

"Dear sir," said Grandfather, quite ashamed of Bikku, "be so kind as not to mind how the boy talks; he is not used to being with people."

"Don't worry about the boy's talk, he is right, guarding the soldier's cap. Listen, Bikku, do you want to become a soldier like your Grandfather?" said the Gentleman.

"Grandfather says it depends upon whom I am to fight," said Bikku.

"That is right," said the gentleman, "and you certainly are not lacking in courage."

"That, Captain, is because he wears trousers for the first time today, and that gives courage."

"Rather say it is the old uniform that gives courage," said the General (for now he was a general). "Much gunpowder and much honor are hidden in that old uniform and the memories of it pass from generation to generation. But this is a new age and the boy may live to serve his country in many ways. Are you strong, little man?" Bikku did not answer, but held out his arm and showed his muscles.

"Yes," said the General, "I see you will be as strong as a bear when you are a little older. Will you go with me and eat soft bread and drink milk every day, and cakes and candy you may have too, if you are good?"

"And shall I have a horse to ride on?" said Bikku.

"Yes, of course," said the General.

Bikku thought it over a while, his little blue eyes flew from the stranger to Grandfather, and from Grandfather to Grandmother, and back to the stranger again. At last he crept upon the old woman's knee and said, "I will stay with Grandfather and Grandmother."

"But, dear Bikku," said the old soldier, with tears in his eyes, "Grandfather gives you only hard bread, water and herring. Don't you hear that the gentleman offers you soft bread, milk, and other good things and a horse to ride?"

"I want to stay with Grandfather, I won't leave Grandfather," cried Bikku, hardly able to keep the tears away.

"You are right," said the General, and stroked Bikku's round cheek. "Stay with your Grandfather, and none of you shall suffer want, and when you grow to be a man, come to me. You shall have fields to plow and forests to hew. But whatever work you do, it is all the same, you will be an honest and loyal son of your country. Will you not, Bikku, my little man?"

"Yes," said the boy, standing straight and tall.

"God bless you, child," said Grandfather and Grandmother, moved to tears. "And God bless our beloved country, and may He give it many loyal sons like you, little Bikku. Honor thy father and thy mother that thy days may be long upon the land which the Lord thy God giveth thee."

"That's written in my primer," said Bikku Matti softly.

"Yes, but it must be written in our hearts also," said the General, and once more he kissed the boy.

Master of All Masters
JOSEPH JACOBS

A girl once went to the fair to hire herself for a servant. At last a funny-looking old gentleman engaged her, and took her home to his house. When she got there, he told her that he had something to teach her, for that in his house he had his own names for things.

He said to her: "What will you call me?"

"Master or mister, or whatever you please, sir," said she.

He said: "You must call me 'master of all masters.' And what would you call this?" pointing to his bed.

"Bed or couch, or whatever you please, sir."

"No, that's my 'barnacle.' And what do you call these?" said he, pointing to his pantaloons.

"Breeches or trousers, or whatever you please, sir."

"You must call them 'squibs and crackers.' And what would you call her?" pointing to the cat.

"Cat or kit, or whatever you please, sir."

"You must call her 'white-faced simminy.' And this now," showing the fire, "what would you call this?"

"Fire or flame or whatever you please, sir."

"You must call it 'hot cockalorum,' and what this?" he went on, pointing to the water.

"Water or wet, or whatever you please, sir."

"No, 'pondalorum' is its name. And what do you call all this?" asked he, as he pointed to the house.

"House or cottage, or whatever you please, sir."

"You must call it 'high topper mountain.' "

That very night the servant woke her master up in a fright and said, "Master of all masters, get out of your barnacle and put on your squibs and crackers. For white-faced simminy has got a spark of hot cockalorum on its tail, and unless you get some pondalorum high topper mountain will be all on hot cockalorum!" . . . That's all.

THE MOON*
VACHEL LINDSAY

The Moon's the North Wind's cooky.
He bites it, day by day,
Until there's but a rim of scraps
That crumble all away.
The South Wind is a baker.
He kneads clouds in his den,
And bakes a crisp new moon,
    that greedy
North. . .Wind. . .eats. . .again!

*Taken from *The Congo*. Copyright, by The Macmillan Company.

THE OWL AND THE PUSSY-CAT
Edward Lear

The Owl and The Pussy-Cat went to sea
In a beautiful pea-green boat:
They took some honey, and plenty of money
Wrapped up in a five-pound note.
The Owl looked up to the stars above,
And sang to a small guitar:
"O lovely Pussy, O Pussy, my love,
What a beautiful Pussy you are!"

UP ONE PAIR OF STAIRS

Pussy said to the Owl, "You elegant fowl,
How charmingly sweet you sing!
Oh! let us be married! too long we have tarried;
But what shall we do for a ring?"
They sailed away, for a year and a day,
To the land where the bong-tree grows:
And there in a wood a Piggy-wig stood,
With a ring in the end of his nose.

"Dear Pig, are you willing to sell for one shilling
Your ring?" Said the Piggy, "I will."
So they took it away, and were married next day
By the Turkey who lives on the hill.
They dined on mince and slices of quince,
Which they ate with a runcible spoon;
And hand in hand, on the edge of the sand,
They danced by the light of the moon.

413

Thumbelisa

HANS CHRISTIAN ANDERSEN

There was once a woman who had the greatest
longing for a little tiny child, but she had no idea
where to get one; so she went to an old witch and
said to her, "I do so long to have a little tiny child.
Will you tell me where I can get one?"

"Oh, we shall be able to manage that," said the
witch. "Here is a barley corn for you; it is not at
all the same kind as that which grows in the peasant's
field, or with which chickens are fed; plant it in a
flowerpot, and you will see what will appear."

"Thank you, oh, thank you!" said the woman, and
she gave the witch twelve pennies, then went home
and planted the barley corn. A large, handsome
flower sprang up at once; it looked exactly like a
tulip, but the petals were tightly shut up, just as if
they were still in bud. "That is a lovely flower,"
said the woman, and she kissed the pretty red and
yellow petals. As she kissed it the flower burst open
with a loud snap. It was a real tulip, you could see
that; but right in the middle of the flower on the
green stool sat a little tiny girl, most lovely and delicate. She was not more than an inch in height, so
she was called Thumbelisa.

Her cradle was a smartly varnished walnut shell,
with the blue petals of violets for a mattress and a
rose-leaf to cover her. She slept in it at night, but

during the day she played about on the table where the woman had placed a plate, surrounded by a wreath of flowers. A large tulip floated on the water, and on this little Thumbelisa sat and sailed about from one side of the plate to the others; she had two white horse hairs for oars. It was a pretty sight. She could sing, too, with such delicacy and charm as was never heard before.

One night as she lay in her pretty bed, a great ugly frog hopped in at the window, for there was a broken pane. Ugh! how hideous that great, wet toad was; it hopped right down on to the table where Thumbelisa lay fast asleep, under the red rose-leaf.

"Here is a lovely wife for my son," said the toad, and then she took up the walnut shell where Thumbelisa slept and hopped away with it through the window, down into the garden. A great, broad stream ran through the garden, but just at the edge it was swampy and muddy, and it was here that the toad lived with her son. Ugh! how ugly and hideous he was, too, exactly like his mother. "Koax, koax, brekke-ke-kex," that was all he had to say when he saw the lovely little girl in the walnut shell.

"Do not talk so loud or you will wake her," said the old toad; "she might escape us yet, for she is as light as thistledown! We will put her on one of the broad water lily leaves out in the stream; it will be just like an island to her, she is so small and light.

She won't be able to run away from there while we get the state-room ready down under the mud, where you and she are to live."

A great many water lilies grew in the stream; their broad green leaves looked as if they were floating on the surface of the water. The leaf which was farthest from the shore was also the biggest, and to this one the old toad swam with the walnut shell in which little Thumbelisa lay.

The poor, tiny little creature woke up quite early in the morning, and when she saw where she was, she began to cry most bitterly, for there was water on every side of the big green leaf, and she could not reach the land at any point.

The old toad sat in the mud decking out her home with grasses and the buds of the yellow water lilies, so as to have it very nice for the new daughter-in-law, and then she swam out with her ugly son to the leaf where Thumbelisa stood; they wanted to fetch her pretty bed to place it in the chamber before they took her there. The old toad made a deep curtsy in the water before her, and said, "Here is my son, and you are to live most comfortably with us down in the mud."

"Koax, koax, brekke-ke-kex," that was all the son could say.

Then they took the pretty little bed and swam away with it, but Thumbelisa sat quite alone on the green leaf and cried because she did not want to live with

the ugly toad. The little fish which swam about in the water had no doubt seen the toad and heard what she said, so they stuck their heads up, wishing, I suppose, to see the little girl. As soon as they saw her, they were delighted with her, and were quite grieved to think that she was to go down to live with the ugly toad. No, that should never happen. They flocked together down in the water round about the green stem which held the leaf she stood upon, and gnawed at it with their teeth till it floated away down the stream, carrying Thumbelisa where the toad could not follow her.

Thumbelisa sailed past place after place, and the little birds in the bushes saw her and sang, "What a lovely little maid!" The leaf with her on it floated further and further away and in this manner reached foreign lands.

A pretty little white butterfly fluttered 'round and 'round her for some time and at last settled on the leaf, for it had taken quite a fancy to Thumbelisa. She was so happy now, because the toad could not reach her and she was sailing through such lovely scenes; the sun shone on the water and it looked like liquid gold. Then she took her sash and tied one end round the butterfly, and the other she made fast to the leaf which went gliding on quicker and quicker, and she with it, for she was standing on the leaf.

At this moment a big May-bug came flying along. He caught sight of her and in an instant he fixed his claw round her slender waist and flew off with her, up into a tree. But the green leaf floated down the stream, and the butterfly with it, for he was tied to it and could not get loose.

The May-bug settled on the largest leaf on the tree, and fed Thumbelisa with honey from the flowers, and he said that she was lovely although she was not a bit like a May-bug. Presently all the other May-bugs which lived in the tree came to visit them; they looked at Thumbelisa, and the young lady May-bugs twitched their feelers and said, "She has only got two legs! What a poor appearance that makes!" "She has no feelers!" said another. "She is so slender in the waist, fie, she looks like a human being." "How ugly she is," said all the mother May-bugs, and yet little Thumbelisa was so pretty. That was certainly also the opinion of the May-bug who had captured her, but when all the others said she was ugly, he at last began to believe it too, and would not have anything more to do with her. She might go wherever she liked! They flew down from the tree with her and placed her on a daisy, where she cried because she was so ugly that the May-bugs would have nothing to do with her; and after all, she was more beautiful than anything you could imagine, as delicate and transparent as the finest rose-leaf.

Poor little Thumbelisa lived all the summer quite alone in the wood. She plaited a bed of grass for herself and hung it up under a big dock-leaf which sheltered her from the rain; she sucked the honey from the flowers for her food, and her drink was the dew which lay on the leaves in the morning. In this way the summer and autumn passed, but then came the winter. All the birds which used to sing so sweetly to her flew away; the great dock-leaf under which she had lived shriveled up leaving nothing but a dried yellow stalk, and she shivered with the cold, for her clothes were worn out. It began to snow and every snowflake which fell upon her was like a whole shovelful upon one of us, for we are big and she was only one inch in height. Then she wrapped herself up in a withered leaf, but that did not warm her much; she trembled with the cold.

Close to the wood in which she had been living

lay a large cornfield, but the corn had long ago been carried away and nothing remained but the bare, dry stubble which stood up out of the frozen ground. The stubble was quite a forest for her to walk about in; oh, how she shook with the cold! Then she came to the door of a Field-Mouse's home. It was a little hole down under the stubble. The Field-Mouse lived so cosily and warm there, her whole room was full of corn, and she had a beautiful kitchen and larder besides. Poor Thumbelisa stood just inside the door like any other beggar child and begged for a little piece of barley corn, for she had had nothing to eat for two whole days.

"You poor little thing," said the Field-Mouse, for she was at bottom a good old Field-Mouse. "Come into my warm room and dine with me." Then, as she took a fancy to Thumbelisa, she said, "You may with pleasure stay with me for the winter, but you must keep my room clean and tidy and tell me stories, for I am very fond of them," and Thumbelisa did what the good old Field-Mouse desired and was on the whole very comfortable.

"Now we shall soon have a visitor," said the Field-Mouse; "my neighbour generally comes to see me every week-day. He is even better housed than I am;

his rooms are very large and he wears a most beautiful black velvet coat; if only you could get him for a husband you would indeed be well settled, but he can't see. You must tell him all the most beautiful stories you know."

But Thumbelisa did not like this, and she would have nothing to say to the neighbour for he was a Mole. He came and paid a visit in his black velvet coat. He was very rich and wise, said the Field-Mouse, and his home was twenty times as large as hers; and he had much learning but he did not like the sun or the beautiful flowers; in fact he spoke slightingly of them for he had never seen them. Thumbelisa had to sing to him and she sang both "Lady-bug, Lady-bug, fly away home," and "A monk, he wandered through the meadow."

The Mole had just made a long tunnel through the ground from his house to theirs, and he gave the Field-Mouse and Thumbelisa leave to walk in it whenever they liked. He told them not to be afraid of the dead bird which was lying in the passage.

The Mole took a piece of tinder-wood in his mouth, for that shines like fire in the dark, and walked in front of them to light them in the long, dark passage. When they came to the place where the bird lay, the Mole thrust his broad nose up to the roof and pushed the earth up so as to make a big hole through which the daylight shone. In the middle of the floor lay a swallow, with its pretty wings closely pressed to its sides, and the legs and head drawn in under the feathers. Thumbelisa was so sorry for it; she loved all the little birds, for they had twittered and sung so sweetly to her during the whole summer; but the Mole kicked it with his short legs and said, "Now it will pipe no more; it must be a miserable fate to be born a little bird! Thank heaven! no child of mine can be a bird!"

Thumbelisa did not say anything, but when the others turned their backs to the bird, she stooped down and stroked aside the feathers which lay over its head, and kissed its closed eyes. "Perhaps it was this very bird which sang so sweetly to me in the summer," she thought; "what pleasure it gave me, the dear, pretty bird."

UP ONE PAIR OF STAIRS

The Mole now closed up the hole which let in the daylight and conducted the ladies to their home. Thumbelisa could not sleep at all in the night, so she got up out of her bed and plaited a large, handsome mat of hay and then she carried it down and spread it all over the bird, and laid some soft cotton wool which she had found in the Field-Mouse's room close 'round its sides, so that it might have a warm bed on the cold ground.

"Good-bye, you sweet little bird," said she, "good-bye, and thank you for your sweet song through the summer when all the trees were green and the sun shone warmly upon us." Then she laid her head close up to the bird's breast, but was quite startled at a sound, as if something was thumping inside it. It was the bird's heart. The swallow was not dead but lay there stiff with cold, and, now that it had been warmed, it began to come to life again.

In the autumn all the swallows fly away to warm countries, but if one happens to be belated, it feels the cold so much that it falls down to the ground and remains lying where it falls till the snow covers it up. The bird was very, very big beside her—Thumbelisa who was only one inch high—but she gathered up her courage, packed the wool closer round it, fetched a leaf which she had used for her own coverlet and laid it over the bird's head. The next night she crept down again to it and found it alive but it could only just open its eyes for a moment to look at Thumbelisa who stood with a bit of tinder-wood in her hand, for she had no other lantern.

"Many, many thanks, you sweet child," said the Swallow to her; "you have warmed me beautifully. I shall soon have strength to fly out into the warm sun again."

"Oh!" said she, "it is so cold outside; it snows and freezes; stay in your warm bed and I will tend you." Then she brought water to the Swallow in a leaf, and when it had drunk some, it told her how it had torn its wing on a black thorn bush, and therefore could not fly as fast as the other swallows which were taking flight then for the distant warm lands. At last it fell down on the ground, but after that it remembered nothing, and did not in the least know how it had got into the tunnel.

It stayed there all the winter, and Thumbelisa was good to it and grew very fond of it. She did not tell either the Mole or the Field-Mouse anything about it, for they did not like the Swallow.

As soon as the spring came and the warmth of the sun penetrated the ground, the Swallow said good-bye to Thumbelisa, who opened the hole which the Mole had made above. The sun streamed in deliciously upon them, and the Swallow asked if she would not go with him. She could sit upon his back and they would fly far away into the green wood. But Thumbelisa

knew that it would grieve the old Field-Mouse if she left her like that.

"No, I can't," said Thumbelisa.

"Good-bye, good-bye then, you kind, pretty girl," said the Swallow, and flew out into the sunshine. Thumbelisa looked after him and her eyes filled with tears, for she was very fond of the Swallow.

"Tweet, tweet," sang the bird, and flew into the green wood. Thumbelisa was very sad. She was not allowed to go out into the warm sunshine at all. The corn which was sown in the field near the Field-Mouse's house grew quite long; it was a thick forest for the poor little girl who was only an inch high.

"You must work at your outfit this summer," said the mouse to her, for their neighbour, the tiresome Mole in his black velvet coat, had asked her to marry him. "You shall have both woolen and linen, you shall have wherewith to clothe and cover yourself when you go to live with the Mole." Thumbelisa had to turn the distaff and the Field-Mouse hired four Spiders to spin and weave day and night. The Mole paid a visit every evening and he was always saying that when the summer came to an end, the sun would not shine nearly so warmly (now it burnt the ground as hard as a stone). Yes, when the summer was over he would take her to his home. But Thumbelisa was not at all pleased, for she did not care a bit for the tiresome Mole. Every morning at sunrise and every evening at sunset she used to creep out to the door, and when the wind blew aside the tops of the cornstalks so that she could see the blue sky, she thought how bright and lovely it was out there and wished so much to see the dear Swallow again; but, it never came back; no doubt it was a long way off, flying about in the beautiful green woods.

When the autumn came all Thumbelisa's outfit was ready. "In four weeks you must be married," said the Field-Mouse to her. But Thumbelisa cried and said that she did not want to go and live with the tiresome Mole.

"Fiddle-dee-dee," said the Field-Mouse; "don't be obstinate. You are going to have a splendid husband; the queen herself hasn't the equal of his black velvet coat; both his kitchen and his cellar are full."

So the Mole had come to fetch Thumbelisa; she was to live deep down under the ground with him, and never to go out into the warm sunshine, for he could not bear it. The poor child was very sad at the thought of bidding good-bye to the beautiful sun; while she had been with the Field-Mouse she had at least been allowed to look at it from the door.

"Good-bye, you bright sun," she said as she stretched out her arms towards it and went a little way outside the Field-Mouse's house, for now the harvest was over and only the stubble remained. "Good-bye, good-bye!" she said, and threw her tiny arms round a little red flower growing there. "Give my love to the dear Swallow if you happen to see him."

"Tweet, tweet," she heard at this moment above her head. She looked up; it was the Swallow just passing. As soon as it saw Thumbelisa it was delighted; she told it how unwilling she was to live with the ugly Mole deep down underground where the sun never shone. She could not help crying about it.

"The cold winter is coming," said the Swallow, "and I am going to fly away to warm countries. Will you go with me? You can sit upon my back! Tie yourself on with your sash, then we will fly away from the ugly Mole and his dark cavern, far away over the mountains to those warm countries where the sun shines with greater splendor than here, where it is always summer and there are heaps of flowers. Do fly with me, you sweet little Thumbelisa, who saved my life when I lay frozen in the dark earthy passage."

"Yes, I will go with you," said Thumbelisa, seating herself on the bird's back with her feet on its outspread wing. She tied her band tightly to one of the strongest feathers, and then the Swallow flew away, high up in the air above forests and lakes, high up

427

above the biggest mountains where the snow never melts; and Thumbelisa shivered in the cold air, but then she crept under the bird's warm feathers, and only stuck out her little head to look at the beautiful sights beneath her.

At last they reached the warm countries. The sun shone with a warmer glow than here; the sky was twice as high, and the most beautiful green and blue grapes grew in clusters on the banks and hedgerows. Oranges and lemons hung in the woods which were fragrant with myrtles and sweet herbs, and beautiful children ran about the roads playing with the large, gorgeously-coloured butterflies. But the Swallow flew on and on, and the country grew more and more beautiful. Under magnificent green trees on the shores of the blue sea stood a dazzling white marble palace of ancient date; vines wreathed themselves 'round the stately pillars. At the head of these there were countless nests, and the Swallow who carried Thumbelisa lived in one of them.

"Here is my house," said the Swallow; "but if you will choose one of the gorgeous flowers growing down

428

there, I will place you in it, and you will live as happily as you can wish."

"That would be delightful," she said, and clapped her little hands.

A great white marble column had fallen to the ground and lay there broken in three pieces, but between these the most lovely white flowers grew. The Swallow flew down with Thumbelisa and put her upon one of the broad leaves. What was her astonishment to find a little man in the middle of the flower, as bright and transparent as if he had been made of glass. He had a lovely golden crown upon his head and the most beautiful bright wings upon his shoulders; he was no bigger than Thumbelisa. He was the angel of the flowers. There was a similar little man or woman in every flower, but he was the king of them all.

"Heavens, how beautiful he is!" whispered Thumbelisa to the Swallow. The Swallow seemed a perfect giant of a bird to the little Prince, he who was so small and delicate, but when he saw Thumbelisa he was delighted; she was the very prettiest maiden he had ever seen. He therefore took the golden crown off his own head and placed it on hers. He asked her name, and if she would be his queen of the flowers! So she said yes to the beautiful Prince, and out of every flower stepped a little lady or a gentleman so lovely that it was a pleasure to look at them. Each one brought a gift to Thumbelisa, but the best of all was a pair of pretty wings from a large, white fly; they were fastened on to her back, and then she too could fly from flower to flower. All was then delight and happiness, but the Swallow sat alone in his nest and sang to them as well as he could, for his heart was heavy; he was so fond of Thumbelisa himself, and would have wished never to part from her.

"You shall not be called Thumbelisa," said the angel of the flowers to her; "that is such an ugly name, and you are so pretty. We will call you May."

"Good-bye, good-bye," said the Swallow, and he flew away again from the warm countries, far away back to Denmark. There he had a little nest above the window where the man lived who wrote this story, and he sang his "tweet, tweet" to the man, and so we have the whole story.

HIAWATHA'S CHILDHOOD*

Henry Wadsworth Longfellow

By the shores of Gitche Gúmee,
By the shining Big-Sea-Water,
Stood the wigwam of Nokómis.
Dark behind it rose the forest,
Rose the black and gloomy pine-trees,
Rose the firs with cones upon them;
Bright before it beat the water,
Beat the clear and sunny water,
Beat the shining Big-Sea-Water.
 There the wrinkled, old Nokómis
Nursed the little Hiawátha,
Rocked him in his linden cradle,
Bedded soft in moss and rushes,
Stilled his fretful wail by saying,
"Hush! the Naked Bear will hear thee!"
Lulled him into slumber, singing.
 At the door on summer evenings
Sat the little Hiawátha,
Heard the whispering of the pine-trees,
Heard the lapping of the water,
 Saw the fire-fly, Wah-wah-tay'-see,
Flitting through the dusk of evening,
With the twinkle of its candle
Lighting up the brakes and bushes,

*Reprinted by the courteous permission of the publishers, Houghton Mifflin Company.

431

And he sang the song of children,
Sang the song Nokómis taught him:
"Wah-wah-tay'-see, little fire-fly,
Little, flitting, white-fire insect,
Little, dancing, white-fire creature,
Light me with your little candle,
Ere upon my bed I lay me,
Ere in sleep I close my eyelids!"
    Saw the moon rise from the water,
Rippling, round from the water,
    Saw the rainbow in the heaven,
In the eastern sky, the rainbow,
Whispered, "What is that, Nokómis?"
And the good Nokómis answered:
" 'Tis the heaven of flowers you see there;
All the wild-flowers of the forest,
All the lilies of the prairie,
When on earth they fade and perish,
Blossom in that heaven above us."
    When he heard the owls at midnight,
Hooting, laughing in the forest,
"What is that?" he said, "Nokómis?"

And the good Nokómis answered:
"That is but the owl and owlet,
Talking in their native language,
Talking, scolding at each other."
   Then the little Hiawátha
Learned of every bird its language,
Learned their names and all their secrets,
How they built their nests in Summer,
Where they hid themselves in Winter,
Talked with them whene'er he met them,
Called them "Hiawátha's Chickens."
Of all beasts he learned the language,
Learned their names and all their secrets,
How the beavers built their lodges,
Where the squirrels hid their acorns,
How the reindeer ran so swiftly,
Why the rabbit was so timid,
Talked with them whene'er he met them,
Called them "Hiawátha's Brothers."

433

Beyond the Toll-Gate*

SARAH ORNE JEWETT

Barbara was not a very large girl, and she had seen only a little of the world; but she was much pleased with what she had seen, and was always interested in everything new and strange. All the first years of her life had been spent in the heart of the town, and there she had been kept most of the time in the house with her mother. But Barbara did not think it was stupid to stay in the house so much; her mother talked to her a great deal and could always think of some way to amuse her. Mrs. Snow sewed all day except when she was working about the house, and sometimes Barbara sewed too, for she was already clever with her needle, and sometimes she played with her doll. Every day she had to read two pages and to learn a spelling lesson, and sometimes she wrote on a slate "Barbara Snow," "Barbara Snow,"—a whole slateful of Barbara Snows, in queer, tumble-about letters, but her father thought she would make a good plain writer in time. He used to set the copies on the slate after Barbara had gone to bed, and sometimes in the morning she would find, "Will you take a walk to-night?" and would copy it just as carefully as she

*Taken from *Play Days*, published by Houghton Mifflin Company.

could, for she was always delighted when she could have a walk with her father and mother.

One night, a while before my story really begins, Mr. Snow had come home looking very much pleased about something, and after supper he told Mrs. Snow and Barbara that he had something to show them. Barbara could not think what it was, and was more and more puzzled when they first walked some distance, and then took a horse-car and rode a long way. But at last they stopped at the pleasantest-looking shady side street, and Mr. Snow presently stopped again before a pretty gray house, unlocked the front door, and asked them to walk in. It was a little house, and the trees in the street shaded it, and there was a little garden at the back with a tree of its own, and a grapevine by the kitchen window, and a grass plot, and there was a seat under the tree. Barbara's father asked if they really liked the house after they had seen it all, and Barbara's mother said it was the nicest house she ever saw for three people like themselves; so you can

imagine how proud Mr. Snow was to tell them that he had bought it that very day, and had almost money enough to pay for it, and that he thought he could save enough to pay the rest by the last of the summer.

Barbara and her mother were as happy as queens, they went about to see everything again and to look into each of the rooms. Barbara found that the window of hers overlooked the little garden, and that she could put her hand out and catch the leaves of the tree. At last they had to lock the door and come away, though they would have liked to stay much longer. Barbara thought it was great fun to have a ride in the horse-car so late in the evening. They kept passing other cars with bright red lights, and her father let her have the money to pay her own fare, and the conductor smiled pleasantly at the little girl, and the bells on the horse-cars sounded like something saying "Barbara's new house—Barbara's new house—Barbara's tree—Barbara's tree—" all the way home.

It was very soon after this that they moved, and soon it seemed to Barbara as if she had always lived in the new house. It seemed home-like at once when the furniture was put in its place; but I know you will believe me when I tell you that every day Barbara found something new. Once it was a lady's delight in bloom in the garden; and another day some scarlet-runner beans, which her mother had given her to plant, came up long before she expected them; and one morning a woman, who lived alone in the next house but one, gave her a dear gray kitten. Mrs. Snow was very busy all the first week getting the house into good order, and Barbara helped her whenever she could, and learned to keep her own bit of a room as neat as wax. It was too bad that her father could only be at home in the evening, but that could not be helped, and he was as happy as they, and whistled and sang merrily; and he put up shelves and mended the cellar stairs and the grape-vine trellis, and drove nails somewhere or other until it was too dark to see. And he kept saying that Barbara was growing rosy, and it was worth everything to all of them to live in that fresh air. He was so glad he had bought the house, and a man felt like somebody when he had earned a home of his own like that.

Barbara could go out doors as much as she chose, for the streets were so quiet; and she used to like to walk up and down and look at the other houses. There did not seem to be any children living very near except two or three little babies. Two girls and a boy used to go by every day to and from school, and Barbara used to wish they would stop and say something to her; she was very shy with other children, and would not have thought of speaking to them. She was to go to school herself when the next term began in September.

One day when she had been living in the new house

about three weeks, she took a longer walk than usual along a street which she had never followed before, and she came to a place where there was a gate across the road. She walked close up to it, and could not think what it meant. The road looked very pleasant beyond, and there were some teams not far ahead which had surely got past the great gate somehow. And Barbara wondered about it and stood still watching until a woman drove up in a rattling wagon. She seemed in a great hurry, and an old man came out of the little red house at the side of the gate; then the woman gave him some money, and he opened the gate and she went through. The toll-keeper was just going into his house again when he saw Barbara. "Did you want to go through, little girl?" said he; and our friend answered sadly, "No, sir; I was only looking." And then with great bravery she asked, "How much would it cost?"

"Only a cent for you, dear," said the toll-keeper, who seemed to be a very kind old man. "Perhaps I shall go in some day," said Barbara, and he smiled at her as if he should be as glad as she if that ever happened. "You just call 'Gate' if you don't see anybody, for these warm days I don't sit by the front window. But I don't keep folks waiting." And then he nodded and went in.

There was a little red seat at the side of the house, and Barbara sat down there and watched the people

GLEN KETCHUM

who drove and walked through the gate, and a great black and white cat came and rubbed against her, and once a hand-organ man came and played three tunes, and the toll-keeper himself came out to listen to him. You don't know what a good time Barbara had that afternoon.

And after this she thought of nothing so much as this toll-gate and the pleasant toll-gate man; and she went there three or four times to sit on the bench by the house and watch the people. Her father told her all about it; that it was a turnpike-road and they made people pay who went that way, because it took a great deal of money to keep it in repair. There were some bridges farther on. Somehow or other Barbara believed it was much pleasanter the other side of the gate than it was on the side she lived, and she wished with all her heart that she could go through and see for herself what was there. In all, four hand-organ men had gone that way and she had never seen any come back, and there were not nearly so many people coming out from this beautiful country as went in; but you see that Barbara was always there in the afternoon, when people were all coming out from town.

When the gate swung wide open she could see some gardens, and there were children playing about and shouting and calling to each other. And one hot afternoon a breeze came through and over the gate as if it were very cool and comfortable beyond. By little and little, Barbara made up her mind that everything pleasant was to be found the other side of the toll-gate, and that she could never be quite satisfied until she could see that part of the world about which she thought so much by day and sometimes dreamed at night.

One day she had been to do an errand for her mother, and she saw a bit of money on the ground which proved to be a silver three-cent piece. Barbara looked up the street and down, but could not see anybody, so she shut her hand and went home as fast as she could run.

"I suppose you can have it," said her mother; "it is not much, and if we hear of the owner I will pay it back. I don't believe you could find the owner, there are so many people passing back and forth all day."

"I hope it did not belong to a little girl," said Barbara gravely, "for she will be so sorry about it. Can I spend it all at once?"

"What for?" asked her mother, smiling.

"To go through the toll-gate with one cent, and to

come back with one cent, and to spend the other in there. I would truly be back before it was late. Oh please, mother!"

Little Barbara was in real earnest about her plan and her mother smiled the more. "What a funny girl you are," said she. "I wonder why you care about doing that?"

"It is so pleasant there," said Barbara. "I wish I could go." And so Mrs. Snow said she might, but she must not wander too far, and must keep on the same side of the street all the way and not trouble anybody.

So that very afternoon Barbara brushed her hair smooth and put on her best dress and the hat she wore to church, and kissed her mother good-by as if she were going on a long journey. Indeed she felt as if she were, and her heart failed her for a minute as she went back to see if there was any milk in the kitten's saucer, but she would not have given up going for all the world, and went away bravely down the street.

Barbara hurried, she was so anxious to get to the gate, and the old toll-keeper looked surprised when she came up to his window and reached up her hand with the three-cent piece. "I'm going through to-day, sir," said she, and the old man nodded as

he gave her the two cents in change. "I hope you will have a good time, my dear," said he kindly; then Barbara took two or three of her short steps, and was fairly on the other side of the gate.

It was a little strange that the street and the houses and the people were after all very much like those she had always seen. It was very pleasant, but it was not as different as she had supposed it would be, though there were fewer houses and a great many more fields; and she picked some flowers that were growing by the side of the road, and these were worth coming for; she had thought there would be some flowers. Once some ladies drove by in a pretty low carriage, and they smiled at Barbara, who was standing there just then, and who smiled at them, but they did not know she was a little girl who had half hoped to find fairy land and all the beautiful things she knew about, on that side of the toll-gate.

Barbara could not help growing sorry; it had been better to think all those treasures were there and not to go through the gate, than it was to be here and find everything so much like what she had seen before. There seemed to be no place to spend her cent, and it would have been very hard if she had not had the flowers.

But by and by, when she had walked out into the country a long way, or so it seemed to her, she came to a small house with rose-bushes all in bloom 'round

it, and vines growing on strings that were fastened to the low eaves,—morning-glories and scarlet runners; and such a pretty cat sat in the doorway. So Barbara stopped to speak to her. Just then somebody came to the door, and when she saw our friend she said: "Don't you want to come in and see the pussy?" So Barbara went in.

"Whose little girl are you?" and Barbara told her. Then the woman asked if she had been sent on an errand, and Barbara told her about wishing to see what was beyond the toll-gate; that her mother knew, and she might go as far as she liked, only not cross the street for fear of the carriages.

443

"You have walked a good way," said the new friend. "I think you had better come in to see me a little while, and play with the cat; perhaps I can find something else to show you."

Barbara was really getting tired, and she was glad to unlatch the little gate, and go into the house with her, for she seemed so kind; and in the room at the right of the door what should she see but another old woman who looked exactly like the first, and Barbara looked first at one and then the other with great wonder.

"Why, you're just alike!" said she, while they both laughed.

"We are twin sisters," said the first one she had seen, "and this is Miss Rhody Brown and I am Miss Ruthy."

Barbara looked at them very hard, and saw that one had a black bow on her cap and the other a green one, and one had a rounder face. This was Miss Rhody, and she told her sister to fetch the kittens while she briskly went into the next room and came back with a little chair just large enough for Barbara. The kittens and the old cat played together with some spools, and the old sisters and their little visitor watched them, and laughed a good deal at their frolics. Barbara got rested and had such a pleasant time. She told Miss Ruthy and Miss Rhody about her father and mother and the new house, and it was so strange to think they knew the old toll-gate man very well. She picked up their balls of yarn whenever they

dropped them, and they said to each other afterward how thoughtful and good she was for such a little thing, and so well-mannered. And they gave her a picture of a boy with a dog, and showed her a great many other pictures, besides a large box full of shells which their brother had brought home from sea a great many years before, and these Barbara would have liked to play with for hours.

And at last Miss Ruthy, the black-bowed sister, disappeared for a few minutes, and when she came back she asked them to come out into the kitchen; and there was a little round table spread with a feast for Barbara. There was a China mug with a rose on it, full of milk, and a plate of gingerbread cakes cut in ever so many different shapes,—a star and a heart and a leaf and a cat; and there was a crisp turn-over with a crinkly edge.

Barbara did not know what to say, it was such a surprise to her. She shyly sat down in the chair which Miss Ruthy had placed for her, and she wished her mother knew what a good time she was having. She was really very hungry, and everything was so good, while the old sisters smiled at each other and were so pleased, and Miss Rhody said two or three times

445

that she thought when she was making that turn-over that it was a pity some little girl couldn't have it.

It would have been very sad to say good-by if they had not told Barbara so many times that she must come and see them whenever she could, and that sometimes she must come and stay all day, if her mother was willing. Miss Ruthy meant to walk part way home with our friend, but just as she was getting her bonnet a man stopped at the door with a wagon, and after he had finished his business the sisters asked him if he could take a little passenger as far as he went? And presently, after Barbara had kissed both her kind friends good-by, and had patted the cat and each of her kittens, and had put one of each kind of the cookies into her pocket, she was lifted to the high wagon-seat and drove away in state. It was growing late in the afternoon, and the sunlight was growing yellow, and the birds were flying about; the shadows of the trees and of the people they met were very long on the turnpike-road. Barbara's flowers had wilted, but she had them still, and the old ladies had picked some bright red roses for her, and she kept taking a sniff of these every little while, because they were so sweet. The man was very kind; he told her that he had a little girl at home who went to ride with him in that very wagon almost every day. He stopped just before they came to the toll-gate, and he took Barbara out carefully and gave her two cents, so she

446

could come that way again some day, which was very kind.

And it seemed as if a great deal had happened since she had seen the old toll-keeper before. He knew her at once, and looked glad to see her. He took the cent she gave him, but when he had done talking he took another cent out of his own pocket and gave it to her for a present.. So Barbara went home both rich and happy. There was a great deal to tell her mother; and do you think that Mrs. Snow had known the two old sisters herself, years ago, before she was married, and she said she must go to see them very soon. Barbara made each of the old ladies a spool-bag; a black silk one and a green silk one, like the bows on their caps. And Barbara often went to see the toll-keeper, and though now she had been through the gate, and could not make up any more stories about what was there, she could make up stories about other things. She spent so many pleasant days that summer beyond the toll-gate, and she thought everybody there tried to make her have a good time.

THE PEDDLER'S CARAVAN*
WILLIAM BRIGHTY RANDS

I wish I lived in a caravan,
With a horse to drive like a peddler-man!
Where he comes from nobody knows,
Or where he goes to, but on he goes!

His caravan has windows two,
And a chimney of tin, that the smoke comes through;
He has a wife, with a baby brown,
And they go riding from town to town.

Chairs to mend, and delf to sell!
He clashes the basins like a bell;
Tea trays, baskets ranged in order,
Plates, with alphabets 'round the border!

With the peddler-man I should like to roam,
And write a book when I come home;
All the people would read my book
Just like the travels of Captain Cook!

*Used by the courteous permission of John Lane Company.